BOATS AND BAD GUYS

An Isle of Man Ghostly Cozy

DIANA XARISSA

❀ Created with Vellum

For all of Fenella's fans.

AUTHOR'S NOTE

Welcome to the second book in the Ghostly Cozy Series. I have to say, writing about a ghost is a lot of fun! I hope you are enjoying reading about her. As with all of my series, the books move along in alphabetical order (because I love to read series books, but I'm a bit obsessive about reading them in order). My characters do develop and change as the series progresses, but each story should stand on its own if you would prefer to only read a single title.

If you're a fan of Bessie and/or the Markham sisters, this series is a little bit different. As my main character is a transplanted American, the book is primarily written in American English. I hope my readers in the UK and further afield don't mind.

Like the Bessie books and my romances, it is set in the Isle of Man. The island is a unique and wonderful place and I urge everyone to visit it, but not all at once!

This is a work of fiction. All of the characters are products of the author's imagination. Any resemblance to actual persons, living or dead, is entirely coincidental. Similarly, the restaurants, shops, and other businesses in the story are fictional. I've taken considerable liberties with locations within the story, adding shops and restaurants where they are convenient to the story, rather than where any shops actually exist. The historical sites and other landmarks on the island are all real; however, the events that take place within them in this story are fictional.

I urge everyone to sign up for my newsletter so that you can keep track of release dates. I also run an occasional contest and try to answer some of the questions I get asked the most. You can find a sign-up link on my website; its address is given in the back of the book. I truly love hearing from my readers. Please do get in touch. All of my contact details are also in the back of the book.

"**O**ne more round?" Peter asked as Fenella swallowed her last sip of wine.

"Oh, go on, then," Shelly replied. "It's Friday, and Fenella's the only one who has to get up tomorrow."

Fenella laughed. "I'm glad you're thinking of me," she said. "But I will have one more, thank you," she told Peter. "I don't expect I'll be drinking at all when I'm in England. I may as well have fun tonight."

"There are pubs in England," Peter told her a moment later as he delivered the fresh drinks. "Some of them even sell good wine."

"As good as this?" Fenella asked, raising her glass.

Peter frowned. "Maybe not quite as good as that," he admitted. "But the Tale and Tail is a very special pub."

"It is," Fenella agreed, looking around the huge room. New owners had converted what had once been the private library in the home of a very wealthy family into a pub some years earlier. Shelves and shelves of books still lined the room and Fenella had already given up on ever having the time to read even the titles of all of them.

She and her friends were settled comfortably on couches around a small table on the upper level of the pub. One of the pub's handful of official pub cats was stretched out on the couch next to Peter, enjoying having his ears scratched. Fenella settled back in her seat and sighed. Moving to the Isle of Man had been something of a whim, she could admit to herself, but so far it seemed as if it had been an excellent decision.

"So what are your plans for next week?" Peter asked.

"I'm being met tomorrow by a researcher that I've been corresponding with for the last six months," Fenella said. "He's kindly offered to put me up tomorrow night and then drive me down to London on Sunday. I have a busy week full of places I want to see, and then I'm going to take the train back to Liverpool to catch the ferry back."

"How much do you know about this researcher?" Shelly asked, frowning.

"Rather more than I'd like to, actually," Fenella said with a laugh. "He's a distant relative of some sort and he and my oldest brother went to school together when they were young. They've always kept in touch, at least with birthday cards and the like, and now, in the Internet age, they're social media friends. Once I moved over here, I added him to my social media account. Since then, I've seen way too many pictures of the man's grandchild, I can tell you that."

Shelly laughed. "Okay, so at least you know he's not some creepy stalker."

"You can't be accused of stalking your own grandchild, can you?" Fenella asked. "I mean, the poor baby has this sort of permanently startled looked on his face, no doubt because there's always a flash going off in front of him."

"First grandchild?" Peter asked.

"Yes, and I'm sure he's hoping it isn't the last," Fenella replied.

"You've only been here what, six weeks, but it's going to be strange not having you around," Shelly said.

"You'll have Katie to keep you company," Fenella reminded her. "You can still have her, right?" She hadn't planned on adopting a stray kitten, but the kitten had more or less moved in with her without asking. Now that Fenella had her, though, she couldn't imagine life without the small ball of fur and attitude.

"Of course I can still have Katie," Shelly said. "I'm looking forward to it. Maybe she can help me make up my mind about getting a kitten of my own."

"You should," Fenella replied. "Then our kittens could play together while we have coffee."

Shelly nodded. "I'm just a little worried about becoming a sad and lonely widowed woman with too many cats," she said a little sheepishly.

"We won't let that happen," Peter said firmly. "One cat isn't a problem, though, if you'd like the company."

"I think I might," Shelly said. "We'll see how it goes, looking after Katie."

That third glass of wine was really one too many for Fenella. She'd never been much of a drinker, and while she'd already developed a habit of going to the Tale and Tail on a regular basis, she rarely had more than a single drink. As she sipped her wine, she began to feel quite sleepy.

"I think I should head for home," she told her friends. "As you said, I do have to be up in the morning."

The others quickly finished their drinks and then the trio made their way to the elevator at the rear of the building. The winding staircase in the center of the pub was best used only for going up when fully sober.

The large apartment building where they all lived was only a few doors away. The lobby seemed too brightly lit to Fenella, and she worried that she might have a migraine coming on.

"Is it just me, or is it brighter in here than normal?" Shelly asked as the group made its way to the elevators.

"It's very bright," Peter said. "The management said something in the last newsletter about installing new lighting, but I didn't really pay attention."

"You read the newsletter?" Shelly asked.

"There's a newsletter?" Fenella demanded.

Peter laughed. "It's emailed to residents every month. If they don't have an email address for you, you won't be getting it," he told Fenella. "And yes, I read the newsletter, or a least I skim through the newsletter. Sometimes there is some quite good information in there."

"Hmmm," Shelly replied. "I'll take your word on that."

Everyone laughed as the elevator stopped on the top floor. Fenella followed the others into the corridor.

"Like Shelly said, it's going to seem strange not having you here," Peter said as they reached his door. He looked like he wanted to say something more, but then he simply gave Fenella a quick hug and let himself into his apartment.

"What's going on with you two?" Shelly asked as the door shut behind Peter. "You went out to dinner a few times and I thought maybe there was going to be a bit of a romance there, and now, nothing."

Fenella shrugged. "We went out a few times, but Peter seems quite content for us to just be friends. I'm not going to push for more, not while I'm still recovering from my last relationship."

Shelly nodded. "Well, I think you two would be great together, if you ever did decide to push for more. There's nothing wrong with being friends, though."

Fenella thought about Peter. He was a handsome man in his early fifties, just about the right age for her as she sped toward fifty herself. He had salt-and-pepper hair and lovely blue eyes, but he also had two ex-wives, one of whom was significantly younger than Fenella. Shelly was right. They might well be better off staying just friends.

"Good night, dear," Shelly said now as she gave Fenella a hug. "I'll see you in the morning when you bring Katie over."

"Yes, I'll be over around eight, sorry."

"No need to be," Shelly assured her. "As long as you don't mind that I won't look quite this fabulous."

Fenella laughed as she looked her friend up and down. Shelly was wearing a bright green top with a hot pink skirt. The combination, especially when paired with the woman's red hair, was striking to say the least. The longer Fenella knew her, the less she noticed what Shelly was wearing. No matter how loud Shelly's outfits were, her personality was always bigger and better. Shelly insisted that Fenella's Aunt Mona had been instrumental in pulling Shelly out of her depression when Shelly's husband had died suddenly. Apparently Mona had encouraged the bright colors and the dyed hair that now seemed inextricably Shelly.

Fenella opened the door to her own apartment, a smile still on her face. She'd left a few lights on for Katie, and the kitten looked up at her from her favorite spot on a couch in the living room.

"Merow," she said softly.

"Hello, Katie," Fenella replied. "I know it's late, but I was having fun with my friends."

"Yes, well, it's high time that little kitten was in bed," a voice said from the kitchen.

Fenella shook her head. "Aunt Mona, you know as well as I do that Katie sleeps whenever and wherever she likes. She couldn't care less what time I go to bed."

"That isn't true," Mona argued. "She waits up for you every time you go out."

Fenella sighed. Mona would know, she supposed. As Mona was either a ghost or a figment of Fenella's imagination, Mona was nearly always in the apartment. Fenella didn't think her imagination was all that good, so as time went by and Mona didn't show any signs of leaving, Fenella was coming to believe that the semi-transparent woman who seemed to pop in and out at random really was the ghost of her recently departed aunt.

"Well, I'm home now, so I'll just get off to bed," Fenella told Mona. "You will keep an eye on things while I'm gone, won't you?" she asked over her shoulder as she turned toward her bedroom.

"Oh, I'll be watching," Mona replied. "I can't do anything if burglars break in, for instance, but I'll be watching for them."

"And then you can describe them to me and I can tell the police," Fenella said. "Although how I'll explain how I know what the burglars looked like to the police, I don't know."

"I don't think you have anything to worry about," Mona told her. "This building is very safe."

"There have been rather a lot of burglaries in Douglas in the last few weeks, though, haven't there? According to the local papers, that's quite unusual."

"Yes, well, perhaps a gang of criminals has moved in from across or something," Mona said. "They'll soon find that there isn't much to steal in most people's houses here and move on again."

Fenella glanced around her comfortably furnished apartment. "I'd hate for anyone to take anything from in here, except maybe that lamp," she said after a moment.

"The lamp your mother bought me," Mona laughed. "You really don't like it, do you?"

Fenella wrinkled her nose. "It just isn't to my taste, although nearly everything else is."

"You know you don't have to keep it," Mona said. "You own the flat and all of its contents. You can redecorate the entire place if you want to."

"That wouldn't feel right, not with you still being here," Fenella said. "I mean, even if you went, I probably wouldn't do much. As I said, most of it is exactly right."

"Yes, well, as I understand it, it's mostly computer equipment and jewelry that are being stolen in these break-ins. Items that are small and valuable and are easy to sell on the street. The furniture in here should be safe enough, and you can lock up your jewelry in the safe before you go."

"I meant to do that," Fenella exclaimed. "Thank you for reminding me."

In the master bedroom, behind a lovely watercolor painting, was a wall safe. Fenella opened it and put her small jewelry box inside.

"Are you wearing those earrings to England?" Mona asked.

Fenella put a hand to her ear and then shook her head. "These are too nice," she said, taking the small diamond studs out of her ears. "I'll wear some simple gold hoops while I'm away." She dropped the studs into the safe with the jewelry box and fished out a pair of plain gold hoop earrings.

"I was thinking about changing my appearance again," Mona said from where she was standing in front of the full-length mirror. "But then, I can't see myself in the mirror if you aren't here, so maybe it isn't worth the bother."

"I thought you liked being around thirty," Fenella said. "What were you thinking of changing to?"

"Oh, I don't know," Mona sighed. "I'm just bored, I think."

"I hope you won't be too bored while I'm away," Fenella said, looking at her aunt with concern.

"It's strange being here all the time," Mona said. "I miss my exciting life and I really miss the Tale and Tail. Maybe it's time to move on to the next phase of my being dead."

Fenella swallowed hard. There were times when she thought it would be nice to have her apartment to herself, but she also knew she'd miss Mona once the other woman moved on to whatever was next. "You have to do what's best for you," she said after a moment.

"Yes, I suppose I do," Mona mused. "It doesn't seem as if I'm helping much with your love life, either, does it? Of course, you don't actually have a love life, so that might be the problem."

Fenella thought later that it was good that she'd had that extra drink. She didn't even bother to argue with her aunt. She just stuck her tongue out at her and then went into the master bathroom and shut the door. Her love life was not something she wanted to discuss with Mona or anyone else for that matter, even if Mona was mostly right. There really wasn't anything to talk about on the subject.

She washed her face and brushed her teeth. She'd recently found an excellent hairdresser on the island, and even now, three weeks after her last cut, she loved the way she looked. Her grey was now covered under a rich chestnut brown, with enough blonde highlights sprinkled throughout to make her feel, and she hoped look, younger. Her eyes were somewhere between blue and green and they weren't doing too badly. She'd worn contact lenses for many years and she knew she was going to need reading glasses or bifocals soon, but she was fighting the idea for the moment.

After she slipped into her nightgown, she switched off the bathroom light. In the bedroom, Katie had taken up her position right in the center of the bed. Fenella shook her head at the cat and then went into the kitchen to fill up Katie's water bowl, just in case the kitten got thirsty during the night.

Her alarm seemed to ring only a few minutes after she'd turned off the bedroom light. "It can't be morning already," she said to Katie as the kitten yawned and then snuggled back down into the duvet.

Fenella sighed and slid out of bed. She had a ferry to catch. As she stood under the shower, she began to feel a tiny bit of excitement. She'd quit her job and moved halfway around the world for a new beginning. Part of that new beginning included writing the book that she'd been thinking about for years. A fictional autobiography of Anne Boleyn had sounded like a great idea when she'd been a hard-working university professor, teaching history to bored undergraduates, but now that she had all the time she needed to get the book actually written, it was proving harder than she'd anticipated. This trip was supposed to inspire her. She was planning to visit several of the most important sites in Tudor history.

Thoughts of Hever Castle and Hampton Court Palace filled her brain as she got dressed and put on a little makeup. It only took her a few minutes to finish packing, which meant she was ready to go as soon as she dropped Katie off next door. She looked at the tiny kitten, who was still in bed, and sighed. She hadn't wanted a pet, but she was really going to miss Katie while she was away.

"It's only a week," she reminded herself sternly as she double-checked the list of instructions she'd written out for Shelly. "And Shelly will spoil her rotten," she added, knowing that her neighbor would fuss over her little furry guest at every opportunity.

Sighing deeply, she scooped the kitten up from her nap, earning herself a "meeeooowww" of protest.

"Hush, now," she said. "Shelly will take good care of you and you'll have a whole new apartment to explore. It will be like having a vacation."

Katie blinked at her and then snuggled into her arms. "You aren't making this easier," she muttered as she carried the kitten into the corridor. Katie's contented purr just made Fenella feel worse.

"Ah, there's my new flatmate," Shelly cooed as she opened her door only a few seconds after Fenella's knock. "I've been waiting for you. I've bought you a new toy for each day that Fenella will be away and I've bought a box of special kitty treats and special bottled water, designed just for kittens."

"Bottled water for kittens?" Fenella echoed faintly.

Shelly flushed. "It was on sale in the pet shop," she said. "The shop assistant said it was much better for their tiny digestive systems than tap water."

Fenella couldn't help but smile. "As soon as I get back, we're going to go to a shelter somewhere to get you a kitten," she told her friend.

Shelly beamed. "I think that's a good idea," she said. "Otherwise I might be tempted to keep Katie."

Fenella gave the top of Katie's head a quick kiss and then handed the seemingly unconcerned animal over to Shelly. "I'll be back next Sunday," she reminded the other woman. "And I will want Katie back."

Shelly grinned. "I know. I promise not to get too attached."

As Fenella turned away, she heard Shelly whispering to Katie about all of the fun they were going to have. Her neighbor definitely needed a cat of her own. Back in her apartment, Fenella grabbed her suitcase and headed for the door. The Sea Terminal was only a short walk away, and a glance out of the huge windows at the front of her apartment showed her that the sun was coming up on a lovely spring morning.

"I just hope it stays like this," she said to herself as she walked out of her building and turned along the promenade. The sea journey from Douglas to Liverpool took over three hours and she understood that if the wind picked up things could get quite rocky on the boat. The last thing she wanted was to arrive in Liverpool having been seasick for several hours.

She'd walked past the Sea Terminal many times in the weeks she'd lived on the island, but she'd never had an occasion to go inside. The reservations for today's journey had been made online and she'd been able to print her ticket herself. Inside the building, she found the check-in desk and waited in line behind an older gentleman and a young couple.

"We'll be boarding in just a few minutes," the girl behind the desk was telling the man. "You can wait in our lounge, just through those doors."

"I want to be in the quiet lounge on the boat," he shouted at the girl. "I like things nice and quiet and I don't want any children underfoot."

"Yes, sir, you've booked a seat in the quiet lounge," the girl told him.

"Pardon?" he yelled.

"I said, you're booked into the quiet lounge," the girl repeated herself more loudly.

"Right, well, I'll just go and wait then, shall I?"

"Yes, that's right," the girl said. "Through those doors." She pointed to a set of double doors to the man's right.

"Through there?" he asked.

"Yes, sir. Right through there," she said loudly.

As the man headed off, slowly dragging his small suitcase behind him, the young couple approached the desk.

"Wasting his money on the quiet lounge, with his hearing that bad," the man muttered as he felt around in his pockets for his ticket.

"But at least he'll be away from children," the woman with him said. "That does sound like a good idea. The last time I took the ferry, a small child wanted to talk to me for most of the journey."

The man grimaced and looked at the woman behind the desk. "Are there any more seats in the quiet lounge?" he asked.

The girl grinned. "Plenty," she said. "It's only the middle of April, so it's fairly quiet today. I don't think you'll have to worry about noisy children anywhere on board, but if you're really worried, you can pay for reserved seats in the quiet lounge."

The pair had a quick conversation and Fenella lost interest. She looked through the doors where the older man had disappeared. The small waiting area reminded her of every airport she'd ever been in, with uncomfortable-looking chairs arranged in clusters. The room was only sparsely populated and Fenella didn't know anyone among the passengers.

That was hardly surprising, considering she'd been on the island for less than two months, but she still found herself looking at everyone as if expecting to recognize a familiar face. Often, she found herself smiling at someone who looked familiar, only to realize, as they stared blankly at her, that they resembled someone she'd known back in Buffalo, New York.

"How can I help you?" the woman behind the desk called as the young couple made their way through the waiting room doors.

"Oh, I'm sailing to Liverpool," Fenella said. She handed over her printed ticket.

"Okay, we'll be allowing foot passengers to board very soon," the girl said. "And I see you've booked a cabin. You'll need to stop at customer service once you've boarded and they'll be able to give you the key and tell you how to find your cabin."

"Excellent, thank you," Fenella said.

"You can wait in our waiting room," the girl told her. "Listen for the boarding announcement soon. They're just loading up the last of the freight. Then they'll load car passengers and foot passengers."

Fenella nodded and walked through the doors into the waiting area. A quick look around confirmed that she didn't know a soul. Not feeling like making new friends, she dropped into a seat and pulled out a book. Within minutes she was miles away, joining a detective who was hunting a killer through the Florida Everglades.

"Good morning, passengers. At this time, we'd like to invite all of our foot passengers to make their way on board for today's sailing to Liverpool." The announcement interrupted an exciting part of the story, but Fenella was eager to get underway, so she didn't mind. She was going to have over three hours in her cabin on the ferry to read, anyway. Saving the book for later was probably a good idea.

All around her, everyone was getting to their feet and gathering up their belongings. Fenella picked up her handbag and began the long walk from the building to the ferry, dragging her suitcase behind her. She was surprised when she arrived at a security desk.

"Please put your suitcase and handbag on the belt and walk through the metal detector. Thank you," the man at the desk told Fenella.

Thinking that this was even more like flying than she'd realized, Fenella was quick to comply. As she collected her bags after their trip through the x-ray machine, the man she'd been behind at the check-in desk tottered up.

"This is a lot of bother," he complained loudly. "You aren't making the car passengers go through all of this and they could have anything in their cars, you know."

"Yes, sir," the man behind the desk said with a long-suffering smile.

Fenella gathered up her belongings and continued along the long corridor. In the distance, she could see the ferry, seemingly bobbling up and down gently in the sea. Just watching it made her feel slightly seasick. Reserving a cabin had seemed like an extravagance when she'd made her reservations, but now she was glad she'd done so. At least she'd have the space to lie down if she did feel sick and her very own bathroom if she needed it.

She slowed her walk and looked down at the long line of cars that were snaking their way onto the ship. If this was a quiet sailing, she wondered how busy they could get. There seemed to be an awful lot of cars filing into the belly of the boat. Maybe, if she ever learned to drive a stick shift, one day she could bring Mona's fancy sports car with her on the ferry. Then she wouldn't have to rely on friends or the train for getting around in England. Driving a stick shift on the wrong side of the road still seemed like an almost insurmountable challenge to her. The racy red sports car was a huge temptation, though. Fenella had always dreamed of owning something like it, although she couldn't imagine that she'd ever have bought it herself.

It's your imagination, she told herself firmly as she stepped onto the ferry and immediately began to feel as if the ground was shifting under her feet. They were still solidly anchored in Douglas Habour, so the boat was barely moving, she thought.

Having no clear idea of where to go, Fenella settled for following the handful of other foot passengers who were ahead of her. They climbed a flight of stairs and went through some doors. On their heels, Fenella found herself in a large room with windows all along the outside. There were several spacious seating areas, a small and partly closed off children's play area, a café with its own row of tables and chairs, a small gift shop, and exactly what Fenella was looking for, a customer service desk.

"How can I help you today?" the girl behind the desk asked, giving Fenella a bright smile.

"I have a cabin reserved," Fenella told her, pulling her ticket out of her handbag.

The girl took the sheet and studied it for a moment. "Yes, Ms.

Woods, let me see here." She turned, still holding the paper, and began flipping through some cards on the desk.

"We've half our summer staff in here doing training," she said after a moment. "They keep moving things around and not putting them back where they belong. The cleaning staff isn't any better. Someone managed to spill a cup of coffee all over the desk this morning, and when the cleaning crew came to sort it out, they just started binning everything that was on the desk. I had to spend an hour going through the rubbish looking for the papers I actually need."

"Oh, dear," Fenella murmured. "How unfortunate for you."

The girl sighed deeply. "I wasn't even meant to work this morning, you know," she said in a confiding whisper. "But someone pulled a sickie at the last minute and management knows they can always ring me and I'll come in. I should start saying no, really I should. Maybe they'd appreciate me more if I wasn't so available."

I'd appreciate you more if you'd give me my cabin key, Fenella thought, swallowing hard as the ship tipped slightly to one side. Or maybe it didn't, as she seemed to be the only one who'd noticed.

"Ah, here we are," the girl said, pulling a large folder out from under a pile of papers. "The cabin assignments for the journey. Let me see where they've put you."

Fenella watched impatiently as the girl ran her perfectly manicured finger down the short list of names. Eventually she found Fenella.

"Ah, you're in 206," she announced. "Now, where have they moved the key tray to?" The tray was unearthed a few minutes later, as Fenella's stomach lurched and the line of impatient passengers grew behind her.

"206, let's see," the girl said. She frowned. "No keys for 206 here. I wonder what's happened to them."

She dug around on the desk again, flipping through dozens of small scraps of paper, each of which seemed to have only a few words jotted on them.

"Here it is," she exclaimed after a moment. "The sink in 206 is out of service. Well, that's no good. They aren't supposed to just make a note of it and leave it. They're supposed to make sure that no one is booked into that cabin for the next journey and..." she sighed and trailed off. "The good news for you," she said to Fenella, "is that we aren't very busy today. I can move you to another cabin."

"Excellent," Fenella said. "I'm looking forward to sitting down and relaxing."

"Yes, well, let me see which cabins are empty." The girl went back to her list and then back and forth between the list and the key tray. "It doesn't look as if very many passengers have picked up their keys yet," she said after a moment.

Fenella glanced at the long line of passengers waiting behind her. It was hardly surprising that no one had their keys yet.

"I'll put you in 212," the girl said eventually. "No one is booked into it and you're traveling alone, right?"

"I am," Fenella agreed.

"That's good, because for some reason I only have one key for that cabin. I'm sure the other will turn up in one of the cleaner's pockets or something, but for today, it won't matter." She handed Fenella a key and then turned a huge fake smile on the next person in line.

"And how can I help you?" she asked.

"I'm sorry," Fenella spoke quickly. "But where am I going?"

The girl's smile faltered as she glanced back at Fenella. "Up the stairs and follow the signs," she said in a bored tone.

Fenella grabbed her bags and walked away as quickly as she could. The cold stares she got from the rest of the passengers who were waiting suggested that they blamed her for the long delay. She shook her head and looked around for a staircase. Luckily there were signs and she followed one now that said "Cabins," which led to a door that opened into the promised flight of stairs.

The stairs were steep and awkward with her suitcase, but Fenella was feeling quite desperate to sit down or maybe even lie down. At the top of the stairs arrows pointed out which way to go for which cabins. She made her way along a short corridor, happy to find cabin 212 in the middle of the hall. Her key turned in the lock and she pushed the door open.

Getting the suitcase through the fairly narrow doorway was a bit of a struggle, but she managed it. There was a restroom on the right as she walked in, and she smiled as she spotted the tiny porthole in the far wall. A few steps into the room, she stopped and stared. There were four berths, although one of the top ones was folded up against the wall. The second top berth, however, was occupied.

"Hello?" she said cautiously, taking a step closer to the man. Standing on her tiptoes, she took a better look and then shuddered. The man was staring at the cabin's ceiling with lifeless eyes, a thick rope around his neck. There was no doubt in Fenella's mind that he was dead, and it looked as if he'd been strangled.

❦ 2 ❦

She tripped over her suitcase walking backwards as quickly as she could. Nearly falling to the floor, she caught herself by grabbing onto the ladder that was neatly hung on hooks near the door.

Oh, goodness, I've just left my fingerprints on the ladder, she thought to herself as she fumbled with the doorknob. Those same fingerprints would be all over the door as well, she realized, as she wrestled her case back into the corridor and pulled the door shut behind her. For a minute she simply stood in the corridor, breathing deeply. An elderly couple appeared at the top of the stairs and let themselves into one of the other cabins as Fenella tried to think. After several minutes, she realized that the ferry was getting ready to sail. That wasn't a good thing.

Her mobile phone was, as always, lost somewhere in the bottom of her bag. She found it with shaking hands and then punched in a number from her speed dial. The phone rang twice before a familiar voice spoke.

"Fenella? I thought you were sailing this morning," Daniel Robinson said in her ear.

Tears sprang into Fenella's eyes at his friendly tone. "Oh, I am," she replied. "But there's a dead man in my cabin."

The short pause that followed had Fenella picturing the man on the other end of the line. No doubt he was wondering if he'd heard her correctly. As a senior police inspector with the Douglas Constabulary, Daniel Robinson had seen his fair share of dead bodies, but Fenella doubted he was used to getting calls about them from his friends.

If they even were friends, she added to herself. The man was attractive, in his late forties, with light brown hair and gorgeous hazel eyes. He and Fenella were both fairly new arrivals to the island, and in the last few weeks they'd started spending the odd Friday or Saturday evening together at the Tale and Tail. Recently, Daniel had suggested that they exchange mobile numbers so that they could let one another know when they were going to be at the pub, but the relationship hadn't progressed beyond that point as yet. Fenella kept reminding herself that she was still getting over her last boyfriend, a man she'd been with for a great many years, but she really liked the handsome policeman.

"Are you sure he's dead?" Daniel asked after a moment.

"Quite sure," Fenella answered.

"I suppose you'd know," the man replied.

Fenella winced. She'd met Daniel over a different dead body only six weeks earlier and then encountered him again when she'd found a second dead man a few days later. If someone had told her before she moved to the island that she'd be finding three dead men in less than two months, she never would have believed them.

"Has the ferry sailed yet?" Daniel asked.

"I don't think so," Fenella replied. "I can't actually tell for sure from here, and I'd rather not go back into the cabin to look out the porthole. I can go downstairs, if you want me to."

"No, I'd like you to stay exactly where you are and make sure that no one goes in or out of that cabin. Do you think the man died of natural causes?"

Fenella could hear the hope in his voice. "Only if being strangled by a rope is now classified as a natural cause," she said tightly.

Daniel sighed. "Hold the line," he said. As Fenella stood in the corridor with her heart racing, she could hear the rumble of Daniel's voice as he spoke to someone else. Unable to make out the words, she tried to imagine what he might be saying. After a moment she shook her head. She really didn't want to think about what he might be saying about her, not now.

"Where are you exactly?" Daniel's voice startled her.

"In front of cabin 212," she replied.

"Are you alone?"

"Well, there isn't anyone else in the corridor at the moment," Fenella said. "I saw a couple going into one of the other cabins, though."

"What about the cabin you found the body in? Are you sure there wasn't anyone inside it? Maybe in the loo or the closet?"

Fenella gasped. "I don't know," she said after a moment. "I wasn't looking for anyone. I was just happy to get to my cabin. I was looking forward to sitting down and relaxing."

"Right, so there might be someone in the cabin," he said. Fenella got the feeling he wasn't actually speaking to her.

"Stay on the line with me," Daniel told her. "We've help on the way."

"I'm not going anywhere," Fenella said. "Although I'd quite like to go just about anywhere right now."

Daniel chuckled. "Hang in there. We're trying to stop the ferry from sailing."

Fenella sighed and leaned back against the wall. Another older couple emerged at the top of the stairs and let themselves into one of the neighboring cabins. The man gave Fenella a curious look, but the woman with him grabbed his arm and pulled him into their cabin.

"So, how was the pub last night?" Daniel asked a moment later.

"Oh, it was fine," Fenella said, feeling confused by the change of subject.

"Did Shelly and Peter both go with you?"

"They did, and we all missed you," Fenella said, knowing for certain that she'd missed the man, anyway.

"Duty called," he told her. "I had to cover for Inspector Harrison. Maybe next time."

"That would be good," Fenella said.

"May I have your attention, please," a voice came over the public address system. "Due to a security issue, our sailing for today has been delayed. We ask for your patience as we deal with the matter. The ship should be on its way within the hour."

"We're going to be on our way within the hour," Fenella told Daniel.

"Not if you're right about what you've found," he told her. "And I have no reason to doubt you."

"I'm not going to be very popular with the other passengers," she remarked.

"It isn't your fault," he said sternly. "Unless you killed the man, that is."

"Of course I didn't," Fenella snapped. "I don't even know who he is."

Another person appeared at the top of the stairs, and Fenella was pleased to see that it was a uniformed police constable this time. The man looked terribly young with his sandy brown hair and matching eyes.

"Good morning," he said politely.

"This simply won't do," a plump, dark-haired man in the ferry company's uniform said from behind the constable. "We need to get underway. This ship is due to get across and then back again today. We don't have time for this nonsense."

"Just give us a few minutes," the constable said in a soothing tone. "An inspector is on his way to investigate what was reported to us. Once he's had a chance to do that, we can work out what happens next."

"You have ten minutes and then we're sailing, with you and your inspector on board if need be," the man snapped. He spun on his heel and stomped off back down the corridor.

"He's not happy," the constable said to Fenella with a grin.

"Yes, well, I see his point," Fenella said. "If I hadn't found the body, I'd be eager to get underway as well."

"Are you talking to me?" Daniel asked in her ear.

"Oh, sorry, no. There's a constable here now," she explained.

"Excellent. I'm nearly there. Stay on the line, just in case, but you can chat with Constable Hopkins while you wait for me."

"You look quite pale," the constable said, looking concerned. "Are you okay?"

"Not really," Fenella admitted. "I don't think I'm a very good sailor."

"The ferry hasn't even left the dock yet," the man said. "It gets a good deal rougher from here. You should try some sickness tablets. My mum swears by them whenever we have to sail."

"Maybe I will," Fenella said. "I'm just glad I forgot to have any breakfast this morning."

The man nodded. "You're American, aren't you? What brings you to the island?"

"I was actually born here," Fenella replied, ready to tell the same story she felt like she'd told a hundred times since she'd arrived. "My family moved to the US when I was only a toddler and I grew up there. Recently, my aunt passed away and she left me her entire estate, including a lovely apartment right on Douglas promenade. I decided it was time for a major change in my life, so I quit my job, dumped my boyfriend, and moved everything I could carry over here to start again."

When she finished speaking, she blushed. She didn't usually blurt out all of those details all at once like that. Clearly finding a dead body had rattled her nerves.

"Your aunt? You aren't Mona Kelly's niece, are you?"

"I am," Fenella admitted, pretty sure she knew what was coming next.

"Ah, Mona was a character," he told her, repeating what everyone said about the woman. "She was larger than life, was Mona. I remember on one of my very first days on the job, I stopped her for speeding. She told me to ring the Chief Constable and ask him about the ticket. I was terrified, but she was very persuasive. In the end, I ripped up the ticket to get out of ringing the man."

Fenella laughed. "She certainly was a character," she agreed.

"A few days later I got a note from the Chief Constable," he added. "He told me to never worry about ringing him if I needed to, but that maybe I should just let Mona off with a warning if I ever stopped her again. I've heard her flat is the most luxurious in the whole of Promenade View Apartments."

"I don't know about that," Fenella said. "But it is very nice."

"So where were you going today?" the man asked.

Fenella opened her mouth to reply, but stopped when she heard voices on the stairs.

"You're wreaking havoc with our schedule." The ferry employee was back, this time with Daniel Robinson following behind him. "I must insist that you conduct this investigation with great speed and get off the ferry within the next ten to fifteen minutes."

"If this is a false alarm, we'll be happy to oblige," Daniel said. "If our witness did see what she thinks she saw, however, I'm afraid the ferry isn't going anywhere today."

"That's impossible. I'll ring the governor if I have to," the man snapped. He spun around and headed for the stairs. Just before he reached them, he turned back. "On second thought, I think I'll stay and see exactly what's going on here," he announced.

"Suit yourself," Daniel said. He looked over at Fenella and smiled. "You don't look like you're feeling very well," he said softly.

Fenella blushed. "I'm feeling a bit seasick," she admitted. "And upset." She nodded toward the cabin behind her and then shuddered as an image of the dead man flashed through her mind.

Daniel nodded. He slipped gloves onto his hands and then reached for the doorknob. "Who has the key?" he asked when the door wouldn't open.

Fenella reached into her pocket and found the key that she'd dropped into it earlier. She held it out and he frowned.

"I suppose your fingerprints are all over this," he said with a frown.

"Yes, and all over the door and the ladder inside," she said apologetically.

He raised an eyebrow but didn't ask any questions. Instead, he took the key and turned it carefully in the lock. Fenella leaned against the opposite wall as the inspector, the uniformed constable, and the man from the ferry company all made their way into the cabin.

"Oh, but he's..." the man from the ferry company exclaimed,

dashing out of the cabin. Fenella just got a glimpse of his pale face, with his hand covering his mouth, as he ran for the stairs.

Daniel wasn't far behind him. "I'm sorry, but you aren't going anywhere today," he said, his face grim. "And I'm going to have to ask you stay right here for a short while longer. It's going to take some time to get the people I need down here."

"I'm fine," Fenella lied. "You focus on your job and I'll work on not throwing up."

Daniel frowned and dug around in his pockets, eventually pulling out a small plastic bag. "It's an evidence bag," he explained as he handed it to her. "If you feel sick, try to get sick in there. It's the best I can do for now. The last thing we want is anything contaminating the crime scene."

Fenella nodded weakly and leaned back against the wall. Her head was starting to ache and if the headache turned into a migraine, she would be sick for sure. The third glass of wine from the night before seemed to be sloshing around in her stomach as she closed her eyes and tried to force herself to breathe steadily and slowly. Surely it wouldn't be too long before someone else from the police arrived. And once that happened, they would have to let her off the ferry, wouldn't they?

Although it felt like many hours passed with Fenella standing in the corridor, when she checked her watch as the police escorted her and the rest of the cabin passengers off the ferry, it had only been forty minutes since she'd rung Daniel.

"We'd like you all to please wait here," one of the uniformed men told the small group. "Inspector Robinson will be coming to take statements from you shortly."

"Statements? What sort of statements? What's going on, anyway?" a young woman demanded.

"The inspector will tell you whatever he can when he arrives," the man said. "I'm not authorized to say anything about anything."

Fenella sank into the first chair she came to and rested her head against the back, closing her eyes tightly. The world still seemed to be rocking back and forth slightly as she breathed in and out. When she opened her eyes, she could see the ferry, still bobbing gently in place.

While she watched, the cargo doors opened and a few cars began to emerge from the interior of the ship.

"Ms. Woods? Inspector Robinson would like to speak with you, please," Constable Hopkins said at her elbow.

Fenella blinked a few times and then stood up slowly. Feeling as if her legs were still trying to cope with the rocking of the boat, she stumbled as she followed the young man across the room. She could feel the eyes of all of the other cabin passengers on her as she went.

The constable led her through a door marked "Staff Only" which led to a short corridor. He stopped at the second door on the right and tapped lightly on it.

"Come in," a voice called.

The constable pushed the door open and then stepped back to let Fenella walk into the room.

"Ah, yes, right," Daniel said from a chair that was behind the cheap metal desk in the center of the room. "I'm just waiting for someone to find me a couple more chairs."

Fenella nodded and looked around the room. The walls were bare, and aside from a small and badly battered filing cabinet in one corner, the desk and Daniel's chair were the only things in the room. There were no windows, and the fluorescent bulb in the ceiling fixture flickered several times as they waited.

"It's a spare office," Daniel explained after a moment. "The ferry company isn't using it at the moment, so they said we could talk to sus, er, witnesses in here."

"You can say suspects," Fenella told him. "Having just been through this twice, I know I'm a suspect."

"Actually, you might not be," he replied. "We'll have to see what the coroner says about an estimated time of death, but the victim had certainly been dead for more than a few minutes when I arrived on the scene."

"And the killer wasn't hiding in the bathroom to make things easy for you?" Fenella asked.

"Unfortunately, no." Before he could continue, someone else tapped on the door.

"You needed chairs?" the tall man in the doorway asked.

"Yes, please, two if you can," Daniel replied.

The man nodded and then pushed the door open as far as it would go. He carried in two hard-looking plastic chairs and set them in front of the desk.

"Was there anything else?" he asked.

"No, that should be good for now," Daniel said. "Thank you."

The man shrugged and then turned and walked out of the small room.

"Have a seat," Daniel suggested to Fenella.

She sat down on the seat and wiggled around, trying to get comfortable.

"They aren't the nicest chairs I've ever seen," Daniel said sympathetically.

"They're less comfortable than they look," Fenella replied.

"I'm not sure that's possible."

"Oh, it is."

Daniel opened his mouth to speak again, but another knock interrupted him. "Come in," he called.

"You wanted me?" the man who stuck his head into the room asked.

"Yes, I do," Daniel said. "You'll take notes, please, while I interview people."

"Yes, sir," the man said smartly. "And how are you, Ms. Woods?" he added, smiling at Fenella.

"I'm fine, Constable Corlett," she replied to the young man. His dirty blond hair needed a trim and his green eyes looked tired. "I heard that the baby arrived. Is that right?" she asked.

She'd first met the man six weeks earlier, when she'd found a dead body in the alley behind her apartment building. At that time he'd been eagerly awaiting the arrival of his first child.

"Oh, aye, he has," the man replied. He reached into his pocket and pulled out his mobile phone. "I can show you a picture if you like," he said, glancing at the inspector.

"Oh, yes, please," Fenella said quickly.

Five minutes later Fenella had admired several dozen photos of the bald and toothless baby boy. She'd heard all about how he ate constantly, could hold up his own head for several seconds at a time and always greeted his father with a huge gummy smile at the end of the day.

"I mean, they aren't supposed to be smiling yet, you know? But he's going to be a smart one, our little Odin," the constable said.

"You've named him Odin?" Fenella asked, trying not to sound as surprised as she felt.

"Oh, aye, well, that was the wife's idea. She loves the whole history of the island and everything. She reckons she has Viking heritage, so she wanted to give him a Viking name," the man replied, flushing.

"It's very unusual, at least," Fenella said.

"It isn't really," the man told her. "At least not on the island at the moment. Viking names are all the rage. She goes to a mums' group and there's another Odin, an Orry and an Olaf there."

"Really? And probably no Fenellas," she said.

"I don't think so," the man replied. "Fenella is a rather old-fashioned name, really."

As opposed to Odin, Fenella thought but didn't say.

"I hate to interrupt," Daniel said. "But we really do have a case to work on."

Fenella flushed and the constable quickly slipped his phone back in his pocket. "Sorry, sir," he said quietly.

"It's fine," the inspector assured him. "I was waiting for a text anyway, but now I have it, so we can go ahead."

The constable sat down next to Fenella and pulled out a notebook. Daniel had a similar one on the desk in front of him already.

"Ms. Woods, we'll be taking notes and recording this interview, if that's okay with you," Daniel said formally.

"Of course it's fine. I'll do anything I can to help you get this case solved. You know that."

Daniel nodded. "All I need for right now is a statement from you about finding the body. If you could walk me through your day, please, starting with what time you woke up and going on from there."

Fenella sat back in her chair, wincing as the hard plastic pushed on her tailbone. She closed her eyes and tried to relax her mind. "I had my alarm set for six-thirty," she said after a moment. Without opening her eyes, she slowly took the two men through her day, from getting out of bed right up to looking at Constable Corlett's baby photos. When she was finished, she exhaled deeply, feeling as if a weight had been lifted from her for some reason.

When she opened her eyes, she watched as Daniel wrote something in his notebook. From where she was sitting, it looked as if Constable Corlett had filled several pages in his.

"Please take me through last night," Daniel said after a moment. "Maybe from six o'clock onwards?"

Fenella nodded and then told the men about the sandwich she'd had for dinner before her trip to the pub with Shelly and Peter.

"And you went home alone?" Daniel checked.

"All alone. Katie didn't even wait up," Fenella replied.

"You still have the cat, then?" Constable Corlett asked.

"I do. No one ever came looking for her," Fenella said. "I can't imagine why they didn't, but I've become quite fond of her since she strolled into my apartment and made herself at home."

"Are you quite certain you don't know who the victim was?" Daniel asked her.

"He didn't look familiar," Fenella replied. "But I only glanced at him and from a weird angle. It's possible I might know him, I suppose, but I don't know very many people on the island, really."

"What makes you think he was from the island?" Daniel asked.

Fenella frowned and thought for a minute. "I suppose I was just assuming that he was travelling from the island to Liverpool, the same as me. Surely the body can't have been there from a previous journey? The cleaning crew would have found it, if that was the case."

"We aren't ruling out anything at this stage," Daniel said. "You said that the woman at customer service told you that they have all sorts of staff training going on, getting ready for the busy summer season. From what I've been told, no one seems exactly sure who cleaned which cabin when this morning."

"Oh, dear," Fenella said softly.

He had her repeat the conversation she'd had with the woman at customer service a second time.

"She told you there was only one key to the cabin?" he checked.

"That's what she said," Fenella replied. "She blamed the cleaning staff for misplacing the second."

"Surely they have master keys," Constable Corlett said.

Daniel made another note in his notebook. "Did you happen to notice the customer service woman's name?" he asked.

Fenella thought back to the large and chaotic room where the desk had been located. She remembered seeing a nametag on the woman's jacket, but no matter how hard she tried, she couldn't recall what the tag said.

"Is it possible that it was blank?" she asked the inspector after a moment. "I know she was wearing a tag with the Isle of Man Ferries company logo on it, but I can't for the life of me picture any letters on it."

Daniel made another note. "Anything is possible," he said. "I'm sure once we've questioned all of the staff, we'll find her and her story will match yours," he said.

"Does someone have to question all of the passengers as well?" Fenella asked. "There must be hundreds of them."

"And they'll all be questioned, at least briefly," Daniel said. "We're hoping we can use the video footage of the ship being loaded to rule out most of the passengers, though. Most, if not all, of them boarded after the man was killed."

"Do you know who the man was?" Fenella asked.

"If I did, I couldn't tell you," he said. "But I don't, at least not yet. Once the crime scene team has taken all of their photos and gathered initial evidence, they'll search him for identification. I'm hoping he'll have his passport or driving license in his pocket, but that seems unlikely."

"He wasn't staff?" she wondered.

"He might have been. At this point, we don't know anything about him at all." Daniel finished the last few words on his feet. "As I said, I can't tell you anything anyway," he added as Fenella stood up. "And it's probably best if we don't socialize during the investigation. I'm sure you understand."

Fenella did understand, but that didn't stop her from feeling a pang of something she wasn't sure she wanted to identify. The look that flashed over Daniel's face looked suspiciously like relief to Fenella, which didn't help with the feeling in the pit of her stomach.

You're still seasick, she told herself as she followed Constable Corlett back down the corridor. That sad and slightly sick feeling is just a result of being rocked back and forth on that miserable boat for so long.

"If you could just wait here for a little while longer," the constable said to her as he ushered her back into the waiting room. "The inspector might have some more questions for you shortly."

Fenella thought about arguing. She'd answered all of the questions she'd been asked, and Daniel knew exactly where to find her if he needed to talk to her again. Knowing everyone else was watching her made her bite her tongue. She wasn't about to start arguing with a police constable in front of an audience of strangers. Instead, she nodded and made her way back over to the same chair she'd been sitting in earlier. Settling back, she shut her eyes again.

"I'm sorry that we're keeping you all waiting," the constable said loudly to the group. "Inspector Robinson will be talking to each one of you shortly. We greatly appreciate your patience as we begin our investigation."

"But what's happened?" a woman called out. "What's being investigated?"

"I'm sorry, but I can't answer any questions," the man replied. "The inspector will share what he can with you when he speaks to you."

"But..." the woman began again.

Constable Corlett held up a hand. "I really need to get back to work," he said. "Thank you for your patience."

He turned and walked out of the room, leaving an uncomfortable silence behind him. Fenella breathed deeply and tried to think about happy things. She was just contemplating buying Katie a new collar with sparkles and glitter when an angry voice shouted across the room.

"Hey, you've spent time with the police already," the man yelled, making the words sound like an accusation. "Tell us what's going on."

❧ 3 ❧

F enella sat up, startled. "I'm sorry, were you talking to me?" she asked.

"Yeah," the man replied. He stood up and Fenella got a good look at him. He didn't look much older than twenty in his torn jeans and slightly grubby sweatshirt. His dark brown hair looked like it needed washing. It hung in an untidy mop around his face, which also would have benefited from the application of some soap and water. A few stray whiskers dotted his chin and the top of his upper lip. "You must know what's going on. Come on, talk."

Fenella shook her head. "I'm sorry, but I really don't know anything and even if I did, I don't think I'm supposed to talk about it."

"You're American," the man said, spitting out the last word as if it were a curse.

"I grew up in America," Fenella corrected him. "But I was born on the island."

"I think that's quite enough bickering," a woman said from one of the other chairs. "We're stuck together for now. We should all get to know one another better."

People glanced around at the other occupants of the room and then resumed looking out windows or down at the floor. The woman who had spoken stood up and cleared her throat.

"I'll start," she announced. Fenella looked at the grey-haired woman. She must have been somewhere in her sixties. Her hair was short and her clothes were sensible and looked comfortable, but they were not stylish.

"I'm Charlotte Masters," the woman continued. "I retired last year and I try to travel as much as I can afford. Unfortunately, I'm a miserable sailor, so I always book a cabin and spend the entire journey lying down. You can go next," she said encouragingly to the young man who was still standing up at his seat.

"Me?" the man gulped. "I don't think..."

"Oh just indulge the woman," another woman called. "We've nothing else to do, after all. Sitting in silence isn't exactly enjoyable, is it?"

The man nodded and then shook his head, frowning. "Okay, whatever," he said eventually. "I'm Justin Newmarket. I'm twenty-four and I'm going to Liverpool to spend a weekend with some of my mates."

"Do you get seasick, dear?" Charlotte Masters asked. "Is that why you booked a cabin?"

The man turned scarlet. "No, of course not," he said indignantly. "I booked a cabin because, well, I was hoping, that is, I thought I might meet a young woman on board. I thought a cabin would give us a place to spend some quiet time together, if you know what I mean."

Fenella knew exactly what he meant and the idea made her feel slightly ill. Or maybe that was just seasickness. Suddenly very glad that she wasn't in her twenties anymore herself, she waited to see whom Charlotte would interrogate next.

"Right, next," Charlotte said, shifting her gaze to the woman who'd encouraged young Justin to speak.

"Oh, I'm Brenda Proper, and this is my husband, Nick," she said. Brenda was a plump woman with very short grey hair and thick glasses. Her husband was thin and bald. He was wearing reading glasses while he flipped his way through a newspaper he'd brought with him off the ferry. When his wife said his name, he glanced up and nodded briefly before returning to the paper.

"We're both retired," Brenda said. "We're going across to Manchester to visit my daughter and her husband and Nick's son. We were both married before, you see. We both have grown children from our first marriages."

"Which one of you gets sick on the ferry?" Charlotte asked.

Fenella wondered what the woman's fascination with other people's stomachs was all about. It seemed very odd to her.

"Oh, neither of us has a problem with sailing," Brenda replied. "We just prefer having peace and quiet for the journey. The lounges are always full of small children and loud teenagers. We like to have a space all to ourselves where we can just relax."

Charlotte nodded and then glanced around. Her gaze landed on another couple who were sitting together and holding hands. Fenella's first thought was that they were father and daughter. He was bald and pot-bellied and he reminded Fenella of her long-dead grandfather. The woman was much younger, probably in her mid-twenties, with long blonde hair caught in a simple ponytail. She was wearing a little dress that wasn't really appropriate for April.

"Oh, I'm Harry Hampton, and this is my wife, Sherry," the man said when he realized that everyone was staring at him. "We're just off across to visit some family, that's all. I'm not a great sailor, so I thought a cabin would be a good idea, even if they are quite expensive."

"Oh, Harry, they aren't at all," Sherry said. "I mean, really, you can afford it. I don't understand why you worry so much about every little expense. We've oodles of money in the bank."

"Thanks to many years of hard work by myself and my dearly departed first wife," Harry said tartly. "I'd rather not spend every penny of it in the first year of my retirement. It needs to last a good long time, you know."

The girl shrugged and then tossed her head. "Yes, dear," she said patronizingly.

Charlotte smiled tightly, perhaps beginning to regret ever starting the conversation. "Right, whom haven't we met?" she asked, looking around the room.

"I'm Sarah Grasso," a thirty-something woman who was sitting on her own said. Her brown hair was held back in a clip and her green eyes looked tired. Fenella thought she looked like someone who'd worked hard all of her life.

"My husband Robert and I are going across on a short holiday," she continued. "I can't imagine where he's disappeared to, though. He was meant to go straight to the ferry after work. He works nights. We were going to meet in our cabin when I arrived, but he wasn't there yet." She sighed. "He probably got held up at work and missed the boat. I suppose it doesn't really matter, as we aren't sailing anyway."

"Why book a cabin, if you don't mind my asking?" Charlotte said.

"Oh, we won the holiday in some prize draw at Robert's work," Sarah explained. "And the prize included a cabin for the sailing."

"How lucky for you," Charlotte said.

"Yes, we never win anything," Sarah said. "We were both thrilled."

"I'm Florence March, and this is Stanley, my husband," the last woman left introduced herself and the man with her. "We're both retired and our children are long since grown up and flown the nest. We were just taking a short break to do some shopping and dining out, that sort of thing. We always book a cabin. We have since the children were small and we needed to keep them where we could see them."

Fenella smiled at the woman. There was something about the pair that whispered "money" to her as she studied them. Maybe it was Florence's beautifully cut hair or impeccable makeup. Their clothes certainly looked as if they'd been expensive, but in a deliberately inconspicuous way.

"I suppose that just leaves our American friend," Charlotte said, turning to Fenella. "Tell us all about yourself," she urged Fenella.

Fenella opened her mouth to reply, but was interrupted when the door suddenly swung open.

"Where are the police?" the man now standing in the doorway demanded. "They can't do this. I simply won't allow it."

Everyone stared at the man. He was probably sixty, with grey hair that looked as if he'd been running his hands through it vigorously for hours. Fenella studied his uniform, which was that of the ferry company. From the looks of the various ribbons and braids, whoever he was, he was important.

"The police have simply left us here," Stanley March said after a long silence. "We haven't seen anyone for several minutes."

The man shook his head. "Unacceptable," he snapped.

"And who are you?" Charlotte Masters called out.

The man glared at her for a moment and then took a deep breath. "I'm so upset, I'm behaving badly," he said. "I do apologize. I realize none of this is your fault. I am Captain Matthew Howard. I'm in charge of the ferry that we've all just been escorted off of, and the police have no right..." he stopped suddenly, as his volume had been increasing dramatically.

"It certainly isn't our fault," Charlotte jumped in. "We're all suffering, too. I can't imagine what's happened to cause the sailing to be cancelled like this. It's simply appalling behavior by the police."

"I'm sorry you feel that way," Daniel Robinson said from the doorway on the opposite wall. Everyone had been so intent on Captain Howard that they hadn't noticed his arrival.

"Oh, I, that is, well," Charlotte said. "I do hope you've come to explain yourself and then let us all back on the ferry so we can get on with our day."

Daniel shook his head. "I'm awfully sorry, but that simply isn't possible yet," he said. "I will explain everything to you as quickly as I can, but investigations take time. For the moment, I'd like to have a word with Sarah Grosso, please."

The young woman blinked a few times and then stood up slowly. "With me?" she asked. "But I haven't done anything wrong."

"No one is suggesting that you have," Daniel assured her. "If you could come with me, please."

The woman nodded and then walked slowly toward Daniel, still looking uncertain. "If you could just tell me where Robert is, I'd feel better," she said when she reached Daniel's side. "He must be worried about me. I've rung his mobile a dozen times, but he isn't answering."

"If you could just come with me," Daniel repeated himself. "I'll try to answer your questions for you."

Sarah glanced back at the others in the room before following Daniel out through the door. As the door shut behind them, Fenella blew out a breath. There was no doubt in her mind that the body she'd found was that of the missing Robert Grosso. She didn't envy Daniel the job of telling poor Sarah that her husband was dead.

"Well, that was odd," Charlotte said. "I do hope Sarah isn't in any trouble."

"Do you know her?" Stanley March asked.

"I just met her now, when she introduced herself," Charlotte replied. "But she seems like a lovely young woman, so worried about her husband. I suppose, under these strange circumstances, that isn't surprising."

"Captain Howard, does this happen regularly?" Stanley asked.

"I've been sailing for over thirty years and this is the first time the police have had the audacity to interfere with a sailing. I'm not having it. I shall make sure that someone loses their job over this, see if I don't," the man replied.

"That suggests that something serious has happened," Stanley remarked. "Any idea what it could be?"

The man frowned. "It doesn't matter," he insisted. "We have our own security staff that can handle whatever arises."

"Drugs," Charlotte announced. "We all know the drug situation is getting out of control on the island. No doubt they found a huge stash of drugs on one of the container lorries."

"The ferry was leaving the island, not arriving," Nick Proper pointed out. "Or are you suggesting that someone is growing drugs here and exporting them to Liverpool?"

"Who knows what they're getting up to in the north of the island," Charlotte said. "I wouldn't be surprised if there were people growing all manner of substances up there. With the prison in Jurby, there's a steady supply of customers for them, as well."

"I hope you aren't suggesting that the men and women in prison in Jurby are being given access to illegal drugs," Stanley said.

"Well, as I understand it..." Charlotte began. She stopped when Stanley held up his hand.

"If it isn't drugs, what else might it be?" he asked.

"People trafficking," Charlotte suggested. "I was reading an article last week about just that. Young girls are being snatched right off the street and turned into sex slaves for wealthy Russian oligarchs. It's horrible. One of my friends, Susan, her daughter disappeared and the police didn't believe her that it was people trafficking. But when Chloe finally managed to get free and come home, she wasn't the same person at all. Oh, she told her mum that she'd run off with her boyfriend but it hadn't worked out, but I could tell that she was so traumatized by what had really happened that she'd made that story up."

"Did the boyfriend disappear too, at the same time?" Stanley asked.

Charlotte nodded. "He did. No doubt he was trafficked as well. They take boys, too, you know." She added the last sentence in a whisper.

"How old were they when this happened?" Florence asked.

"Oh, she was nineteen and he was twenty-two," Charlotte said.

"So rather older than the average age for someone trafficked," Captain Howard said. "I'd suggest her story about running away with her boyfriend was probably more likely."

"You seem to know a lot about people trafficking," Charlotte said, her tone accusatory.

The man nodded. "It's part of my job. It's highly unlikely that anyone is being taken from the Isle of Man to the United Kingdom or vice versa, but I used to sail on the Channel and I learned a lot there, none of it pleasant."

"If it wasn't drugs or people trafficking, what might have stopped the sailing?" Stanley asked.

"Murder," Charlotte said dramatically.

"Murder?" Captain Howard echoed. "I think that's highly unlikely. Perhaps some sort of accident where someone died is more likely."

"Would the police come to investigate an accident like this?" Stanley asked.

"Maybe," the captain shrugged. "It depends, I suppose, on what happened and how the police were notified. Whenever anything out of the ordinary happens on board, I'm meant to be notified first. Then I decide how to deal with the matter. I can only assume that whatever happened, someone rang the police directly and dragged them in without giving the proper procedures a single thought."

Fenella felt herself blushing at his words. He was absolutely right,

of course. She'd never even considered that there were "proper procedures" when finding a dead body on the ferry. If she hadn't known
Daniel Robinson personally, she might have reported what she'd found
to a member of the ferry's crew, though, which would have meant that
the captain would have been informed. And goodness knows how that
would have ended up, she thought. He didn't seem like the type to
want to have the police on his ship. And there was no way she'd want
to entrust a murder investigation to whatever security the ferry
company offered.

"Surely you've had accidents on board before," Stanley said. "The
police can't always stop a sailing just because of an accident."

The captain shrugged. "I once had a passenger have a heart
attack on a sailing across the Channel. There was an investigation
when we arrived in Calais, but his wife told us that he'd had heart
trouble for years. The police barely spent any time on the boat at all
that time."

He glanced out the window when he finished speaking. A huge
number of police cars were still visible, parked along the road leading
to the ferry. Clearly there was still a large police presence on the boat.

"I don't suppose there's any chance the ferry itself is the problem?"
Stanley asked. "All of its safety checks are up-to-date, are they?"

"Of course," the captain snapped. "I can assure you that the ferry is
perfectly safe and was ready to sail as scheduled. You won't be getting
any compensation from Isle of Man Ferries for the delay."

"Well, that remains to be seen," Stanley said.

"Oh, Stanley, do stop being a bother," his wife said. "I'm sure
everyone is doing their best to sort everything out as quickly as they
can. If even the captain doesn't know what's going on, the delay
certainly can't be the ferry company's fault."

Stanley opened his mouth to reply, but the door at the back of the
room swung open noisily. Daniel Robinson smiled tightly in the
doorway as he surveyed the group.

"Captain Howard, perhaps it would be best if we started with you,"
he said after what felt like several long minutes.

"And it's about time," the captain said crossly. "I don't appreciate
the way this has been dealt with at all. You can be quite certain that I

will be complaining to the Chief Constable and the Governor about your behavior."

"Yes, sir, that's certainly your right," Daniel replied calmly.

"And when will we be able to resume our trip?" Stanley called from his seat. "Florence and I have better places to be than this horrid little room."

Daniel nodded. "I do understand," he said. "I'll be speaking with each of you in turn and I hope to have everyone's full cooperation. Once I've spoken to you, you'll be free to go. I understand the ferry company is working on bringing in another ferry to cover while this one is temporarily out of service."

"So there is a problem with the ferry," Stanley said triumphantly.

"That's not what I said," Daniel replied. "At any rate, I believe Isle of Man Ferries is hoping to have everyone who still wants to sail on their way in another four hours or so. It will take that long to get another vessel here, and that gives me plenty of time for my questions."

"Four hours?" Stanley repeated. "That's totally unacceptable."

"Now, Stanley," Florence said, patting his arm. "Stop being silly. It isn't as if we have a choice. We'll wait and we'll be nice and patient, too." She addressed the last sentence to Daniel, who smiled gratefully at her.

"Thank you," he said. "I'll get started with my interviews, then."

He turned and walked out of the room with Captain Howard following behind him. As the door swung shut, Charlotte cleared her throat.

"I imagine there is something wrong with the ferry," she said loudly. "No matter what the captain tried to say about drugs and people trafficking, problems with the ferry seems the most likely thing, doesn't it? My friend Mabel told me that she heard that the safety inspections are only done about half as often as they're meant to be done. She heard that sometimes ferry captains bribe the inspectors to sign off on their inspections without even coming on board."

"I'm surprised you're prepared to sail with them, if that's the case," Justin said.

"Yes, well, I'm on a fixed income, you know. I can't afford to fly back and forth when I want to get across," the woman said stiffly. "But I always make sure I know where the lifeboats are as soon as I get on the vessel. I doubt most people bother. If we ever did have an emergency at sea, I'd probably end up alone in a lifeboat while everyone else drowned."

Maybe that would be preferable, Fenella thought to herself. She didn't want to try to imagine what it might be like to be stuck in a small boat adrift at sea with the woman she was finding increasingly unlikable.

"Oh, but you never told us about yourself," Charlotte said, turning to Fenella.

Disliking Charlotte even more, Fenella forced herself to smile. "I'm Fenella Woods," she said. "After living in the US for many years, I've recently taken a very early retirement and settled back in my ancestral homeland."

"Why?" Charlotte demanded.

"Oh, I, er, well, I, that is," Fenella stammered. She took a deep breath, trying to decide how much she wanted to share with this group of total strangers. "I came into a small inheritance," she said eventually.

"Lucky you," Justin said. "I keep hoping a convenient aunty will drop dead and leave me millions, but I haven't had any luck so far."

"I had no idea I was going to inherit anything," Fenella replied. "I had a full and happy life in the US before my aunt died."

"So why give that all up to come here?" Justin demanded. "I'd love to live in the US. I watch a lot of American telly and it looks amazing."

Fenella laughed. "It isn't all like on television," she said. "I was a professor at a large university and nothing exciting or glamorous ever happened to me."

"Well, I hope you didn't come over here hoping for excitement or glamor," Justin told her. "There isn't a more deadly dull place in the world than the Isle of Man. Nothing ever happens here."

"Except today you're caught up in a police investigation," Fenella pointed out.

"Yeah, it'll turn out to be a false alarm or something," he said dismissively. "Nothing ever happens here."

The door at the back of the room swung open again. Constable Hopkins walked into the room and looked around at everyone.

"I've been given a list of names for who is in here," he said loudly. "We're going to work our way through the list, one person at a time. The inspector would like to start with Harry Hampton, please."

Harry looked around, his face flushing. "I can wait, if you'd like to start with someone else," he said quickly.

"I'm sorry, sir, but the inspector asked for you first. If it makes you feel any better, I think he's simply going in alphabetical order," the constable replied.

"Oh, well, I mean, of course. I just thought some of the others might like to go first," Harry said. He stood up and looked down at his wife. "Hang in there, darling," he told her. "I won't be far away."

Sherry yawned and looked at her fingernails. As Harry walked out, he cast a nervous look back at her, but she was busy touching up her lipstick and didn't notice.

As soon as the door shut behind Harry and the constable, Justin moved over to sit next to the very pretty blonde. She frowned at him when he first sat down, but within minutes the two were having what looked like an intense conversation.

Charlotte sighed deeply, giving the young couple a disapproving look before glancing around the room. Fenella quickly looked out the window to avoid catching Charlotte's eye. She didn't approve of Justin's behavior either, but she wasn't about to let Charlotte know that.

"So, from whom did you inherit your fortune?" Charlotte asked after a moment.

"It's hardly a fortune," Fenella protested. "Just enough money to allow me to make a change in my life. I must say, so far I'm really enjoying the island. Castle Rushen is amazing and I'm looking forward to seeing Peel Castle and all of the other incredible historical sites."

"Castle Rushen is one of the finest medieval castles in the whole of the British Isles," Charlotte said. "We're lucky to have it and fortunate that it's been kept in such good repair over the years."

"It's a pile of old rocks that takes up far too much space in a crowded town," Stanley said. "They could flatten it tomorrow and build houses for first-time buyers. That would be a much better use of prime real estate."

Fenella nearly drew blood as she bit her tongue. This was not the time or the place to argue about the importance of historical properties. Charlotte didn't seem to agree.

"Flatten it?" Charlotte echoed, her voice angry. "What a preposterous notion. Do you have any idea of the historical significance of that building? Why it was built..." She was interrupted when the door at the back opened again.

Constable Hopkins stuck his head into the room and looked around. "If I could have Charlotte Masters, please," he said.

"I thought you were going in alphabetical order," Charlotte said as she stood up.

"Just following orders," the constable replied.

"Yes, well, this is highly irregular," Charlotte complained. "You should talk to Harry's wife next. She'll want to get back to him as quickly as possible."

The constable glanced over at Sherry Hampton, who was busy whispering something into Justin's ear. When she realized she was being watched, she moved a few inches away from the young man.

"We have friends in common," she said quickly.

"More like common friends," Charlotte muttered just loudly enough to be heard by everyone.

Sherry flushed, but didn't reply. Justin looked from Sherry to Charlotte and back again, an angry look on his face. When he opened his mouth to speak, Sherry shook her head. After a moment the constable broke the silence.

"Ms. Masters, if you'd like to follow me, please," he said, turning to go.

Charlotte shrugged and crossed the room, disapproval etched on her face. In the doorway, she turned and looked back at the others, staring for a moment at Sherry, before she walked away. The door banged shut behind her.

As it did so, it seemed to Fenella as if everyone let out a sigh of relief. She sat back in her chair and inhaled deeply. Perhaps under different circumstances, she might not have disliked Charlotte so much, but with visions of the dead man haunting her, she'd had a difficult time being polite to the nosy woman.

"Well, that's cleared the air," Justin said loudly.

The door swung open again, catching everyone by surprise.

"Ah, good afternoon," the young man in the doorway said. "I'm Constable Corlett. In an effort to get the questioning done more quickly, I'm going to start taking some preliminary statements from you each in turn. I'd like to start with Sherry Hampton, please."

"Oh, must you?" Sherry asked. "I'm quite enjoying relaxing in here. I'm certainly not in any hurry to get on another ferry."

The constable smiled. "The other ferry is still some hours away," he said. "But your husband is quite insistent that we talk to you and then let you both get on your way."

Sherry sighed deeply. "Harry is like that," she said, sounding tired. She rose to her feet and then bent back down to whisper something to Justin. He smiled and nodded at her. Fenella was sure that his eyes were glued to the woman's bottom as she swayed out of the room on incredibly high heels.

Apparently the police effort to speed things up was successful. It didn't seem very long at all before Constable Corlett was back to ask Nick Proper to join him, and Nick's wife, Brenda, followed soon after that.

No one left behind to wait seemed to want to make conversation, which suited Fenella. She sat back in her seat and tried to guess which one of the remaining people would be called for next. When she got tired of that game, she started wondering if any of the people she'd met in this waiting room had actually killed the victim. That got her exactly nowhere, so she thought about Robert Grosso instead. He was the only person that she could imagine as the victim, which proved nothing at all, but gave her something to consider. Poor Sarah would be devastated if Fenella was right.

"Justin Newmarket?" Constable Hopkins asked from the doorway.

"Oh, yeah, that's me," the young man said. He rose to his feet and quickly walked to the doorway. "Bad news for you lot, I suppose," he said with an obnoxious smile. "You're stuck waiting even longer."

He turned and walked away, following the constable down the

corridor. The door banged shut behind him, leaving Fenella alone with only Stanley and Florence March for company.

"We'd better be next," Stanley said crossly after a moment.

"It's fine," Florence said softly. "The police are just doing their job, after all."

"Harassing innocent civilians isn't their job," Stanley snapped. "Whatever has gone wrong on that damn ferry, it's nothing to do with us."

"Yes, dear," Florence said.

When the door opened again several minutes later, Constable Corlett smiled at them all. "If I could have Florence March, please," he said.

"Oh, no, you aren't talking to my wife without me being there," Stanley said. He rose to his feet. "And depending on what's going on, I might want an advocate as well."

The constable smiled. "Of course, sir," he said patiently. "Why don't you ring your advocate while I arrange transportation."

"What sort of transportation?" Stanley demanded.

"Transportation down to our Douglas station," the constable explained. "We've only just borrowed a tiny office here, and there's no way we can accommodate both you and your wife and an advocate in that space. We have much larger rooms at the station. Have your advocate meet us there in half an hour or so."

"That's absurd," the man shouted. "I won't be treated like this."

"I'm trying to accommodate you," the constable said patiently.

"You can interview us in here," Stanley said. "There's plenty of room for us and our advocate."

"I'm afraid Isle of Man Ferries needs this space back as soon as possible," the constable told him. "They have customers to accommodate."

"Oh, Stanley, do stop being silly," Florence interjected. "I'll go and answer all of the man's questions, and then you can have your turn and we can be on our way. Let's not drag things out any longer."

"I don't want you alone with that police inspector," Stanley said.

"Why ever not?" Florence demanded. "What are you afraid I'm going to tell him?"

Stanley flushed. "I'm your husband," he said. "It's my job to look after you in difficult situations."

"You're the one making this difficult," Florence retorted. "Let me go see what this is all about. If I feel like I'm in over my head, I can always refuse to say anything further without my advocate."

Stanley looked like he wanted to argue more, but after a moment he sat back down. "Just watch out for tricks," he told his wife. "If you aren't careful, you'll end up confessing to all manner of things."

"I'm not a small child," Florence replied. "I think I can answer a few questions without getting flustered enough to confess to anything."

On that she walked away, through the door and down the corridor. Stanley watched her go, his face a picture of misery. The door had barely closed behind Florence when it swung open again. This time Constable Hopkins pushed it open.

"Ah, Stanley March? We're ready for you," he announced.

"About bloody time," Stanley muttered loudly. He crossed the room in only a handful of steps and swept out, leaving the constable to follow him.

As the door shut yet again, Fenella sat back in her seat and swallowed hard. Suddenly alone, she felt sad and a little bit lonely. She could only hope that Daniel would get to her before too much longer.

❧ 4 ❧

With nothing else to do, Fenella watched the clock as the hands moved slowly around the face. She had her bag with the books she'd packed for her journey, but for once reading didn't appeal. Twenty-six minutes and fourteen seconds after he'd left with Stanley March, Constable Hopkins was back.

"Ah, thank you so much for waiting patiently," he said to Fenella. "Inspector Robinson is ready to see you again now."

Fenella walked down the short corridor behind the constable, pulling her suitcase. She was eager to get the meeting over with and get home. The door to the office Daniel was using was ajar. Daniel was sitting behind the desk, taking notes in one of his ever-present notebooks, when the constable knocked and then pushed the door open.

"Hello, Fenella," Daniel said. He smiled at her when he looked up.

"You look tired," she said as she sat down in the chair he'd indicated. Constable Hopkins slid into the second chair behind the desk.

"I am tired," the inspector admitted. "Many of our witnesses have been less than cooperative, which doesn't help."

"They were an odd group of people," Fenella said. "I won't mind if I never see any of them again."

Daniel smiled. "I expect I'll be seeing them all again, but anyway, let's get down to business."

Fenella sat up straighter in her chair and folded her hands in her lap, suddenly feeling like she'd been called before the dean of her department after a student complaint or something.

"We've identified the body," he told her.

"Robert Grosso," Fenella guessed.

"I should have left an officer with you in that waiting room," Daniel said. "I wasn't worried about everyone talking together, as you were the only one who knew about the body and I knew you wouldn't mention it. I didn't think about Sarah Grosso talking about her missing husband."

"So it was him?" Fenella confirmed.

"Yes, it was. His wife positively identified the body for us," Daniel replied.

"That poor woman," Fenella said. "She was worried about him and so happy to be having a vacation with him."

"Yes, we're checking into that," Daniel said. "I have to ask whether you had ever met or even seen either him or his wife prior to today?"

"No, I don't think so," Fenella replied. "I don't know what he did for a living, or what his wife does for that matter. It's possible I might have come across one or the other of them in a shop or restaurant or something, but neither looked familiar."

"Sarah Grosso is a nurse at Noble's," Daniel said.

"Well, fortunately I haven't had to visit the local hospital, yet," Fenella said. "What did Robert do?"

"He worked for an import and export business," Daniel said. "That meant that he travelled a great deal, both by ferry and by plane."

"So, no, I doubt very much I'd ever seen them and I know I'd never met either of them," Fenella said.

"And you didn't see Sarah Grosso on the ferry at any point?" Daniel asked.

Fenella tried to think. "Give me a minute," she requested. She shut her eyes and sat back, mentally walking back through her morning. "I'm sorry," she said eventually. "I simply wasn't paying that much attention. I don't think I saw her, but there were a lot of people rushing around every which way. I think the only person I actually remember seeing is the girl who was behind the customer service desk, and I'm not one hundred percent certain I could pick her out of a lineup."

Daniel nodded. "Sarah was a car passenger, so she wouldn't have been waiting with you inside the terminal. I assume you don't remember seeing any of the other cabin passengers before you found the body?"

Fenella shook her head. "They were probably all behind me in the line at customer service, but I felt so bad about how long it took for the woman to give me the key to my cabin that I sort of slunk away without looking back."

"And you'd never met any of them before today?" Daniel asked.

"No, I hadn't. And as I said, I won't be in a rush to see them again."

"You mentioned seeing two different couples in the corridor after you found the body," Daniel said.

"Yes, and now I can tell you that they were Nick and Brenda Proper and Stanley and Florence March, thanks to the round of introductions that Charlotte Masters had us go through."

"Was anything said in the waiting room while you and the other cabin passengers were waiting that you think might be relevant to our investigation?" was the next question.

"Charlotte had us all introduce ourselves," Fenella told him. "That was about it, really."

"Just introductions?" he pressed.

"Once Captain Howard arrived there was a discussion about why the ferry had been stopped from sailing," Fenella recalled. "Stanley March in particular seemed to want answers as to what might have caused the delay."

"And what answers did anyone come up with?"

"Charlotte was the only one who offered any ideas. She suggested drugs, people trafficking, and murder as the most likely explanations."

Daniel made a few notes. "And what did everyone else think?"

"Mostly it seemed like they thought she was being overly dramatic. Stanley seemed to think the problem was with the ferry itself."

"Isle of Man Ferries is bringing in another ferry. All scheduled passengers will be permitted to travel later today, if they so desire," Daniel told her. "I'd like to ask you to postpone your journey for a few days, if you don't mind, however."

"I don't mind," Fenella said emphatically. "I'm in no rush to get on another boat, that's for sure. I might have to look into flying instead."

"Under the circumstances, you'll be able to get a full refund from the ferry company if you choose not to travel," he told her. "They're being as cooperative as they can be, all things considered."

"Do you have a particular reason for suspecting the cabin passengers?" Fenella asked. "I mean, your questions have focused on them."

"Right now we have to consider every person who was on the boat as a suspect," Daniel replied. "We don't have enough evidence of anything to force anyone to stay on the island while we investigate, unfortunately. I do suspect that the killer was most likely another cabin passenger, but at this point that's little more than one possible scenario."

"It seems impossible," Fenella said. "There were so many people on the ferry, between passengers and staff. How will you ever sort through them all?"

"It won't be easy, but it's my job," Daniel replied. "In a case like this we'll have to start with motive and work from there, I think, considering how many people may have had the opportunity."

"Sarah Grosso seemed like such an ordinary person," Fenella said. "I can't imagine why anyone would want to kill her husband."

"That's the question we need to answer," Daniel replied. "And that's why I have to be on my way. At this point in time, I know next to nothing about Robert Grosso. By the time I go to bed tonight, I need to know him as well as his best friend does."

Fenella nodded. "I don't envy you the job," she said.

Daniel stood up. "I may have more questions for you as the investigation continues," he said. "That's why I asked you not to travel. I'll be in touch."

Fenella only had time to nod before Daniel swept out of the room. She looked over at Constable Hopkins. "I guess I can go home, then," she said.

"You can," he confirmed. "I'll take you, if you don't have a car here."

"I don't. I was a foot passenger. But I walked here and I can walk home just as easily."

He shook his head. "I'd rather give you a ride, if you don't mind," he said. "You don't want to have to walk through the pack of reporters who have gathered outside."

"There are reporters outside?" she asked.

"The police stopping a ferry from sailing is big news," he told her as they both got to their feet. "And Inspector Robinson has refused to answer any questions all morning. They're probably getting frustrated by now."

"I'm surprised no one has told them what's going on," Fenella said. She pulled up the handle on her suitcase for what felt like the hundredth time that day. "There are so many people who were supposed to be on the ferry. Surely one or two of them must have been willing to talk to the press after their police interview."

"I understand that most of them are still in the building," the constable told her as he escorted her out of the room. He took the suitcase from her before he continued. "Isle of Man Ferries has been providing food and drinks to everyone who is waiting for the replacement ferry, which has encouraged many people to simply stay here and wait. I understand they're showing movies in one of the waiting areas as well."

"They are being helpful, aren't they," Fenella remarked.

"They want their ferry back as soon as possible," the constable said. "I'm sure they were hoping we would wrap this all up within an hour or two."

"I didn't get the impression from Daniel that you were anywhere near wrapping things up," Fenella said.

"Inspector Robinson is doing everything he can, but short of an unexpected confession, the investigation will take time," he replied.

While they'd been talking, the constable had led her through the Sea Terminal and out a door at the back that led to a small parking lot.

"This one is mine," he said as he stopped next to a small car that was at the end of a row. He unlocked the car and put her bag in the back before he held the passenger door open for Fenella. She slid inside, and once she'd fastened her seatbelt, the constable pushed the door shut.

"You weren't kidding about the press," Fenella said a moment later as the constable steered the car through the lot and out toward the main road. What looked like several dozen people were clustered in front of the Sea Terminal building, taking pictures and talking on mobile phones. As the police car drew near them, a few people broke away from the group and began to walk toward the car.

"Sorry about the noise," Constable Hopkins said as he pressed a button on the dashboard. The wail of a police siren cut through the air and caused the approaching men to take a few steps backwards. Traffic on the main road came to a halt because of the sound, allowing the constable to slide into traffic easily.

"If I had that, I'd use it all the time," Fenella said as the man drove sedately down the promenade toward Fenella's apartment building.

"The rules about using it are pretty strict," he told her. "But that was all about protecting a witness from potential press harassment."

"For which I'm hugely grateful," Fenella assured him. "I certainly didn't want to talk to them."

"Inspector Robinson doesn't either, but he's going to have a press conference in a few hours anyway," the man said.

"Poor Daniel," Fenella remarked.

"It comes with the job," the constable shrugged. "That's part of why I'm not in any hurry to move up to inspector."

Fenella smiled. "It's such a difficult job, any job in the police. I'm sure the rest of us aren't nearly as grateful to you all as we should be."

"Here we are," the man said as he pulled to a stop in front of Promenade View Apartments. He stopped the car and switched off the engine. Before he climbed out, he put a "Police" sign on the dashboard.

"If I had one of those, I'd abuse that, too," Fenella said, pointing to the sign that was letting the man park illegally.

"Again, there are rules," the man replied. "But in this case, Inspector Robinson instructed me to escort you to your flat, so I'm covered."

"That really isn't necessary," Fenella said as she watched the man drag her suitcase out of the back of the car.

"He's the boss," the man retorted. "You can argue with him about it, if you want."

"I will, the next time I see him," Fenella replied.

The man nodded, and then Fenella led him across the lobby and into a conveniently open elevator. While they rode up, she dug her keycard out of her bag. It felt odd to be walking back toward her own apartment again so soon, but Fenella felt tired, sad, and eager to get home.

"This is me," she said as she stopped at her door. She waved the key in front of the lock and then pushed the door open. The constable followed her through the door, still dragging her suitcase behind him.

"Oh, you can just leave that anywhere," Fenella said.

"What on earth?" Mona gasped, getting up from the couch with a surprised look on her face.

Fenella opened her mouth to reply and then quickly bit her tongue. Constable Hopkins couldn't see Mona. He would think Fenella was crazy if she started talking to her.

"Are you okay?" the young man asked, glancing around the large room with its floor-to-ceiling windows that looked out at the sea.

"I'm fine," Fenella assured him. "I'll have to reschedule my trip at some point, but for now I'm ever so glad to be home."

The man nodded. "I'll get out of your way, then," he said cheerfully. At the door, he stopped and reached into his pocket. "Here's my card. Please don't hesitate to ring me if you need anything."

"That's very kind of you," Fenella replied. "I hope I never have an occasion to use it, though."

The man nodded. "No one ever wants to need me," he said. "I'm good with that."

Fenella chuckled as she let the man out, quickly locking the door behind him as he disappeared down the corridor.

"What are you doing back here?" Mona demanded as soon as the door was shut.

"I must call Edward and tell him I'm not coming," Fenella said, holding up a hand to stop Mona's questions.

There was no one home at Edward's house, so Fenella left a message on the answering machine, simply saying that the ferry had been cancelled and that she'd be in touch when she'd made other arrangements. With that out of the way, she sank into a chair and sighed deeply.

"What's happened?" Mona asked, sitting down next to Fenella.

"I found another body," Fenella said after a moment.

"You what?" Mona asked.

"I found another body. When I went to my cabin, there was a dead man in one of the berths. He had a rope around his neck. I called Daniel and he came and cancelled the sailing. I'd have been back a long time ago, but I had to wait to be questioned."

"This is getting to be a rather unpleasant habit for you," Mona said sharply.

"It isn't my fault," Fenella snapped back. "The cabin I was supposed to be in had some sort of plumbing issue or something. The girl at customer service just assigned me to a random cabin. It's hardly my fault that someone had hidden a dead body in there."

"So the man wasn't killed there? He was just hidden there?" Mona asked.

"I have no idea," Fenella replied. "And I don't want to talk about it, either."

"Surely you've been talking about it all day," Mona said. "It won't hurt for you to tell the story one more time."

"I'm going to get Katie," Fenella told her aunt. "She won't want to hear all of the morbid details. She'll just be happy to see me."

"But Shelly will want all of the details," Mona said. "At least ring her and have her bring Katie here. Then you can tell both of us what happened at the same time."

Fenella shook her head. "How rude is that? Calling her up and asking her to bring me my cat back? I shall go and get Katie. You can listen in the doorway if you must."

Mona sniffed. "Eavesdrop? How tacky."

"Suit yourself," Fenella replied. She walked to the door and unlocked it, deliberately leaving it ajar as she walked the short distance to Shelly's door. When no one answered, she was hugely disappointed.

"Is no one home?" Mona asked when Fenella walked back into her own apartment a moment later. The woman was sitting on the couch, but Fenella reckoned she looked as if she'd rushed to get there after having been listening at the door a moment earlier.

"I have her spare key, but it would be wrong to let myself in just to get Katie. I'll have to wait until she gets home," Fenella said, annoyed with herself when she heard how sad she sounded.

"I'm sure Katie will survive for a few more hours without you," Mona said. "And while we wait, you can tell me about the body you found."

Fenella sighed. "You aren't going to leave me alone until I tell you, are you?" she asked.

"If you want me to, of course I'll leave you alone," Mona replied. "You know I don't want to be a bother."

Before Fenella could reply, Mona slowly faded away. Fenella dropped into the nearest chair and put her head in her hands. This day was not going at all the way she'd planned and she felt like screaming, crying, and eating chocolate, not necessarily in that order. After a minute, when tears didn't come and shouting felt less appealing, Fenella headed for the kitchen.

As she poked around in her cupboards, she realized that she hadn't had anything to eat all day and it was nearly three o'clock in the afternoon. She also realized that she'd cleared most of the food out of the apartment in anticipation of being away for a week. With a sigh, she pulled a box of chocolate-covered cookies out of a cupboard and opened it. For several minutes, she nibbled mindlessly on one after another, taking comfort in their sugary sweetness.

"Shelly, it's Fenella. The ferry was cancelled. I'll explain when I see you, but basically I'm not going anywhere for a while. I can get Katie back from you when you get this message," she said into Shelly's answering machine a short time later. She needed to go grocery shopping, but she couldn't muster up the energy. Too full of cookies to really care at the moment, she decided she could get pizza delivered later and deal with her shopping needs another day.

She was reconsidering that decision a while later as she pottered around her apartment. She couldn't seem to find anything to do.

Reading didn't appeal, there was nothing to watch on the television, and she didn't want to go out. Sighing deeply, she glared at her reflection in the mirror in her bedroom.

"You should have just told Mona the whole story," she said to her mirror image. "Maybe retelling it would have chased it out of your head."

When her doorbell rang a short time later, Fenella couldn't answer it fast enough. Even a life insurance salesman would be welcome at the moment, she thought as she turned the knob and pulled the door open.

"Are you sure you don't just want me to keep her?" Shelly asked as she held Katie out to Fenella.

"Oh, quite sure," Fenella said. She took the animal from Shelly and buried her face in Katie's back. The kitten squirmed as Fenella burst into tears.

"Oh, good heavens," Shelly exclaimed. "Are you okay?"

Fenella nodded and then shook her head while Shelly gently pushed her backwards into the apartment. Shelly shut the door behind herself and then pulled Fenella over to the couch.

"Sit down and tell me what this is all about," Shelly instructed Fenella as they sat down next to each other.

Katie let out a soft "meow" that interrupted Fenella's tears.

"I shouldn't cry all over you, should I?" Fenella asked the kitten.

"Merrooww," Katie replied. Fenella smiled in spite of herself and gave Katie a hug. "Off you go, then," she said, putting Katie on the floor.

The kitten ran off, straight to the kitchen. Fenella had already filled the water and food dishes in anticipation of Katie's return.

"Now, what's happened?" Shelly asked, taking Fenella's hand.

"I found a body," Fenella said. She took a deep breath and shook her head. "I didn't mean to just blurt that out," she added as Shelly gasped and stared at her.

"You poor thing," Shelly said after a moment. "After last month, I thought you'd found your body quota for the rest of your life."

"Yeah, me too," Fenella told her. "I mean, I'm nearly fifty and I'd never found a dead body, ever. Finding two in less than a week was pretty traumatic, but I was feeling like I was getting over it. I can't really get my head around the idea that I found another one."

"Was it a man or a woman?" Shelly asked.

"A man."

"And had he had a heart attack or something?"

Fenella shook her head. "He was strangled," she whispered.

Shelly looked shocked as she sat back in her seat. "How awful," she said.

"It really was," Fenella agreed.

"Who was he?"

Fenella wondered for a moment if she was allowed to say, but she knew she could trust Shelly not to repeat what she was told. Anyway, Daniel was having a press conference soon. Surely he'd tell everyone the dead man's identity. "His name was Robert Grosso," she told Shelly. "Daniel said something about him working in imports and exports, whatever that means."

"It can mean everything from being the owner of a huge multinational trading company to smuggling," Shelly told her with a wry grin. "If the man ended up dead, maybe he was more towards the smuggling end of things."

"Would it be wrong of me to hope he was involved in something criminal?" Fenella asked. "Only it seems like that would be easy for Daniel to discover; it gives someone a good solid motive, and maybe it means they'll be able to find the killer very quickly."

"How old did he look?" Shelly asked.

"Oh, I haven't any idea," Fenella replied. "He was lying on the top berth, and his face was all purple and," she stopped and shuddered. After a deep breath, she continued. "His wife looked to be in her mid-thirties, anyway."

"He had a wife? Oh dear, the poor woman. Unless she killed him, of course. Did she seem devastated?"

"When I saw her, she was still wondering what had happened to the man," Fenella explained. "They were supposed to be having a short vacation, I gather, but as far as she knew at that point, he'd never turned up for the ferry."

"That's sad," Shelly said. "They were planning a holiday together and now she has to plan a funeral instead."

Fenella surprised them both by bursting into tears again. Shelly jumped up and found a box of tissues, handing them to Fenella as she tried to get herself under control.

"I'm sorry," she said eventually. "It just sounded so sad when you put it that way."

"I'm an idiot," Shelly told her. "I knew you were upset. I should be changing the subject and talking about the weather or politics or something."

Fenella shook her head. "I think I need to talk to someone about it," she said. "My brain won't settle and I felt a little crazy before you got here."

"Well, talk away," Shelly urged her. "I won't ask any more questions, but I'm happy to listen if you want to tell me anything."

"There was a problem with my cabin assignment," Fenella said after a moment. Some considerable time later she'd taken Shelly through her entire morning, from boarding the ferry to her last conversation with Daniel Robinson. "So that's what happened," she said, blowing out a long breath. "And you must be bored to pieces. I am sorry."

"I'm fascinated," Shelly corrected her. "Possibly more so because I know a few of the people in the story."

"Really? Which ones?"

"Justin Newmarket, for a start," Shelly replied. "Although I haven't seen him in years, I had him in school when he was younger." Shelly had been a teacher before she retired.

"What was he like?" Fenella asked.

"Oh, disagreeable," Shelly replied, laughing. "I would never have admitted that at the time, of course, and if you repeat it to anyone I will deny saying it, but he wasn't a very nice child."

"In what way?"

"He was mostly just lazy," Shelly said after a moment's thought. "He didn't want to do any of the work, but he still expected high marks. I tried to tell him that he needed to study for his exams, but he seemed to think that his natural abilities would see him safely through."

"And did they?"

Shelly chuckled. "Well, he passed everything, but only just barely.

He was planning on some sort of technical school after his exams, but I don't think he ended up getting a place there. I'm sure his marks weren't strong enough, although I do remember his mother coming to the school and attempting to argue with the head about them. She seemed to think that we should be able to change all of his grades to whatever it was he needed to get accepted to the school. I recall her being very upset when she was told that wasn't going to happen."

"Parents who do that sort of thing aren't really doing their children any favors," Fenella remarked. "We saw them at my university all the time. The parents would pull strings or argue with high school teachers to get their kids the grades they needed to get into the university, but once the kids were there, on their own, they couldn't handle the workload, or the pressure, or the freedom. Often they couldn't cope with all three. Of course, then the parents would be in our offices, arguing with us to raise their child's grades again."

Shelly shook her head. "Maybe I'm glad I never had children," she said.

"Children aren't the problem," Fenella said dryly. "It's the parents who cause all of the trouble."

Shelly laughed. "Anyway, Justin was never a favorite of mine, but I am sorry to see him tied up in a murder investigation."

"You don't think he could have had anything to do with it?"

"I doubt it," Shelly replied. "Killing someone takes effort, and I can't see Justin bothering, quite frankly."

"Who else do you know, then?" Fenella asked.

"I'm not sure, but I think I know Sherry Hampton," Shelly said. "She was another student of mine, if I'm thinking of the right person. She was Sherry Kelly in those days, though, but I do remember hearing that she'd married a much older man for his money."

"Which is deeply unpleasant."

"Yes, but I do think most women who marry for money end up having to earn it," Shelly replied. "Unless their dear hubby dies right after the wedding, of course."

"Harry Hampton didn't look as if he is going to be dying any time soon," Fenella told her.

"Then Sherry will probably have to work hard to keep him happy.

From what you said, they didn't seem to be getting along terribly well."

"No, they weren't. She did seem to enjoy Justin's company, though."

"They'll have been in school together," Shelly remarked. "Although they aren't the exact same age and they probably didn't have any classes together, they'll still have probably known each other."

Katie walked back into the room and jumped up on the couch next to Fenella, who was more than happy to give her a cuddle and scratch behind her ears.

"So what are you going to do about your trip?" Shelly asked.

"I don't know," Fenella told her. "I have to admit that I hated the ferry and it made me feel quite sick. I think I might have to look into flying instead, although I hate to spend the extra money."

"You should pop down to the chemist and get some tablets," Shelly told her. "They'll settle your stomach for you, no problem."

"Really?"

"Yeah, I take them whenever I have to sail. They do a great job, as long as it's a reasonably smooth crossing. If you have a cabin and can lie down, you should be fine, even if it isn't the smoothest."

"I told Daniel that I wouldn't go anywhere for now," she told her friend. "I'll have to think about what I want to do, but for now I'm quite happy back at home."

"But you haven't any food in the house, have you?" Shelly asked. "Would you like me to drive you to the grocery shop so you can do some shopping?"

Fenella didn't really feel like shopping. She really wanted to curl up in a ball with Katie and cry. But she needed food, and the offer of a ride was too good to pass up. Being afraid to try driving Mona's fancy sports car, she nearly always walked to the nearest grocery store to get what she needed.

"Are you sure?" Fenella asked.

"Of course I'm sure. While we're there, we'll get the ingredients for my world-famous cottage pie, and then when we get back here, I'll whip that up for us both for dinner. We can get a nice bottle of red wine to go with it and something chocolate for pudding."

Fenella felt tears welling up in her eyes. "That sounds wonderful," she said after she'd swallowed hard.

S helly went back to her apartment to get her keys and handbag while Fenella quickly got ready to go out.

"I've decided to be gracious and not hold it against you," Mona said as Fenella walked through the living room on her way to the door.

"What?"

Mona sighed. "My dear, 'pardon' sounds so much better than 'what,' don't you think?"

Fenella blinked at her, feeling as if she'd wandered into the middle of the conversation somehow. "I'm sorry, but what are you talking about?"

Mona shook her head. "Never mind. The important thing is that I'm not going to get angry with you for refusing to tell me what happened and then telling Shelly all about it," she explained. "Even though I am a bit, well, hurt."

"I didn't mean to hurt your feelings," Fenella said. "But I really didn't want to talk about it. I only told Shelly because I had to explain why I was back for Katie so early, that's all."

"Yes, well, you go and get some shopping in. We can talk about it later."

"Sure, yeah, whatever," Fenella muttered. She had no intention of discussing the murder with Mona, or anyone else for that matter, aside from Daniel, and then only when she absolutely had to.

The grocery store felt crowded to Fenella as she made her way through the aisles. She was sure it was just because she was feeling the tiniest bit overwhelmed by everything that had happened that day. She filled her cart with far more than she needed, adding bags of salty snacks and several different varieties of chocolate cookies to the real food, like chicken and rice.

"Oh, my, it's Fenella, isn't it?" someone asked as she was studying the pastries.

She turned her head and forced herself to smile as she recognized Nick and Brenda Proper. "Hello. This is a surprise," she said.

"And not a pleasant one," Nick muttered. "Oh, no offense, but I was hoping to never see anyone from this morning ever again. I've rarely passed a more unpleasant morning anywhere and I'd quite like to put it right out of my head."

"It wasn't that bad," Brenda said, smiling brightly at Fenella. "And anyway, that Charlotte Masters was the main problem. Fancy making us all talk about ourselves like that. I suppose you have the same problem we do now." She glanced into Fenella's shopping cart. "We've no food in our house, either, so we had to rush down here to stock up."

"Yes, I cleared out everything in anticipation of being away," Fenella agreed. "I was offered a spot on the replacement ferry, but I really just wanted to go home."

"Maybe we shouldn't talk about that," Brenda said, glancing sideways at her husband.

"Why not?" Nick demanded. "I don't mind people knowing that you turned down the replacement ferry in favor of completely rescheduling everyone's lives for the next two months."

Brenda flushed. "When I heard that a young man was murdered, well, I felt quite unwell. I thought I might faint, if I'm honest. There was no way I was capable of continuing with our plans at that point."

"I understand," Fenella said. "The whole thing is very upsetting."

"Yes, and his wife seemed so lovely," the woman replied. "She was happy about their holiday and so worried about her husband. I have to say, I did wonder if he'd been in an accident or something when she was saying she didn't know where he was, but I never imagined that he'd been murdered. Did you?"

"I don't think anyone ever expects to hear that someone has been murdered," Fenella said, avoiding giving a direct answer.

"This is the first time I've ever known anyone who's been murdered," Brenda said.

"Except we didn't know him," Nick growled.

"Well, I mean, it's the first time we've been involved in a murder investigation," Brenda corrected herself.

"Except we aren't actually involved," he retorted.

"We're witnesses," Brenda replied.

"To what?" he snapped.

"Well, we must be witnesses to something, or the police wouldn't have kept us all morning, would they?" Brenda argued. She looked over at Fenella. "I was wondering if that Masters woman is actually a policewoman. Maybe she was there to try to get someone to say the wrong thing or something."

"Maybe she's just a nosy old lady," Nick suggested. "Anyway, we should be going. I'm sure Mrs. Woods has better things to do than stand around talking to us, and I know we do as well."

"Here," Brenda said, digging around in her handbag. She pulled out a scrap of paper and a pen and wrote something on the back of the scrap. "Here's my number," she told Fenella. "Ring me if you hear anything interesting, won't you?"

Fenella took the paper and glanced at it. "I suppose so," she said slowly. "Although I can't imagine I'll hear anything."

"Well, give me your number, too," Brenda suggested. "I'll let you know if we hear anything as well."

Unable to think of a reason to say no quickly enough, Fenella wrote her mobile phone number on another fragment of paper that Brenda produced from her bag.

"I'll be in touch," Brenda promised as Nick began to walk away with their shopping cart. "Maybe we could get together for tea one day or something."

Before Fenella could reply, the woman had turned and followed her husband. While Fenella picked out a chocolate croissant and an apple cinnamon muffin, she wondered if Brenda would ever call and what she would say to the woman if she did. The lines at the checkouts were long, and Fenella was happy to find herself behind Shelly.

"I was afraid you were done and waiting for me," she told her friend.

"Not at all," Shelly replied. "I spent rather a long time studying the pastries, and then I got sidetracked by some new things I'd not seen before in the chocolate section. I only just remembered to get everything I needed for tonight's dinner."

In spite of the lines, the pair was out of the store and on their way back to their apartment building before too long. Fenella sighed happily as Shelly pulled her car into the parking garage under their building.

"I should have brought my little wheeled shopping trolley," Fenella said as she tried to gather up all of her bags. "I think I have more than I can carry in one trip here."

"Me, too," Shelly laughed. "But the second trip will be good exercise," she added as they both gathered up what they could easily carry.

"And I shall need it. I bought a lot of things I probably shouldn't have," Fenella replied.

"You've had a very stressful and upsetting day. You deserve a few treats," Shelly replied.

By the time they'd made the second trip, it was getting late.

"Would you rather just come over to my flat once I've prepared dinner?" Shelly asked in the corridor. "Or I can bring everything to your flat and make the meal there. I thought maybe you'd rather do that so you can be comfortable at home with Katie."

"Are you sure you don't mind?" Fenella asked. "I'd much rather be at home, but I don't want to inconvenience you."

"I used to do this all the time with Mona," Shelly told her. "Mona didn't like to cook very much, but she loved my cooking. Sometimes I would cook at my flat and sometimes at hers. Anyway, you've had enough stress for today. Go inside and put on your most comfortable clothes and just relax. I'll be over in a few minutes with everything I need for our dinner."

Fenella didn't have to be told twice. She let herself into her apartment and carried the second lot of shopping into the kitchen. After
quickly putting everything away, except for the muffin that somehow
managed to get eaten while she worked, she changed into a pair of
sweatpants and a T-shirt.

"That's what you're wearing?" Mona asked from the bedroom
doorway.

Fenella glanced into the mirror. "What's wrong with this?" she
demanded.

"It's horrible," Mona told her.

"It's comfortable," Fenella retorted. "I've had a difficult day."

"That's no excuse for dressing sloppily," Mona said. "You can be
comfortable and still look elegant for your guest."

"It's just Shelly."

"You should make more effort for your female friends than for your
male ones," Mona said. "They're the ones who will be there for you
when the men let you down, after all."

"Shelly doesn't care what I wear. She suggested I should get
comfortable," Fenella argued.

"Try something from my wardrobe," Mona suggested. "I have some
lovely and very comfortable loungewear that will be elegant and
suitable."

Fenella opened her aunt's wardrobe and found herself smiling at
the racks of gorgeous clothes inside.

"In the bottom drawer," Mona told her.

Fenella opened the drawer and looked inside. There were several
pairs of beautiful pajamas in bright colors and patterns. She pulled out
the top pair, which had a stunning turquoise and white design all
over it.

"They're incredibly soft," she said as she rubbed the fabric between
her fingers.

"They're silk," Mona replied. "Try them on."

Fenella pulled off her sweatpants and T-shirt and slid on the
pajamas.

"Much better," Mona told her.

Fenella looked in the mirror and smiled at herself. She looked elegant and exotic, but Mona was right. The outfit was incredibly comfortable and the smooth silk felt amazing against her skin.

"Thank you," she told her aunt.

Before Mona could reply, Fenella heard a knock on her door.

"Oh, but that looks lovely on you," Shelly exclaimed. "Mona had such exquisite taste and had such beautiful things." She walked into the room, carrying a huge box.

"Thanks," Fenella replied. "I feel a bit odd, wearing her things, but I think she would approve."

"Oh, absolutely," Shelly agreed. "She'd hate the thought of them just sitting in the wardrobe being neglected."

Fenella followed Shelly into the kitchen with Mona right behind her. Mona settled onto one of the dining area chairs. "I did think about donating all of Mona's clothes somewhere," Fenella said, grinning to herself at the shocked look that flashed over Mona's face.

"Oh, you shouldn't do that," Shelly said. "Everything you've worn of hers has fitted you perfectly, and it's all such wonderful quality. You should enjoy it."

Fenella nodded and then slid into a seat next to Mona, who was clearly invisible to Shelly. She watched as Shelly unpacked her box.

"Is there anything I can do to help?" she asked after a moment.

"No, no, you just sit there and relax. Once I get things started, I'll open the wine. If I don't start first, I might drink too much to finish."

Fenella laughed. While Shelly cooked, the pair chatted about the April weather, local politics, and recent happenings on a few of the television shows they both watched.

"There we are," Shelly said a short time later, as she slid a very full casserole dish into the oven. "Now we just have to wait."

"I'll try to be patient," Fenella said. "But it already smells amazing."

The bottle of wine was nearly half empty when someone knocked on the apartment's door. Fenella glanced down at her outfit and shrugged.

"I'm not sure I'm dressed for guests," she laughed as she crossed the room.

"You look wonderful," Shelly called after her.

Fenella pulled open her door and smiled at Peter. "Hello? What brings you here?" she asked, feeling just the tiniest bit tipsy.

"I thought I heard someone talking in here," he replied. "But you're meant to be across."

"The ferry was cancelled," Fenella explained.

"I heard there was something going on with the ferry today, but I didn't realize they'd cancelled it altogether," Peter said. "It's usually only the weather that does that."

"Fenella found another dead body," Shelly called from the kitchen. "Come in and have some cottage pie with us and she'll tell you all about it."

Fenella frowned, but took a step backwards to let Peter into the room. He walked in, but shook his head. "I'd love to chat for a few minutes, but I won't interrupt your dinner and I certainly don't want to hear about the dead body. I'm sure Fenella is upset enough without having to talk about it."

Shelly blushed. "I'm sorry," she said to Fenella. "I wasn't thinking."

"It's okay," Fenella assured her. "And you're more than welcome for dinner if you'd like to stay," she told Peter. "I would rather talk about other things, though. I'm sure the local paper will be full of the murder tomorrow, with far more details than I have anyway."

Peter patted Fenella's shoulder and then followed her to the kitchen. Shelly was already pouring him a glass of wine. He perched himself on the edge of one of the chairs.

"I really can't stay for long," he said. "I'm meeting a former business colleague for dinner and drinks. He has a proposition for me, apparently."

"Somewhere nearby?" Shelly asked. "Or should I take the wine away because you're driving?"

"We're meeting at the pub on the corner," Peter told her. "I shall be walking, so no worries there."

"It is nice, being so centrally located," Fenella remarked. "I don't know what I'd do if I was further away from everything and had to take taxis everywhere."

"The island's bus service isn't too bad," Shelly told her.

"And you could always learn to drive," Peter added. "I keep meaning to find my friend's card for you. He would have you driving in no time."

"No rush," Fenella said with a laugh. "I'm not in any hurry to get back behind the wheel of a car. I'm enjoying being able to walk everywhere."

"If I were you, I'd be dying to drive Mona's car," Shelly said. "I've always wanted a fancy sports car."

"You should take it for a spin," Fenella said. "I'm sure it isn't good for the car, sitting around unused for months on end."

"Just take a few lessons and get driving," Mona interjected. When Fenella had let Peter in, Mona had moved over to sit in the living room, possibly so that Peter wouldn't sit on top of her when he joined the others. Fenella glanced over at her, but stopped herself just in time from replying.

"Anyway," she said loudly. "I hope it's a successful meeting."

"I'm sure it will be," he replied. "He wants me to invest in a project of his, and I'm quite interested in doing so. He doesn't know that I've already done my research, but I know exactly how much I'm prepared to invest and what I will expect in return for that investment. He'll buy the dinner and drinks and I shall listen politely. Once that's all done, hopefully we'll be able to reach an agreement. He needs me. I'm happy to invest, but I won't feel bad if we can't reach the terms I'm after, either. I have enough on my plate as it is."

"At least you'll get dinner out of it," Shelly said.

"Exactly," Peter agreed with a chuckle.

He finished his glass of wine and rose to his feet. "And on that note, I really must go," he said. "Thank you for the wine. I suspect my meeting will go on for a bit, so I probably won't make it to the pub tonight. Maybe I'll see you both there tomorrow?"

Shelly shrugged. "You know I'm there most nights," she said.

"I certainly don't feel up to going tonight," Fenella told him. "I hope I'll be feeling better tomorrow."

"I hope so as well, for your sake, not just so I have someone to talk to at the pub," Peter said.

Fenella walked with him to the door. Before she opened it, he turned and gave her a brief hug.

"I do hope you haven't been too traumatized by today's events," he said quietly. "I can't imagine what you must think of the island, after everything that's happened to you since you've been here."

Fenella shook her head. "I'm quite taken with the island, in spite of everything," she assured him. "Even though I've only been here for a short time, I'm already struggling to imagine ever living anywhere else again."

"Excellent," he beamed.

Fenella pulled open the door, wondering if the man's approval meant that he was interested in her or if he was just being friendly. Her thoughts were cut short as she looked at the man who was standing just outside her door.

"Daniel?" she said.

He chuckled. "I was about to knock," he said. "I hope you aren't on your way out?"

"No, not at all," Fenella replied. "I was just letting Peter out."

Daniel nodded and then he and Peter exchanged a few words before Peter headed back toward his own apartment.

"I was hoping I could ask you a few more questions," Daniel said to Fenella as they watched the other man walk away.

"Of course you can," Fenella replied. "Come in."

She stepped back and let the man in and then shut the door behind him.

"Oh, hi, Daniel," Shelly called from the kitchen. "Dinner's almost ready. I hope you're hungry."

"I can come back," he said to Fenella. "I don't want to interrupt your meal."

"Stay and join us," Shelly insisted. "I made plenty."

Daniel looked at Shelly and then shrugged. "I'm not really supposed to socialize with susp, er, witnesses," he said apologetically.

"You aren't socializing," Shelly replied. "You're questioning. You just happen to be doing it over a plate of cottage pie."

She pulled the oven door open and the entire apartment seemed to fill with the smell of rich gravy and spices.

Daniel took a deep breath and then sighed. "I can't possibly leave now," he complained. "That smells wonderful."

"It's my world-famous recipe cottage pie," Shelly told him. "You'll love it."

"No doubt," Daniel said.

Fenella and Daniel moved over to the kitchen as Shelly pulled the casserole dish out of the oven. The mashed potato topping was golden brown and Fenella could see dark rich gravy bubbling up around the edges of the potato. Her mouth began to water as she got plates down out of the cupboard.

"Fenella and I are having wine," Shelly told Daniel. "Would you like a glass?"

"Not while I'm working," he said. "If you have milk, that would be great, otherwise, just water is fine."

"I do have milk," Fenella said. "Thanks to Shelly, who took me grocery shopping this afternoon."

She poured milk into a glass for the man and topped up Shelly's wine glass before refilling her own. "I hope it's okay that I'm drinking," she said to Daniel.

"It's fine," he said with a smile. "This visit was only semi-official anyway, and now that I'm joining you for dinner, it's even less than that."

"I hope that means I'm not a suspect," Fenella said.

"Everyone who was on the ferry is a suspect, at least on paper," he told her. "But you come very far down the list."

"I suppose that's better than nothing," Fenella replied.

Shelly spooned generous helpings of cottage pie onto plates while Fenella got out knives and forks.

"Ooh, I love this flatware," Shelly said. "Mona always insisted that we use these, even though I'm sure the set was really expensive."

"Why wouldn't you use them?" Daniel asked.

"They just seem too nice for everyday," Shelly replied. "My husband and I never used the silver service we received for our wedding. We always wanted to keep it nice for something special."

"Every day is special," Fenella replied.

"Yes, I know that now," Shelly agreed. "Mona used to say the same thing. For what it's worth, I use that set every day now, and I feel terrible that my poor hubby never got to eat with it."

"Do men care?" Fenella asked.

Everyone laughed before Daniel replied.

"Speaking on behalf of my entire gender, no," he said. "I didn't even notice the forks. I will admit, now that you mention it, that they seem quite heavy, but I'm not sure why that makes them any better. As long as they get the food safely from my plate to my mouth, I'm happy."

"Well, using them makes me happy," Fenella told him. "They're much nicer than anything else I've ever owned."

The trio chatted about nothing much as they ate the delicious meal.

"Shelly, I can see why your cottage pie recipe is world-famous," Daniel said after he'd cleared his plate twice. "That was the best I've had."

"I'll let you in on a secret," Shelly told him. "It's Delia Smith's recipe."

Even Fenella laughed at that. She'd been on the island long enough to know that Delia Smith was a famous British chef who'd written dozens of cookbooks and starred in several television series about cooking. Some of her cookbooks were on the shelf in the corner of the kitchen.

With the meal out of the way and the wine bottle empty, Fenella and Shelly cleared up the kitchen.

"Let me help," Daniel offered.

"Why don't you and Fenella go into the other room and have your conversation, and I'll take care of the washing-up?" Shelly suggested.

"You did all of the cooking," Fenella protested. "Anyway, most of the things can simply go in the dishwasher."

"I don't mind doing everything by hand," Shelly insisted. "Get the unpleasant questions over with and then we can open a box of biscuits and have them with some tea for pudding."

Unable to argue with that, Fenella followed Daniel into the living room. Mona quickly moved over to a chair in the corner as Daniel headed for where she'd been only a moment earlier. Fenella hid a smile as she sat down on the couch.

"The replacement ferry sailed about five hours late," Daniel told her after a moment. "About three-quarters of the original passengers were on it."

"And the rest of us will get our money back?" Fenella checked.

"Either that or a ticket for a comparable sailing," Daniel replied.

"I think I'll take the money and try flying next time," Fenella said. "Although Shelly recommended some tablets for me to try that are supposed to fight seasickness."

"The tablets are good," Daniel told her. "My ex-wife used to take them and she found them very effective."

Fenella found herself unreasonably annoyed to discover that Daniel's ex-wife had also been prone to seasickness. "We'll see," she muttered. "But what did you want to ask me?"

Daniel flipped open his notebook and turned the pages slowly. "When you found the body, did you notice a mobile phone anywhere?"

Fenella thought about her answer for a moment and then shook her head. "I didn't," she said. "I didn't notice much of anything. I don't even remember really looking around the room. As soon as I spotted the body on the berth, I turned around and left."

"How close did you get to the man?"

"Too close," Fenella said, shuddering. "I went up on my tiptoes to get a good look at him. A quick glance was more than enough to tell me that he was dead."

"Did you touch him?"

Daniel had already asked her most of these questions, but Fenella didn't point that out. "No, although I'm not sure why I didn't," she said. "There was just something odd about even the little bit of him that I could see from the doorway, I guess. His feet were oddly twisted or stiff or something. He didn't look as if he was just sleeping, even before I saw his face."

"Did you see Captain Howard anywhere on the ship before you found the body?"

Fenella shook her head. "I may have, but I didn't notice him," she said.

"And you didn't notice any of the others, either? The people who were in the other cabins?"

"Not that I recall," Fenella said.

"I know I've already asked you all of this before," Daniel said now as he flipped through his notebook again. "But sometimes people's answers change after they've had some time to think."

"I've been trying not to think," Fenella told him. "I've been trying to block out everything that happened today before I got back here thanks to Constable Hopkins."

"I don't have any further questions, then," he said. "I really just wanted to go back over those points."

"I ran into Nick and Brenda Proper at ShopFast," Fenella said as Daniel got to his feet.

He looked at her for a moment and then sat back down. "Did you now? Did you speak to them?"

"I did," Fenella replied. She repeated as much as she could remember of the conversation she'd had with the couple in the grocery store.

"Why did she want your phone number?" Daniel asked when she'd finished.

"I have no idea," Fenella replied.

"I don't want you meeting her," he said in a serious voice. "I shouldn't have to remind you that spending time with murder suspects is dangerous."

Fenella thought back to what had happened the last time she'd been caught up in a murder investigation. "If she does want to see me, I'll make sure we meet somewhere very public," she replied. "And I'll take Shelly with me."

"Oh, thanks," Shelly called from the kitchen. "Because that doesn't sound at all dangerous."

Fenella smiled. "Surely the Propers aren't suspects," she said.

"I told you, everyone is a suspect," Daniel replied. "That's especially true at this point, when we're only just beginning the investigation. For now, I suggest you stay well away from all of the suspects. If any of them contact you, please let me know."

"Have you come up with a motive yet?" Shelly asked as she dropped onto the couch next to Fenella.

"We're working on that," Daniel replied.

"Which means you aren't going to tell me," Shelly said with a grin.

"It's very early days yet," Daniel said. "But at this point, I honestly don't have any idea why the man was killed."

"I've put the kettle on," Shelly told them both. "Once it boils and we have tea and biscuits, maybe we should talk about possible motives."

"I really do need to get back to the station," Daniel said. "And I'd advise you both to simply forget all about the investigation. Let the police handle it. I'm sure you can come up with many other things to talk about."

Fenella walked Daniel to the door while Shelly was making their tea.

"I don't think I'll have any more questions for you, at least not in the short term," he told her in the doorway. "I'd still appreciate it if you'd stay on the island until the investigation is complete. If you do decide to go across, please let me know."

"I will," Fenella promised. "But I'm not in any hurry, really. I think I'll focus on things I can do on the island for a short while and leave trips across for later."

Daniel nodded. "I'll probably see you at the pub one of these days," he said. "It's best if we limit our socializing for the time being, however."

Fenella nodded, feeling as if she wanted to cry. She and the handsome inspector had only just started sending one another the odd text and now they were back to square one. As she pushed the door shut behind him, she banged her head gently against the door's frame.

"That can't feel good," Shelly commented as she carried in a tray with tea and cookies on it.

"I'm just feeling a bit frustrated," Fenella admitted. "I can't quite believe that I found another dead body. The police are going to start suspecting me of something if this keeps up."

"They can't possibly suspect you this time," Shelly told her. "You didn't even know the poor man."

"No, but from what I could tell this morning, neither did anyone else from the other cabins, aside from his wife," Fenella said. "Maybe the killer wasn't someone from one of the cabins, even though that seems to be what Daniel suspects."

Fenella worked her way through a handful of cookies and two cups of tea without saying a word. Her mind was racing in every possible direction. Shelly ate her own cookies and sipped her tea while playing with Katie, who seemed to love the extra attention.

"Are you okay?" Shelly asked as she and Fenella cleared away the plates and cups. "You haven't said a word for the last hour."

Fenella flushed. "I'm terribly sorry," she said. "I'm just a mess, that's all. My brain is running away with me."

"I was going to start a dozen different conversations," Shelly said. "But every time I looked at you, you seemed to be lost in thought."

"I'm sure I was," Fenella said. "I can't stop thinking about poor Robert Grosso, and even more about his wife, Sarah. I hope she has family and friends on the island to help her through this."

"Did you say she works at Noble's?" Shelly asked.

"That's what Daniel told me."

"I have some friends who work there," Shelly said. "I'll ring one of them and check on her, if you'd like."

"I don't want to pry into the poor woman's life," Fenella replied. "But I'm sure I'll feel better if I know she's being looked after by someone."

"I'll go and ring now and then come back over and let you know what I've learned," Shelly offered. "I'd ring from here, but I'd feel awfully self-conscious talking with you listening in."

"I'd appreciate it," Fenella said, hoping that Shelly would find someone who could help quickly. Fenella wasn't sure she'd be able to sleep without knowing that Sarah was okay.

She let Shelly out, leaving the apartment door unlocked so that her friend could let herself back in. While she waited, Fenella settled on the couch and stared out at the sea.

6

"Shelly's cottage pie was always delicious," Mona said from the chair next to her. "Sometimes I miss being alive."

"It was really good," Fenella replied. "But I think when I'm dead, I'll miss chocolate more."

"Tell me everything you can remember about the dead man," Mona suggested. "Maybe we'll be able to come up with a viable motive for his murder."

"I don't want to talk about it," Fenella snapped. "Daniel was right. This is a job for the police, not me."

"The problem with the police is that they don't have any imagination," Mona said. "They'll look for simple and logical explanations for the murder."

"That sounds about right."

"But what if this murder wasn't simple or logical?" Mona demanded. "Maybe the motive is quite complex. It could take Daniel years to work that out. And while we're waiting for that to happen, you aren't allowed to socialize with him, which is criminal in itself."

Fenella shook her head. "I'm sure Daniel won't need years to work it out," she said. "Shelly said the man's business might have involved smuggling. If that's the case, then surely he was killed due to his being tied up in something illegal. Daniel should be able to solve the case quickly, if that's true."

"But what if that isn't it at all?" Mona demanded. "What if he was having an affair with the ferry captain's wife, or maybe he was secretly the heir to a huge fortune and the next in line for the money killed him. Daniel probably hasn't given either of those motives any thought at all."

"I think they're both a bit of a stretch," Fenella said. "But I'm sure Daniel will be very thorough. That's his job, after all. And now I really don't want to talk about it any more."

Before Mona could reply, Shelly walked back into the apartment.

"I spoke to my friend. She actually works with Sarah," Shelly told Fenella. "She was meant to be covering one of Sarah's shifts for her while Sarah was away, but Sarah rang her and told her that she needn't bother. Apparently Sarah is planning on going back to work tomorrow."

"Tomorrow?" Fenella repeated. "But her husband was murdered today."

Shelly shrugged. "My friend said that Sarah told her that she thinks she'll be better off keeping busy. If I've learned anything from losing my husband, it's that everyone mourns differently."

"It still seems odd to me," Fenella said. "But at least Sarah mustn't be too miserable if she's feeling up to working."

"My friend said that when she talked to her, Sarah sounded the same as she always does. She didn't even realize that Robert had died until Sarah actually told her."

"As you say, everyone has to deal with grief in their own way," Fenella said. "At least I know Sarah isn't sitting home crying all alone."

"No, once my friend heard what had happened, she asked Sarah if she needed company. Sarah told her that her parents were there and that Robert's parents were on their way. Maybe that's another reason why Sarah is so eager to get back to work."

Fenella laughed. "I used to put in a lot of extra office hours whenever Jack's mom would come to visit," she admitted. "But then, the woman never liked me and made it abundantly clear that she thought Jack could do much better."

"My mother-in-law was wonderful," Shelly said. "She lived with us for many years, after my father-in-law passed away, and I never once minded having her around. She was retired, but she was busier than I was, even though I was working at the time. I think I was more upset when she died than my husband was."

Fenella opened her mouth to reply, but yawned instead. "Oh, dear, I am sorry," she said.

"Don't be," Shelly told her. "You've had a very long day. I'll just leave you to get some sleep."

Fenella walked her friend to the door and locked it behind her. She yawned again as she made her way into the kitchen to refill Katie's bowls.

"I'm completely worn out," she told the kitten, who'd followed her across the apartment. "I'd like a late start tomorrow, please."

Katie narrowed her eyes at her and then seemed to shrug. "Merrow," she said as she took off out of the kitchen in a sudden dash.

Fenella walked more slowly behind her, switching off lights as she went. In the large master bedroom, Katie was settled in the exact center of the king-sized bed, seemingly already asleep. Fenella washed her face and then studied her reflection in the mirror.

"You really must stop finding dead bodies," she told herself sternly.

"It wasn't my fault," her reflection argued back.

"Talking to yourself is the first sign of madness," Mona said from behind her.

"Talking to a ghost is its own special kind of crazy," Fenella shot back.

Mona chuckled. "If you think that outfit is comfortable for relaxing in, you should try sleeping in it," she told Fenella.

"What a lovely thought," Fenella said. She washed her face and rubbed in some face cream before brushing her teeth. Back in the bedroom she carefully climbed into bed and switched off the light, trying not to disturb Katie. Telling herself to not think about the events of the day, she snuggled down under the duvet and fell asleep almost immediately.

She hadn't thought to set an alarm for the next morning, but Katie was careful not to let her oversleep. Fenella opened one eye as the kitten began patting her on the nose. "It's only just after six," she complained. "Surely you can wait another hour for breakfast."

"Merrow," Katie replied. She jumped off the bed and raced away, no doubt straight to the kitchen to complain over her empty food bowl. Fenella sat up in bed. By the time she'd filled Katie's bowls, she'd be too awake to go back to bed.

Sighing deeply, she slid out from under the duvet and padded after the kitten. Katie was sitting in the middle of the kitchen floor, staring disapprovingly at her bowl. Fenella opened a can of something and dumped it into the bowl before she refilled Katie's water.

"There you are," she said. "That should keep you happy for five minutes."

Hoping to actually get a bit more time than that, Fenella headed for the shower. A short time later she was dressed and ready to face the day. A glance at the clock told her that she was ready for a day that hadn't really begun yet anywhere else on the island.

"It's Sunday," she told Katie. "I'm probably the only person awake on the whole island."

Katie blinked at her and then walked out of the room. Fenella followed and watched as the kitten jumped up on the bed and curled back up in her favorite spot. Within seconds the tiny animal seemed to be fast asleep again.

"You have some nerve," Fenella said to the slumbering animal.

"Oh, leave her alone," Mona said. "She's had a hard morning, eating all that kibble."

Fenella laughed. "It's a tough life," she said.

"What are you planning for your day?" Mona asked her.

"I've no idea," Fenella replied. "I wasn't supposed to be here, after all. Maybe I'll just curl up with a good book and relax."

"We should talk about the murder," Mona told her. "You should try to work out what happened."

"I'm not interested in what happened," Fenella said. "And I don't want to talk about it."

"I thought you would at least ask me if I know any of the suspects," Mona said.

Fenella swallowed a sigh. "Gee, Mona, do you know any of the suspects?" she asked through gritted teeth.

"I do, as it happens," Mona said. "But if you're going to take that attitude, I don't think I want to discuss it with you."

Now Fenella did sigh. "Oh, stop being silly," she said. "Who do you know and why didn't you mention knowing them earlier?"

"You didn't ask," Mona said with a small shrug.

Fenella took one more look at her pet, and was jealous of the animal that was fast asleep. Fenella was tired, and she had to deal with her aunt, who seemed to be in a particularly annoying mood.

"Let's go and sit in the other room," Fenella suggested. "I don't know if you get tired of standing up, but I do."

"I don't get tired," Mona replied. "But I still prefer sitting comfortably."

Fenella didn't question her aunt any further. In the living room, Fenella sat on the couch and waited for Mona to join her. "So, who did you know from the people I met yesterday?" she asked once Mona was settled.

"I didn't know any of them well," Mona began. "But I'd certainly met several of them. Let's start with Sarah Grosso."

"You knew the widow?" Fenella gasped.

"She's a nurse at Noble's," Mona told her. "I wasn't often unwell, but many of my friends suffered with ill health. Sarah used to work in the general medical ward, although she moved to the surgical ward in the last year. Before she moved, I saw quite a lot of her, really. It seemed as though one friend or another was nearly always falling ill with something."

"What did you think of her?" Fenella asked.

"She's a very hard worker," Mona replied. "Some of the nurses act as if doing some little thing for a patient is a huge favor, but she never acted like that, no matter what she was being asked for. She used to take on extra hours whenever they were offered, which is probably why I saw so much of her. She was nearly always there. I know she moved to the surgical ward because it pays better. Money was tight for her and her husband."

"Which was why she was so excited about his winning the trip across," Fenella said.

"I doubt very much he won anything," Mona said. "I met the man once and I didn't like him one bit. He was, well, shifty, I would say. If someone else had died instead of him, he'd be at the top of my list of suspects."

"So you think he might have been involved in something criminal?"

"Undoubtedly," Mona replied. "I always thought it was rather unfortunate that he wasn't more successful, really. Perhaps if he had been, poor Sarah wouldn't have had to work so hard."

"But if he didn't win the trip, how was he paying for it?"

"Perhaps someone needed something taken across and he was being paid to take it," Mona suggested.

"Why would he include Sarah if it was work?"

"Maybe he needed to look innocent," Mona said. "What could be more innocent than a married couple having a short holiday?"

"Could Sarah have known about it?"

"From what I know of the woman, I don't think so," Mona said. "She didn't seem the type to engage in criminal activity. I suspect she was completely in the dark as to what her husband was doing, if he was doing something wrong."

"Can you be married to someone and not know what they're doing?" Fenella asked.

"Perhaps she had her suspicions and chose to ignore them. From what I could see, she was more than a little in love with the man."

"And yet she's planning on going to work today," Fenella said.

"Everyone deals with grief differently," Mona replied. "I suspect she'll bury herself in her work and try to block out everything else. It might even help. She does love her job."

"Who else did you know?" Fenella asked.

"The lovely Stanley and Florence March were, well, acquaintances of mine," Mona said.

"Not friends?"

"Oh, goodness, no," Mona laughed. "I was a woman of questionable morals with no visible means of support. Stanley and Florence were carefully polite when we used to see one another at various charity functions, but they were also carefully distant so as not to seem to be approving of my lifestyle."

"I knew I didn't like them," Fenella said.

"Florence is, well, difficult to like," Mona told her. "Stanley is worse, though. He was quite fond of getting me alone and trying to seduce me."

"Oh, dear," Fenella gasped.

"He's quite a bit younger than I am, or rather than I was, and he seemed to think he was doing me a tremendous honor by even speaking with me. This was all some years ago now, of course, when I was closer to your age and Stanley was in his thirties. He could never understand why I always turned him down."

"Do you think either of them killed Robert Grosso?" Fenella asked.

"If they did, they would have hired someone else to take care of it," Mona told her. "And whoever they'd have hired would have done a better job of it than that. All the killer needed to do was stay with the body until the ferry sailed. Once you were underway, they could have thrown him overboard and no one would have been the wiser."

"Surely the body would have washed ashore eventually?"

"Perhaps, but goodness knows where, or in what condition."

Fenella shuddered. "How horrible," she said.

"I'm afraid I didn't know Justin Newmarket," Mona told her. "But I did know Nick and Brenda Proper."

"You're making me think the island is really quite small," Fenella remarked.

"It isn't all that large and the population was smaller years ago. It's only in the last fifteen or twenty years that we've had an influx of new arrivals from across to work in banking and insurance. That's all thanks to the changes in the tax laws, of course."

"So how did you know Nick and Brenda?" Fenella asked.

"Again, I used to see them at charity events on occasion. Not the fancy ones that Stanley and Florence would attend, but smaller ones for little local charities. I knew them before they were married, actually, when they were both on their first marriages. Nick's first wife was a dear woman who deserved a better husband, if I can be frank."

"Nick didn't treat her well?"

"He cheated on her fairly regularly. Brenda was his last mistress. They started seeing one another after Brenda's husband died, and when Nick's wife died rather suddenly Brenda insisted that he marry her."

"Perhaps they deserve each other," Fenella suggested.

"Yes, I rather think they do," Mona agreed.

"But can you see either of them as the murderer?"

"Perhaps. Although I can't imagine a motive. They're both retired and as I understand it, they spend most of their time visiting their various children in turn. It's an inexpensive way to live, I believe."

"The poor children," Fenella remarked.

"Yes indeed."

"Is that everyone?" Fenella asked, feeling tired of the conversation.

"I also knew Harry Hampton and his first wife," Mona told her. "He was always too frugal to donate much to charity, but his first wife was a keen volunteer on a great many committees. She died rather suddenly as well and Sherry Kelly didn't waste any time seducing him."

"I can't imagine what he sees in her," Fenella said.

"Really?" Mona asked, raising an eyebrow. "I would have thought by your age that you'd understand men better than that."

Fenella flushed. "Well, I mean, I know she's a lot younger and she's really pretty, but he doesn't seem the type to fall for that sort of woman."

"As I said, she was quick," Mona told her. "Mary fell ill quite suddenly and needed care around the clock. Sherry was one of the nursing assistants who came to help look after her. When Mary passed away, Sherry was right there to offer a sympathetic shoulder to poor Harry. And over time, she offered more than her shoulder."

Fenella shook her head. "They didn't seem to be getting along terribly well yesterday," she told her aunt.

"I would imagine they're already getting quite tired of each other," Mona said. "I can't see them lasting too much longer, unless Harry decides he'd rather have to live with her than part with any of his money. We'll see."

"Could either of them have killed Robert Grosso?" Fenella asked.

Mona shrugged. "Again, I can't work out much of a motive for either of them. Perhaps, if Sherry was having an affair with Robert, she might have killed him to keep him from telling Harry about it, but if Robert was having an affair, he had plenty of good reasons for keeping quiet about it himself."

"I don't think I like any of these people," Fenella said, mostly to herself.

"Well, don't waste any energy trying to like Charlotte Masters," Mona said firmly. "She's incredibly disagreeable."

"I thought maybe she was just upset yesterday," Fenella said.

"Oh, no, she's always difficult," Mona told her. "She didn't approve of my lifestyle, either, and she made a point of telling me that every time she saw me. She was always incredibly nosy as well, prying into my personal life and asking all manner of rude questions, and then acting quite put out when I refused to answer."

"Does any of that give her a motive for murder?" Fenella asked.

"I can't imagine that it does," Mona said sadly. "If she'd been the victim, there would be a very long list of suspects, but I can't imagine her killing anyone. Not unless she has some deep dark secret of her own that Robert Grosso discovered and threatened to reveal."

"That's an interesting idea," Fenella said.

"It's certainly my favorite solution to the murder," Mona told her with a grin.

"What about the ferry captain?" Fenella asked. "Did you know him?"

"Captain Howard," Mona said, her voice almost a purr. "I'm sure he came across as ill-tempered and rude, but he's actually a lovely man."

"Is he, now?" Fenella asked suspiciously.

Mona giggled. "I knew his father," she explained. "And his grandfather. Neither of them approved of his chosen career, of course. They were both very successful advocates. Anyway, I knew Matthew from childhood and I can assure you that he had nothing to do with any murder."

"So where does that leave us?" Fenella demanded. "We don't seem to have come any closer to working out who killed Robert Grosso."

"No, but it was an interesting conversation," Mona said. "Now you

<caption>DIANA XARISSA</caption>

can go out and start gathering information about the various suspects, and then we can talk again."

"I'm sure there must be many other suspects," Fenella said. "If the man was dead for some time before I found him, that suggests that he was on the ferry before they were letting passengers board. He must have been killed by some member of the crew, therefore."

"You've been giving this a lot of thought," Mona said approvingly.

"Not too much," Fenella muttered. "But it is on my mind, of course."

"You must ring Daniel and ask him about that very thing," Mona told her.

"I'm not ringing anyone," Fenella said firmly. "I'm not getting involved in another murder investigation."

"Suit yourself," Mona said. "I'll just go and see what I can find out, then."

Before Fenella could speak, Mona faded away.

"You do that," Fenella snapped at the empty air.

Realizing that she was starving, Fenella made herself some toast and spread it liberally with honey. She needed the extra sugar after the stress of the previous day, she told herself, as she nibbled her way through a third slice. After breakfast, she forced herself to sit down with one of the many biographies of Henry the Eighth in her collection and began to read and take notes. By the time noon rolled around, she was thoroughly ready for a long break.

"Lunch and then a walk on the promenade," she told herself as she walked to the kitchen.

"Merow," Katie said conversationally from next to her food bowl.

"Yes, yes, I know. You seem to have run out of kitty munchies, haven't you?" Fenella replied. She filled the cat's food and water bowls and then made herself some soup and a sandwich.

"It's a shame you aren't a dog," she said to Katie as they both ate.

Katie hissed at her.

Fenella laughed. "But wouldn't it be nice to go for a long walk on the promenade with me?" she asked the kitten.

Katie shook her head and then walked out of the kitchen, straight to her favorite chair. She jumped up onto it and turned around several times before curling up in a ball. Again, she seemed to be asleep in seconds.

Fenella sighed and finished her lunch, piling all of the dishes into the dishwasher. Maybe Katie had the right idea. Maybe she should simply go back to bed as well. The warm spring sunshine coming through her windows persuaded her to venture outdoors, though. She walked in the opposite direction from the Sea Terminal, wanting to stay as far away from it as she possibly could. The fresh air and brisk exercise left her feeling refreshed by the time she returned to her apartment building.

Katie apparently hadn't moved while Fenella had been gone, but she did lift up her head to stare at her owner as Fenella walked into the room.

"Did I miss anything?" she asked the animal.

"Mmmmerroowww," Katie said.

Fenella raised an eyebrow. What was Katie trying to tell her? She glanced at her phone on the table and then sighed. The light on her answering machine was blinking. Clearly someone had called while she'd been out and the phone had disturbed Katie.

"So sorry that you were bothered," Fenella said sarcastically.

She pressed the play button and was surprised when the mechanical voice told her she had two new messages. No wonder Katie was annoyed.

"Ah, Fenella, it's Edward Jones. I'm awfully sorry that your plans had to be changed at the last minute. You know my door is always open for John's baby sister. Ring me when you've rebooked and we'll work something out."

Fenella smiled. Surely, at her age, she wasn't anyone's baby sister anymore? The second message wiped the smile off her face.

"Maggie? It's Jack. I was just surfing the Internet and I found an article about a dead man on the ferry there. I'm sure you aren't involved this time, but it's still disturbing. I think it might be best if I came over for a visit. I'll have to see about getting a passport, but once that's taken care of, I'll be on the next flight to London. You'll be able to pick me up there, won't you? Call me back."

Fenella sighed deeply. For such an intelligent man, Jack was surprisingly stupid sometimes. Which was one of the reasons why, after ten years as a couple, she'd been happy to leave him behind. It felt strange to hear him call her Maggie, even though she'd gone by her middle name, Margaret, when she'd lived in the US. Jack was just about the only person in the world who called her Maggie, which she'd never really liked. Sighing again, she reached for her phone.

"Jack, don't come to visit," she said when he answered.

"Oh, Maggie, you don't mean that," he replied. "I miss you and you must miss me. We were good together."

"You don't miss me, you miss having everything done for you," Fenella corrected him. "Now you have to do your own grocery shopping and cooking and laundry, and you hate that."

"Actually, Hazel has been doing my laundry for me," Jack told her. "She said it isn't any trouble, as she never has a full load. Apparently, I'm doing her a favor, which is good, because the first load I did on my own all came out pink for some reason."

Fenella swallowed a sigh. "I'm glad Hazel is taking care of you," she muttered, feeling almost sorry for the other woman whom she'd never liked. "At least as far as laundry is concerned."

"And Sue is doing my grocery shopping," Jack added. "She shops every Sunday for herself and she said she can save a lot of money by buying everything in bulk and then splitting it with me."

"Did she?" Fenella asked.

"But I still miss you," Jack said. "And I'm worried about you. There seem to be a lot of murders happening over there."

"No more so than in Buffalo," Fenella told him.

"But Buffalo is a big city," Jack argued. "I thought the island was tiny."

"Whatever you thought, I'm perfectly safe," Fenella said, hoping she was speaking the truth. "And I'm not your concern anymore, anyway. We split up, remember?"

"Are you seeing other men?" Jack demanded. "I don't like the idea of you seeing other men."

"You're seeing other women," Fenella pointed out.

"I am not," Jack said.

"What about Sue and Hazel? Surely you aren't just letting them do your shopping and laundry without buying them dinner once in a while to thank them."

"Do you think I should?" Jack asked. "I hadn't thought of that."

Fenella sighed again. She'd known when she and Jack were together that both women were interested in the man. No doubt they were finding it frustrating now that he was single that he was so completely clueless as to their intent.

"I'm sure they're both expecting it," Fenella said.

"Oh, dear, maybe I should just do my own laundry and shopping," Jack fretted.

"Or maybe you should ask one of them to move in with you," Fenella suggested.

"But what will you do when you come back?" Jack asked.

"I'm not coming back," Fenella told him.

"I'm going to see what I need to do to get a passport," Jack said. "I think I need my birth certificate, though. I don't suppose you remember where I keep it?"

"I haven't the slightest idea," Fenella said. She could have hazarded a guess that the document in question was in the huge pile of papers that he was always talking about filing but never got around to, but his problems were no longer hers.

"I think I can order a copy," he said thoughtfully. "I wonder how you do that."

"Yes, well, I suggest you stop worrying about it," Fenella said. "You've no reason to visit me, and hotels are very expensive over here. The trip would cost you a fortune."

"I thought I would just stay with you," Jack said, sounding hurt.

"Oh, goodness, no," Fenella said quickly. "The island is very old-fashioned. My neighbors would never approve of me having a man to stay with me, not when we aren't married." She could only hope that Jack would never discover that she wasn't being totally honest with him.

"Maybe we should get married," he said plaintively.

"Marry Hazel or Sue," Fenella told him. "I'm not coming back to Buffalo."

"What is the island like?" Jack asked. "Would I like it?"

"I hardly think so," Fenella said. "But I need to go. Thank you for your concern, but it's misplaced."

"So you aren't involved in this latest murder?" he asked.

"Someone is at my door," Fenella lied. "I have to go." She hung up the phone and put her head in her hands.

"Merrrrrow," Katie said from her chair.

"It seemed a nicer lie than lying about the murder," Fenella tried to justify herself to the cat. "I didn't know what else to say."

"You should stop taking his calls," Mona suggested.

"Sure, and then when he turns up here, you can deal with him," Fenella replied.

"I think I'd quite like to meet him, actually," Mona said. "He seems ghastly when you speak to him. I'm incredibly curious as to what you saw in him for all those years."

"Sometimes I ask myself that very same question," Fenella admitted. "I keep thinking that it was just easier to stay with him than go through all of this. He's having enough trouble dealing with the split and I'm three thousand-odd miles away. I can't imagine what he'd have been like if I'd dumped him but stayed in Buffalo."

A knock on the door interrupted the conversation. "Only a few minutes too late," Fenella muttered as she crossed the room.

"I know we both spent a fortune shopping yesterday, but I can't face cooking tonight," Shelly told her. "I thought maybe I could persuade you to join me for some pizza at that little place a few doors down."

"I love their pizza," Fenella said, her mouth already watering.

"We could eat too much and then go to the Tale and Tail and drink too much as well," Shelly suggested.

"That sounds like the perfect evening," Fenella told her.

Shelly went back to her own apartment to get ready while Fenella changed into something a bit nicer than the jeans and sweatshirt she'd been in all day.

"Wear a dress," Mona urged her. "Or at least a skirt."

Fenella shook her head. "The nights are still a bit chilly," she said. "I'll be more comfortable in pants."

"Trousers," her aunt corrected her. "You don't want to talk about pants in polite company over here."

Fenella nodded. Whoever had said that a common language divided the US and the UK was absolutely correct. She was amazed nearly every day with how many words were different in the two countries.

She found a pair of black trousers and a light red sweater that were warm, comfortable and slightly dressy. After combing her hair, she touched up her makeup and then waited for Shelly. Less than five minutes later, the other woman knocked on her door.

Fenella picked up her bag and was ready to go out when Katie let out a shout.

"MMMeeeoowww," Katie said crossly.

"Oh, dear, I haven't given you your dinner, have I?" Fenella said. "Sorry," she told both Shelly and Katie.

A minute later, Katie was happily munching her way through her dinner, with a full water bowl next to her, and Fenella was ready to try leaving again.

"Let's go before she decides she needs something else," Fenella told Shelly.

"Maybe I don't want a kitten," Shelly laughed.

"You really do," Fenella told her.

"Yes, I suppose you're right."

7

The little Italian restaurant was busy, but then, it was always busy. Fenella and Shelly were shown to a table in the corner. They asked for garlic bread before they'd even sat down. Their waiter laughed.

"Everyone always wants garlic bread," he said. "I'll put that order in while you look at the menus."

"I don't really need to look," Shelly told Fenella after they were settled in. "I'm having pizza. I always do."

Fenella opened her menu and read through the list of pasta dishes and pizzas. As the waiter returned with their garlic bread, she shut the menu and smiled at Shelly. "I looked, but I can't find anything I want more than I want pizza."

Drinks and food ordered, Fenella glanced around the room. The other customers seemed to range in age from an elderly gentleman at the head of a large table to a toddler in a high chair who looked to be covered in tomato sauce.

"I've never been here when it hasn't been busy," Fenella told Shelly.

"It's because the food is so good," Shelly said after she'd swallowed a bite. "And the garlic bread is amazing."

Fenella helped herself to a second slice and grinned. "I won't argue with that," she said.

She looked around the room again, this time paying more attention to the people around her. Having lived on the island for six weeks now, she was starting to feel as if she ought to recognize more people. Logically, she knew that the island was home to around eighty thousand people and that she'd only met a handful of them, but she was still disappointed that Shelly was the only familiar face in the room.

A large group came in and was seated across the room from them. They were laughing and shouting together, and Fenella didn't bother to study them as they all appeared to be in their teens or early twenties.

"Well, there's a familiar face," Shelly said, nodding toward the new arrivals.

"Someone I know?" Fenella asked, surprised.

"Someone you've met, at least," Shelly told her. "It's Justin Newmarket and some of his friends."

Fenella turned in her seat to look at the group again. Shelly was right. Justin was sitting between two beautiful blondes, but he didn't look happy.

"The girls with him are stunning," Fenella commented.

"The one on his left is his sister," Shelly told her. "She's a year or two younger and light years smarter than her brother."

"He doesn't look happy, does he?" Fenella asked.

"Not at all," Shelly agreed. "I wonder what's bothering him."

The waiter returned with their drinks, and their pizzas weren't far behind. The pair ate and chatted, but Fenella found her eyes returning to Justin repeatedly. He was eating and drinking as well, but he didn't seem to be enjoying himself.

"I think I might just use the loo before we leave," Fenella said as she wiped her mouth. "I won't be long."

"Well done for remembering to use 'loo' this time," Shelly laughed.

"I am trying," Fenella told her.

She walked across the room, right past Justin and his friends. Feeling rather foolish, she made a point of catching Justin's eye and nodding at him on her way. A few minutes later, feeling refreshed, she started back across the room to Shelly.

"Hey, hey, aren't you that woman from the ferry?" Justin shouted as she passed his table.

Fenella stopped and smiled at the man. "It was Justin, wasn't it?" she said. She took the handful of steps she needed to stand next to him by the large table. The group had been having a loud conversation when she'd walked out of the bathroom; now everyone stopped speaking and stared at Fenella.

"Yeah," Justin muttered. "But have you heard anything from the police? That's what I want to know."

"I haven't spoken to the police lately," Fenella replied. "But I can't imagine why they would contact me, anyway. What happened on the ferry was nothing to do with me."

"Someone told me you found the body," Justin said.

"Well, yes, that's true," Fenella replied. "But I didn't know the man, or anyone else on the ferry for that matter."

"Don't have many friends, then, do you?" the girl on Justin's right drawled. "Every time I sail, I know at least a dozen people on the ferry, even if I didn't know they were going to be there."

"I've only been on the island for a short time," Fenella told the girl. "I haven't had time to make many friends."

"I heard you and Inspector Robinson from CID were good friends," Justin said, making the statement sound like an accusation.

"Is that the gorgeous new inspector from across?" one of the other girls asked. "I had to pay a parking ticket the other day and he was in the office doing something or other. I was tempted to break some law, just so he could arrest me."

"Oh, come on, Tiffany. He's like forty," the girl that Shelly had identified as Justin's sister scoffed.

"I like older men," the other girl shot back.

"I don't even know how I got mixed up in the whole thing," Justin complained loudly. "I was just trying to get across to visit a friend. You got the whole sailing cancelled, and I missed a great party."

"You could have sailed later in the day," Fenella pointed out.

"Yeah, but by that time I was too fed up to even think about it," Justin replied.

"He means he was too seasick to even think about it," Justin's sister interjected. "He's a terrible sailor. He even has to book himself a cabin so he can just lie flat for the entire journey. Aside from when he's in the loo being sick, that is."

"You have a big mouth," Justin said to his sister. "I don't know why I even bother hanging around with you."

"You hang around with me because I have much cooler friends than you do," the girl told him. "If you weren't with me, you'd be stuck at home with mum and dad, and they'd be nagging you about getting a job and doing something with your life. This is much better, isn't it?"

"Not much," Justin muttered.

"So what did the dead guy look like?" Justin's sister asked. "Was there blood everywhere like on telly when someone gets murdered?"

"I'm sure I'm not supposed to be talking about what I saw," Fenella said. "But it was terribly unpleasant. I can tell you that much."

"I think it would be cool to find a dead body," Tiffany said. "I'd ring up Inspector Robinson and then sob in his arms until we fell into bed together."

Several of the others at the table laughed at that. "Maybe you should kill someone," someone shouted.

"That's a thought," Tiffany said. "Who's most expendable?"

"Surely that must be Justin," his sister said. "No one would miss him."

Fenella took a deep breath. "That's a terrible thing to say about your brother," she said sternly. "Everyone has value and no one has any right to kill anyone else. Even joking about it is in terribly bad taste, especially after what Justin and I went through yesterday. You should be ashamed of yourself."

The woman looked Fenella up and down and then shrugged. "It's easy to see why you're friends with Mrs. Quirk. She was one of my least favorite teachers ever."

Fenella glanced over at Shelly, but she was far enough away that she couldn't have heard the nasty remark. "Murder is no laughing matter," she said.

She turned and walked briskly away from the table, ignoring the rude comments that followed her across the room. When she sat back down next to Shelly, she found that she was shaking.

"What did they say to you that's upset you?" Shelly asked.

"They're just horrible people," Fenella replied. "They were laughing about the idea of murder, and then Justin's sister suggested that he was expendable if one of the other girls wanted to kill someone so that she could meet Inspector Robinson."

"Oh, dear, that does sound like Jennifer," Shelly said. "I usually managed to see some good in all of my students, but I never did find anything to like about her."

"She didn't like you either, apparently," Fenella said dryly.

Shelly laughed. "I suppose I ought to feel bad about that, but really, I couldn't care less. Let's go to the pub, shall we?"

Fenella was happy to agree. They paid their bill and headed for the exit. Fenella pointedly ignored the group that was still eating and drinking and being loud. She and Shelly were only a few steps away from the restaurant when she heard her name being called.

"Fenella? I'm sorry, I don't remember your surname," Justin said as he caught up to them.

"It's Woods, but you're more than welcome to call me Fenella," she replied.

"I just wanted to, well, thank you for trying to stick up for me," Justin said. "Jennifer was just teasing, but she can be, well, difficult."

"She was deliberately mean to you. I'm not sure why you put up with it," Fenella said.

Justin shrugged. "She was right. Her friends are cooler than mine and going out with them is better than sitting at home. My parents, well, they aren't happy with me right now. I would have gone out with just about anyone tonight to get out of the house."

"Are you feeling okay after yesterday?" Fenella asked.

Justin blushed. "The police part wasn't too bad," he said. "I've been questioned by the police lots of times, and the inspector yesterday was better than most. Jennifer was right, though. I do get really seasick. If I could have found the money, I would have flown across for the party, but I barely scrounged up enough to pay for a foot passenger ticket and a cabin."

"And once you got off the boat, you couldn't stand the idea of getting back on," Fenella guessed.

"Yeah," he said. "And I'd already missed my ride from Liverpool to the party anyway. I could have tried to work something else out, but, yeah, getting on another boat when I was already feeling sick didn't sound like fun."

"I know exactly what you mean," Fenella told him.

"I sort of knew the dead guy," Justin said. "He was friends with a mate of mine, at least."

"Robert Grosso? I hope your friend isn't too upset over his death," Fenella said.

"He's angry, more like," Justin said. "He and Robert were doing some sort of business together and now it's all a mess."

"What sort of business?" Fenella asked.

"I think Robert was going to get him some quality items for his market stall," Justin explained. "My friend sells bags, like handbags and suitcases and the like. Robert told him he could get him some designer bags at a really good price. My friend had already paid in advance for some stuff and now he doesn't know if he'll get it or not."

"Designer bags?" Fenella repeated, feeling confused.

"Well, not real ones," Justin told her. "Really good knock-offs, you know."

Fenella nodded. "I hope you told the police about that," she said.

"I didn't know about it when I talked to the police," Justin said. "I just saw my friend last night. He came over to ask me what I knew about the murder, and then he told me about his business deal going wrong."

"You should call the inspector and tell him," Fenella suggested.

"Ah, I don't want to get my mate in any trouble," he said. "I mean, I suppose he hasn't done anything wrong, but you never know. Maybe it would be better if I let him talk to the police. I probably shouldn't have said anything to you, but, well, I sort of needed someone to talk to."

"Yesterday was upsetting for all of us," Fenella said soothingly.

"Yeah, I mean, it's weird. It started out like a normal day. Life is really short, though. I bet Robert Grosso didn't wake up yesterday expecting to be dead before lunch. It's all sort of freaked me out."

"I know exactly what you mean," Fenella told him. While she

wasn't sure she'd have used those exact words, she felt more than a little "freaked out" herself.

"Anyway, I'd better get back to my friends. I'll probably see you around or something," he said. Before Fenella could reply, he turned and walked back into the restaurant.

"Maybe yesterday's events will get that young man to take a good look at his life and make a few changes," Shelly said as she and Fenella continued on their way to the pub.

"He didn't seem like such a bad kid, really," Fenella said.

"He's just lazy and unfocused," Shelly told her. "He never quite worked out what he wants to do with his life."

"I still don't know what I want to do with mine," Fenella replied.

Shelly laughed. "There is that," she said. "I always thought I would teach for a few years and then something amazing would happen, and I'd do something totally different with the rest of my life. As it happened, I retired from teaching, and I'm still waiting for something amazing to happen."

"You met me," Fenella teased.

"That was amazing," Shelly said, laughing again.

The ground floor of the Tale and Tail was about half full of customers.

"Let's go upstairs," Shelly suggested after she and Fenella had taken their first sips of wine. "It might be quieter."

Fenella followed her friend up the steep spiral staircase. As they went, Shelly was busy waving and shouting greetings to various people she knew.

"You're very popular," Fenella said as they sat down together on one of the comfortable couches. A large white cat jumped up and settled himself between the pair, rubbing his head against Fenella until she began to pet him.

"When you teach in the island's largest primary school for your entire teaching career, you meet just about everyone," Shelly replied. "And I'm a friendly person. I love people and I make a point of learning all about them and remembering them."

"Whereas I taught at a huge research university," Fenella said.

"With two hundred undergraduates in a class, I never really got to know anyone."

"I'd hate that," Shelly said.

"I did get to know the research assistants and at least some of the young men and women who majored in history," Fenella told her. "There are even a few I've kept in touch with over the years, but not many."

"The US is such a huge place, though," Shelly said. "The island is so much smaller and more, well, friendly, I suppose."

"It certainly seems quite friendly to me," Fenella said. "At least so far. I lived in the same house for many years in Buffalo and never even met my neighbors. Here, you and Peter have already become good friends."

"Speak of the devil," Shelly said, laughing.

Peter was standing at the top of the staircase, looking around the room. Shelly waved and he smiled and crossed to the couch. He sat down next to Shelly.

"I was wondering if you two were here," he said. "I stopped to see if you were okay," he told Fenella, "but you weren't home."

"Shelly and I went out for pizza before we came here," Fenella explained.

"I really need to stop working so hard," Peter said. "Then maybe I could join you two for pizza once in a while."

"Why were you working on a Sunday, anyway?" Shelly asked.

"I told you about my meeting last night," he replied. "It ended with my being offered something considerably different to what I'd been expecting. I had to do a great deal more research than I'd intended, including talking to a number of people."

"And is it all good?" Fenella asked.

Peter grinned. "It's all very good," he told her "The advantage to doing all of the hard work over the weekend is that now I'll be ready first thing tomorrow morning with my counter-offer."

"I hope it all goes well," Fenella said, wondering what he was talking about, but feeling as if asking him to explain would be a waste of time.

"It all sounds incredibly complicated," Shelly said, putting Fenella's thoughts into words. "I just hope it's profitable for you."

"It should be," Peter said. "As long as I can get the deal I want. It's good either way from my perspective. If they won't agree, I'm happy to walk away."

"I'm sorry, but what do you do?" Fenella felt she had to ask.

Peter smiled at her. "I used to own my own small business," he said. "Or rather, I owned a succession of small businesses. A few years ago I got tired of the day-to-day hassle, so I sold up and started investing in other people's businesses instead. Thus far, I've had pretty good luck in selecting with whom to invest my money, I must say. I don't just invest money, though; I also work with the owners, offering advice and assistance. As I said, so far it's all been very profitable."

"Like the program on telly?" Shelly asked.

"On a much smaller scale," Peter laughed.

Another cat, this one black and white, decided to join them. He jumped into Peter's lap and then surveyed the others. As Peter scratched under his chin, he studied both Fenella and Shelly. After a moment, he stepped off of Peter and snuggled into Shelly's lap.

"Well, that's gratitude for you," Peter said. "While I was giving him a good scratch, he was picking out a better prospect."

"We don't usually attract two cats," Fenella remarked. There were maybe half a dozen animals that called the pub home. For the most part they kept to themselves, lolling around on the various pillows and beds that were scattered around the building. Occasionally one might demand a bit of attention from a willing customer, but to have two sharing the couch with them was out of the ordinary.

"Maybe we smell like pizza," Shelly suggested.

As if on cue, both cats suddenly sat up straight and looked around the room. They exchanged glances and then they both jumped to the floor and raced away, down the stairs and out of sight.

"And that's the end of that," Fenella laughed.

"As my lap is now free, I'll go and get us a second round," Shelly said. She walked away before Fenella could decide whether she wanted to object or not. Peter slid closer to her and took her hand.

"How are you?" he asked. "I hope yesterday's events haven't upset you too much."

"I'm doing okay," Fenella answered. "Shelly has been keeping a close eye on me and keeping me busy."

"I feel as if I'm letting you down somehow," Peter said with a frown.

"You're busy with work. I understand. Besides, it isn't your job to entertain me."

"But you've had a huge trauma. I feel, as your friend and neighbor, that I should be doing something to help."

Fenella felt a pang of something she didn't want to think about as her brain processed his words. "Friend and neighbor" was a long way from potential romantic partner, she thought sadly. "I'm fine, really I am," she said after a moment.

"You must let me take a turn at distracting you, though," Peter said firmly. "You haven't been to Peel Castle yet, have you?"

"No, the only historical site I've managed thus far is Castle Rushen," Fenella said, blushing. "I'm embarrassed to admit that I haven't even been to the Manx Museum, well, aside from the one time I went and it was closed."

"And you call yourself a historian," Peter teased.

"I know. I said I was embarrassed," Fenella replied. She didn't even have a good excuse to offer. She wasn't working and she spent most of her days curled up in her apartment with a good book, watching the sea crashing on the promenade and enjoying not having to be anywhere. Now that she'd had to change her plans for the week ahead, maybe it was time to start exploring her new home a bit more.

"Why don't I take you to Peel Castle tomorrow?" Peter asked as Shelly stepped off the elevator with three very full wine glasses in her hands.

"I thought you had your big deal to sort out tomorrow," Fenella reminded him as she took a glass from Shelly.

"It might be best if I'm unavailable," Peter replied. "I've given them my best offer. It's up to them to decide what they want to do with it."

"But what if they have questions?" Fenella asked, not sure why she was arguing, as she really wanted to see Peel Castle.

"That's one of the things I pay my advocate for," Peter told her. "He's more than capable of answering any questions that might come up. If you don't want to go, you can simply tell me that. You needn't try to find excuses for me to back out."

Fenella shook her head. "I do want to go," she said. "As long as you're sure you can take the time off."

"I'm quite sure," he said firmly, giving her hand a squeeze.

"Where are you going?" Shelly asked from where she'd sat down in Peter's former place.

"Peel Castle," Peter told her. "Would you like to join us?"

Shelly shook her head. "No offense. I'm sure it would be great fun, really, but I took class trips there for many years. Having seen the ruins through the eyes of everyone from five-year-olds who simply wanted to roll down the hills to bored teens who kept trying to sneak away and snog in the crypt, I'm not in any hurry to visit again."

Peter laughed. "I'm sure seeing it with Fenella, through the eyes of a historian, will be fascinating," he said. "But I can understand your not wanting to join us."

Shelly glanced at Fenella and then shook her head firmly. "Thank you for inviting me, but you two should go and have fun."

"We will," Peter said. "We'll have a good look around and then I'll buy Fenella lunch somewhere nice. If my deal has gone through, it will be a celebration, and if it hasn't, she can commiserate with me over something delicious."

"That sounds like a plan," Shelly said.

"It does," Fenella agreed, trying not to mind that Peter had invited Shelly to come along. Clearly the man simply wants to be friends, she told herself. And never mind why he's holding your hand. Maybe it's a British thing.

The trio talked about local news for a short while as they finished up their second round. "I think that's enough for me," Fenella said as she put down her empty glass. "I've been drinking more than I should lately. This pub is just too tempting."

"You can come in and drink something fizzy, you know," Peter teased.

"But the wine is so good," Fenella told him. "And I'm so weak-willed."

Everyone laughed. "It isn't all that late," Shelly said, glancing at the clock as they headed for the elevator. "I'd completely lost track of the time."

"It's only eight," Peter said. "Really too early to be heading home."

"I'm ready for home and bed," Fenella said stoutly. "Katie woke me at six this morning, which is her worst habit, really."

"And I suppose you got up and fed her," Shelly said.

"Of course, otherwise, you'd have heard her complaining in your apartment," Fenella replied.

The walk home was a short one, and Fenella found herself breathing deeply as they walked. "I love the smell of the sea," she told the others.

"The air is especially good for you, too," Shelly said. "I sleep better here, right on the sea, than I ever have anywhere else."

"I usually sleep well here, too," Fenella said. "I hadn't thought about it, but I'm happy to credit the sea air for that."

Katie was chasing her tail when Fenella walked in. She blinked at her owner a few times and then jumped back onto her favorite chair, curled up and went to sleep.

"I suppose that was your idea of quality time with me," Fenella said to the pet. "Or maybe you're just angry because I was petting another cat at the pub."

"Maybe you should take her with you once in a while," Mona suggested.

Fenella jumped. "I didn't know you were here," she said.

"Obviously," Mona replied. "How was your evening?"

"It was good," Fenella said. She told Mona about dinner and the conversations she'd had with Justin Newmarket. "I feel as if I ought to tell the police about the things he told me," she concluded. "But that feels, well, as if I'm betraying his trust or something."

"He didn't ask you not to repeat the conversation," Mona pointed out. "Maybe you'd be doing him a favor, getting the information to the police without him having to be the one who told on his friend."

"Maybe," Fenella said doubtfully. "I don't know what to do."

"Why not ring Daniel and ask him how things are going?" Mona suggested.

"I couldn't possibly," Fenella replied quickly. "Anyway, he won't be at work this late at night, or he shouldn't be."

"You have his mobile number," Mona pointed out.

"That's only so we can let one another know when we're going to be at the pub," Fenella said. "And we aren't doing that right now because of the investigation."

"Maybe you should text him and let him know that you've already been to the pub tonight. If he was thinking of going, then he'll know he can, without having to worry about running into you," Mona said.

"I'm going to bed," Fenella announced.

"It's only eight o'clock," Mona said.

"It's nearly nine," Fenella countered, glancing at the clock that showed eight-twenty.

"And to think, when I left you my estate I thought you'd be having parties in here every night," Mona said with a sigh.

"I'm sorry if I'm a disappointment to you," Fenella snapped. "Maybe if I can go a few weeks without finding any bodies, I'll start to make some friends."

"Yes, I'm sure your reputation is somewhat off-putting for people."

Fenella bit her tongue and shook her head, her eyes prickling with tears she simply would not allow herself to shed in front of Mona. "Good night," she snapped, spinning on her heel and stomping into the master bedroom. She slammed the door and then leaned against it, fighting back tears of frustration. When her phone began to ring a moment later, she took a deep shaky breath.

"Hello?"

"Fenella? It's Dan, er, Daniel Robinson. I just wanted to see how you are."

"Oh, I'm fine," Fenella answered, trying to sound carefree.

"You sound upset," Daniel replied. "What's wrong?"

My aunt is making me crazy, Fenella thought but didn't say. "Yesterday was difficult," she said instead. "And tonight I ran into Justin Newmarket, which didn't help."

"Did you talk to him at all?"

Fenella sighed. "I may as well tell you the whole story," she said. She sat down on the edge of her bed and took a deep breath. When she finished several minutes later, Daniel was silent.

"That's all," she said eventually. "I mean, then I went to the pub with Shelly."

"I asked you to ring me if you spoke to any of the suspects," Daniel said after another awkward pause.

"I was going to ring you tomorrow," Fenella lied. "It seemed too late tonight."

"It's not even nine o'clock," Daniel said. "And I work all hours when I'm in the middle of a murder investigation. Next time, ring me as soon as you can, okay?"

"I'm sorry. I didn't think the chat was important," Fenella said. "And I didn't want to bother you."

"I don't know if it's important or not," he told her. "But everything is relevant at this point in the investigation. I'll need to have another word with young Justin and then I'll need to track down his friend. Thank you for telling me about the conversation."

"You're welcome," Fenella said quietly.

"I'm not meant to socialize with witnesses during murder investigations," Daniel said. "But maybe we could accidentally bump into each other tomorrow around midday? We could get lunch somewhere, I suppose."

"I'm sorry," Fenella said. "But I'm going to Peel Castle tomorrow."

"Oh, that should be fun for you," Daniel said. "Are you going alone or is Shelly taking you?"

"Actually, Peter is taking me," Fenella said. She held her breath, wondering how Daniel would feel about that little detail.

"Peter?" he echoed. "Well, as I said, have fun."

When she'd put the phone back on the desk, Fenella sat on the edge of her bed and tried to figure out why the man had called. His suggestion that they have lunch together had confused her. Was he asking for a date or simply being friendly?

She got ready for bed on automatic pilot and crawled under the duvet before Katie joined her. Men were too darn complicated, she thought as Katie jumped onto the bed and curled up in the center. Feeling as if she was better off with her cat, Fenella fell into a restless sleep.

8

She was falling and she couldn't catch herself. When she hit the water, she began to swim as quickly as she could, but she didn't know which direction she should go. The person who had been chasing her had hit the water right after she had, but Fenella didn't know where he or she had gone.

Heading toward the shore seemed like the best idea, but first she had to get around the ferry. As she swam desperately forward, the ferry seemed to move alongside of her, never allowing her to get around it. She thrashed out, hitting the water as hard as she could.

"Yyyyyooooowwwwww," Katie shouted as Fenella slammed her hand hard into the duvet.

Fenella's eyes flew open and she gasped. Robert Grosso's killer had been chasing her around the ferry, she remembered. With nowhere to hide, she'd jumped off the boat and tried to swim to shore. She rubbed her eyes and looked at the clock. She didn't have to be up for many hours, but the nightmare had left her heart pounding.

"Merrow?" Katie said, rubbing her face against Fenella's cheek.

"It's okay," Fenella told her. "I just had a bad dream."

Katie sat down and began to pat the top of Fenella's head gently. After a minute, Fenella felt a tear run down her face. She took a deep breath and then rolled over on her side. Katie snuggled up against her chest and seemingly fell asleep almost immediately. Not wanting to wake her sleeping pet again, Fenella laid very still, wondering if she'd ever be able to sleep again. When her alarm went off a few hours later, she was shocked to find that she'd slept well and neither she nor Katie had moved.

Katie protested as Fenella switched off the alarm and sat up. "I do have to get up, I'm afraid," Fenella told her. "I'm going to Peel Castle with Peter today."

The kitten stared at her for a moment and then shrugged and jumped off the bed. Fenella laughed as the animal started complaining from the kitchen about her lack of breakfast. It only took a moment to pour some food into a bowl for Katie before Fenella got herself through the shower and into suitable clothes for a day being spent mostly outside.

It was overcast but dry as Fenella turned on her laptop and did a quick bit of reading about the castle she was going to visit. While it was disappointing that the site was mostly ruins, she was excited to read about its Viking heritage. By the time Peter knocked on her door, she'd filled her brain with as much knowledge as she could about their destination.

"Ready to go?" Peter asked when Fenella opened the door.

"I'm so excited," Fenella answered. "I've been reading all about the history of the site and the pagan burial there where they found that fabulous necklace. It all sounds so wonderful."

"Let's go, then," Peter said, smiling at her.

His car was in the garage under their apartment building. Fenella patted Mona's sports car as they walked past it.

"Please remind me to give you my friend's card," Peter said as he unlocked the car. "I promise you he'll have you driving in no time."

"I've discovered that I'll have to take the driving test again," Fenella said. "Which is a very scary thought."

Peter laughed. "We all pick up so many bad habits over the years as we drive. I'm not sure I'd pass again, if I had to do that."

"Yes, well, I'm still thinking about it," Fenella said. "Really, I hate not being able to drive. There are so many places I want to go and things I want to see. I must stop being silly and just get on with it, I suppose."

Peter drove out of the garage and headed for Peel. "If we don't spend too long at the castle, we might have time for the House of Manannan as well," he told her. "It's a modern museum with all sorts of interactive displays. I've been told it does a good job of presenting the island's history."

"You haven't been before?" Fenella asked.

"No, I haven't," he admitted. "I love going around museums when I travel, but when I'm at home, I simply never think about visiting ours."

"I suppose that's fairly typical," Fenella said. "Although as a historian, I intend to visit every museum and historical site on the island at least a dozen times a year."

Peter laughed. "I don't know that you'll want to visit that often," he said. "But from what I understand, they are all certainly worth an occasional visit."

"I would go back to Castle Rushen every day if I could," Fenella told him. "I'd move in, if they'd let me. I simply loved it there."

"Well, Castle Rushen is considerably more habitable than Peel Castle," Peter replied. "Although I'm not sure that I'd use the word habitable to describe Castle Rushen. It would certainly be very cold and damp, if you tried to live there."

"But at least it has a roof," Fenella pointed out.

"That it does," Peter agreed. "And Peel Castle is sadly lacking in that department."

This was Fenella's first trip across the middle of the island, so she looked around with interest as Peter drove. After a short while, he pulled over to the side of the road and pointed past Fenella.

"Tynwald Hill," he announced. "The government of the island still meets there once a year. Everyone from the island can attend. All of the new laws that have been passed over the previous twelve months are read out in English and in Manx. Also, anyone who has a problem or concern can present it to the government on that day."

"Anyone can complain about anything?" Fenella asked.

"There are procedures to follow, but basically, yes. I imagine it's fairly unique to the island, that."

"I would think so," Fenella said. "Presumably they can manage it because the island has a fairly small population. When does this happen?"

"The fifth of July is Tynwald Day," Peter told her. "Although the actual meeting of the parliament can be moved to the following Monday when the fifth is a Saturday or a Sunday."

"I'm going to put that on my calendar as soon as I get home," Fenella said. "Clearly I didn't read nearly enough about the island's history before I moved back here."

Peter chuckled. "I wouldn't worry too much about putting it on your calendar," he said. "You won't be able to miss it. There's a huge, all-day fair out here with music and entertainment."

"How wonderful," Fenella said. "And the new laws are read in Manx? I can't wait to hear that. My mother used to try to teach me a few words in Manx, but I never wanted to learn. Now, of course, I'm sorry, but at the time I wasn't interested."

"The language is having something of a revival," Peter said as he pulled back onto the road. "There's even a primary school where the children are taught entirely in Manx. I believe they start learning English in year three or four."

"Really? I had no idea it was used at all," Fenella said. "Again, I should have done my research, shouldn't I?"

"The same people who run the school also run a handful of nurseries around the island. The idea is to incorporate as much Manx language as possible in their classrooms. The local radio station gives news updates in Manx, and there are a number of different classes in the subject, if you're interested in learning it," Peter told her.

"I don't know," Fenella said. "I've never been good at foreign languages. I just get myself all tangled up very quickly with the grammar rules. They all seem so much more difficult than English."

"Maybe Manx isn't for you, then," Peter said. "It's a Celtic language, so the rules are quite different."

"You seem to know a lot about the subject," Fenella said.

"My first wife took several classes in Manx and even dragged me along to a few," he told her. "After we split up, I quit going, of course, but I keep thinking I might try again one of these days."

"Say something in Manx."

Peter grinned. "Moghrey mie," he said.

"That means good morning," Fenella told him with a smile. "That's probably the only thing I remember from my mother's efforts."

"Very good," Peter said. "And now, on your right, is the aforementioned House of Manannan."

Fenella looked out the side window and gasped. "But it looks as if the boat is sailing right through the front window," she said.

"Yes, it's very cleverly done," Peter told her. "We'll have to try to find time for it this afternoon."

The road to the castle was actually a narrow causeway that connected St. Patrick's Isle, the site of the castle, to the mainland. Peter drove slowly down the causeway and then found a parking space in a small lot overlooking the beach.

"This is lovely," Fenella said as she climbed out of the car. "If a bit windy," she added as the cool breeze hit her.

"It's only a short walk to the castle from here," Peter told her, offering her his arm.

Fenella took it, feeling like an excited child on her way to an amusement park. The outer walls of the castle appeared to be completely intact, and Fenella found herself hurrying as they made their way up the steps and onto the castle grounds.

"Ah, good morning," the young man behind the ticket desk said when Fenella and Peter reached him. "Two admissions?"

"Yes, please," Fenella said. She turned to Peter. "Let me pay for this, as you've driven," she suggested.

"As long as I can buy lunch, then," Peter countered.

"We'll argue about lunch later," Fenella told him with a smile.

"I always recommend the audio tour," the man told her after she'd paid for their admission. "It's included in the price of admission and offers a wonderful narrated tour of the site."

Fenella took the audio guide, which was large and slightly unwieldy, and eagerly began her tour. Peter followed with his own guide.

Several hours later, Fenella had walked around the entire site twice and visited every stop on the audio tour. At some point, Peter had given up and gone to sit on a bench in the sunshine. As the tour concluded, Fenella blinked several times, trying to drag herself back to the twenty-first century. She looked around the vast site and spotted Peter near the outer wall.

"I've just been watching the seals," he told Fenella when she joined him.

"Seals?" Fenella repeated.

"There." Peter pointed toward the sea and Fenella looked down at the rocks and waves below them. A handful of dark heads could be seen bobbing up and down in the water.

"Wow," Fenella breathed. Feeling as if she could watch them all day, she settled onto the bench next to Peter. A moment later her stomach growled loudly.

"Oh, dear," Fenella gasped, blushing. "I've completely lost track of the time. Is it time for some lunch?"

"It's nearly one o'clock," Peter told her. "I'd call that past time for some lunch."

"I am sorry," Fenella said. "I was so caught up in the tour that I didn't even think about the time."

"I'm glad you enjoyed yourself," Peter said. "But I am getting quite hungry. There's an excellent pub just across the street from the House of Manannan. We could get lunch there and then visit the museum after."

"Perfect," Fenella said.

"Would you like to stop in the gift shop before we go?" Peter asked.

"Could we?" Fenella asked. "I promise I won't be long. I'd just like a quick look at the books they carry. I'd love a good history of the island, if they have one."

"I'm sure they do," Peter said. "Let's go and see."

The gift shop was empty, aside from an elderly woman behind the cash register. "Ah, customers," she said brightly when the pair walked in. "I was starting to think that I wasn't going to see another person today."

"Is it usually this quiet?" Fenella asked.

"This time of year, yes," the woman said. "In a few weeks, we'll start getting all the school groups through for their tours before school breaks up for the summer. Summer can get quite busy, and we have special events as well, which are always busy. Then it goes quiet again until we shut in October."

"I think it's a wonderful site," Fenella said. "I plan to come back and visit many more times."

"We're always happy to have visitors," the woman said. "Most of us are volunteers, but the sites still cost a lot to maintain and keep open. Every visitor helps."

Fenella found a nice selection of books about the island and then realized that she wanted to buy all of them. After a few moments of indecision, she selected the four that looked the most interesting to her and reluctantly returned the others to the shelves.

"You've made some good choices if you want to learn the island's history quickly," the woman told her. "The Manx Museum in Douglas has an even better selection. If you haven't been there yet, I highly recommend it."

"It's on my list," Fenella said. "But I haven't managed it yet. I will get there soon, though. I promise."

The woman laughed. "I'll remember that and the next time you come out here, I shall ask if you've been yet," she said.

"I only live a short walk away from the museum. I've no excuse for not getting there, really," Fenella said sheepishly.

"What's the point in requesting days off if they're just going to ring and ask you to come in anyway?" a voice demanded from the shop's doorway.

Fenella thought the voice sounded familiar and she had a smile in place as she turned to see the new arrival. She was surprised when she recognized the woman, however.

"You?" the woman snapped at Fenella. "What are you doing here?"

Her smile faltered, but Fenella forced herself to bite her tongue and count to ten before she replied. "Imagine seeing you here," she said with false cheer. "I've been trying to get out here to tour Peel Castle for weeks, but I never expected to see you here."

"No, I don't suppose you did," the woman said. "I don't believe I mentioned before that I'm a volunteer with Manx National Heritage."

"No, I don't think you did," Fenella agreed.

Peter coughed, which reminded Fenella of her manners. "Oh, yes, of course, Peter Cannell, this is Charlotte Masters," she said quickly. "Charlotte was another of the cabin passengers on the ferry on Saturday," she explained.

"It's very nice to meet you," Peter said, offering his hand.

Charlotte stared at the hand for a moment and then, seemingly grudgingly, shook it.

"Peter is my next-door neighbor," Fenella told Charlotte. "He was kind enough to bring me here to see the castle."

"You don't drive?" Charlotte asked.

"I've not tried driving since I moved here from America," Fenella told her. "I need to take a few lessons and retake my driving test."

"Where were you going on the ferry?" was Charlotte's next question.

"Liverpool," Fenella replied. "I thought that was its only destination."

Charlotte frowned at her. "And what were you going to Liverpool to do?" she asked.

"To visit a friend," Fenella replied, feeling as if she'd had quite enough of the rude woman and her questions.

"You seem to have quite a few friends scattered around the place, considering you've only just arrived," Charlotte said, sounding as if she were accusing Fenella of something.

"I'm a friendly person," Fenella replied as calmly as she could.

"You weren't very talkative in the office at the ferry terminal," Charlotte said. "You didn't seem to want to answer my questions at all."

Fenella took a deep breath and counted to ten again.

"I believe Fenella was under considerable strain that morning," Peter interjected. "She'd only just stumbled across a dead body, after all."

The woman behind the register gasped. "Oh, dear, you poor thing," she said sympathetically.

"You found the body, but you didn't tell any of us what was happening," Charlotte said, ignoring the other woman.

"The police instructed me not to discuss it," Fenella said. "In fact, I'm not supposed to be discussing it now."

"That's convenient, isn't it?" Charlotte sneered.

"Perhaps, but it's also true," Fenella replied, trying hard not to let the disagreeable woman see how upset she was making her.

"How did you know the dead man?" Charlotte asked.

"I think that's quite enough," Peter said. "We came in here to buy a few books. Your questions are quite rude and intrusive."

"I spent several hours in that ferry terminal Saturday morning, and I was questioned by the police. Do you have any idea how distasteful that was? I am not accustomed to being interrogated like a common criminal."

"I'm sure it was a miserable experience for everyone involved," Peter said. "Let's just hope the police can work out what happened quickly. Then you can all forget it ever happened."

"I won't forget," Charlotte said firmly. "I shall be complaining to the chief constable about how the police behaved. There was no rhyme nor reason to the order in which they questioned the witnesses, for one thing."

"No doubt they had their reasons," Peter said. He glanced at Fenella and raised his eyebrows.

"We really need to go," she said loudly. "I'm starving and you have that meeting this afternoon. If we're going to get lunch, we need to hurry."

"Yes, I suppose you're right," Peter said. "Did you get everything you wanted?"

"Not everything I wanted, but certainly everything I can afford, at least for now," Fenella replied.

"I think you'll find, my dear, that it is in very bad taste to discuss money matters with your friends," Charlotte said. "If one were the suspicious type, one might think that you were hinting that Peter ought to help fund your purchases."

Fenella blushed. "That wasn't what I meant at all," she said quickly.

"Of course it wasn't," Peter said. "And the thought never crossed my mind."

Picking up her bag of books, Fenella headed for the door. "It was nice to see you again," she said to Charlotte as she passed her.

"Yes, delightful," Charlotte said sarcastically.

Fenella bit her tongue yet again as she pulled the door open and took a deep breath of the fresh sea air.

"It was very nice to meet you," Charlotte said to Peter.

"Likewise, I'm sure," Peter muttered as he followed Fenella out of the room.

The pair walked a few steps toward the exit and then exchanged glances.

"What an unpleasant woman," Peter said.

"She was rather horrible, wasn't she?" Fenella agreed.

"I can't imagine why she was asking you all of those rude questions."

"I think she's just incurably nosy," Fenella replied. "Maybe she'd have been happier if she'd been the one who found the body, instead of me."

"She does seem the type," Peter said.

"I know I would have been happier if she'd found the body instead of me," Fenella said. "And maybe she would have simply told a member of the ferry staff about it and they would have told the captain. From what I've seen, he would have insisted on sailing anyway. I would be in London now, doing my research, and I'd probably never have even heard of Robert Grosso."

"And his murderer would probably never be found," Peter added.

Fenella frowned. "Well, yes, I suppose that's also true," she said. "I know that bringing Inspector Robinson in to investigate was the right thing to do, even if it wasn't exactly pleasant."

They'd reached Peter's car and Fenella stopped to stare down at the beach for a moment. "It's lovely being near the water all the time," she said.

"My first wife and I had a house in the Douglas suburbs," Peter told her. "It was a nice neighborhood, but I like living by the sea better."

"It seems as if the entire island must be by the sea," Fenella said with a laugh. "The island isn't that big, really."

"It's about fourteen miles across and about thirty-two miles long,"

Peter told her. "We couldn't even see the sea from our house in Douglas, and that's true for large parts of the island."

"I really need to get out and explore the island," Fenella sighed. "I haven't been anywhere, aside from one visit to Castletown. I do walk around Douglas sometimes, but I haven't gone very far. I either need to get driving or start walking a good deal more, I think."

"We do have some excellent taxi firms, as well," Peter said as he unlocked the car. "I can recommend someone to you who can set you up with an account that you can pay monthly, if that interests you."

"It sounds good, but perhaps too tempting," Fenella replied. "I could end up going all over the place and running up a huge bill. I do need to find a good taxi service, though. If nothing else, it would mean I could go grocery shopping once in a while and buy more than I can easily carry."

"You should have said something," Peter said. "I go shopping almost every Sunday afternoon. I'm more than happy to take you along."

"I don't want to impose on anyone," Fenella told him.

"Don't be silly. How can it be an imposition when you live right next door? I don't have to move my car to collect you or to drop you off and I'm already going anyway. No more arguing; starting this weekend, I'll happily take you shopping any Sunday you'd like to go."

Fenella opened her mouth to object, but decided against it. If she wasn't comfortable taking him up on the offer, she simply didn't have to go along.

Peter started the car and began the short journey along the causeway.

"All of the little boats are pretty," Fenella said as they drove.

"I have friends with boats here and in Douglas. Maybe you'd like to go sailing sometime?"

Fenella thought about her short stay on the ferry and shook her head. "I don't think I'm a very good sailor," she said. "I'm probably better off on dry land."

Peter found a parking spot in a large public lot near the pub. "I'll move the car over to the car park for the House of Manannan after lunch," he told her.

That suited Fenella, although the museum was only a short distance away from where he'd left the car. The pub was somewhat dark, especially after being outdoors, so when they walked in it took Fenella's eyes a few minutes to adjust.

"Just sit anywhere," the man behind the bar called. "Order from the bar when you're ready."

Peter led Fenella to a small table in the corner and then went to the bar for menus. He handed her one when he returned, before sitting down opposite her.

"What's good?" she asked.

"If you ever wanted to try kippers, this is the place," Peter told her.

"What are kippers?" Fenella asked.

"Smoked herring," the man replied. "They're a local delicacy. There's an entire section of the museum next door devoted to them."

Fenella wrinkled her nose. "I don't really like seafood much," she said apologetically. "My mother didn't like it, so she didn't ever cook it. My father wasn't one to argue, as long as there was food on the table when he got home from work."

"They do a nice chicken casserole," Peter said. "Or steak and kidney pie."

"Chicken casserole sounds good," Fenella said. "It's just cold enough outside still that something like that will really hit the spot."

"I think you'll find that it never really gets all that hot," Peter told her. "There will probably only be a few days in the summer when something like chicken casserole won't sound good."

"That sounds about right for me," Fenella told him. "Buffalo summers can get very hot indeed. We had air conditioning, which helped, but when it's eighty-five or ninety outside all you want to do is sit in the A/C and sip lemonade."

"I suspect if it ever hit eighty-five over here, the entire island would melt," Peter laughed. "With all this water around us, I'm not even sure it's possible."

"Does that mean that our apartments don't have air conditioning?" she asked.

"They do, actually," Peter told her. "Or so I'm told. I've never actually tried to use it, but there is a switch on the temperature controls to turn it on and off."

Peter went back to the bar to order their drinks and food while Fenella surveyed the room. It was small, with only a dozen or so tables. Another ten people could sit at the bar, although at the moment only one person was taking advantage of that fact.

"I can't imagine a place this small doing well in Buffalo," she said to Peter when he rejoined her. "They don't have enough room to do very much business."

"You'll find lots of small businesses like this all over the island," he replied. "They don't need a lot of staff, so they can keep their overhead low."

"They still have to pay for heat and electricity and the like," Fenella argued.

"In this case, the man behind the bar is also the owner. He and his wife live in the flat above the pub. Their daughter helps out behind the bar some nights and on weekends in the summer. I'm sure they aren't getting rich, but they make enough to get by."

Peter had brought back their drinks. "Did they not have ice?" Fenella asked as she sipped her soda.

"Did you want ice?" he asked. "I didn't think to ask, but I'm sure they'll have it if you want it."

"You have to ask for ice?"

"Well, yes," Peter said. "And now that you mention it, I do recall visiting New York City once and being surprised that everywhere I went I was given a huge amount of ice in every glass."

"It's ice," Fenella said. "It belongs in cold drinks. But what were you doing in New York City?"

"Working," he replied. "Which is pretty much what I do all the time, everywhere. I'm trying to cut back, but, well, I love what I do, which makes it hard to stop."

"Why stop if you love it?"

"My doctor wants me to cut back," he said, waving a hand. "He worries about my blood pressure and how much stress I have in my life."

Before Fenella could ask any more questions, the man from behind the bar appeared, carrying two very full bowls.

"Two chicken casseroles," he said, setting the plates on the table. "Give me a shout if you need anything."

"I think I need a hungry friend," Fenella said as she looked at the enormous serving she'd been given.

"You can always take the extra home for Katie," Peter suggested.

"I don't think people food is good for Katie," Fenella replied. "But I might take the extra home for me."

Peter laughed and then the pair concentrated on eating. The food was excellent and while they ate they chatted about television and movies and nothing much. When both bowls were empty, Peter grinned at her.

"How about pudding?" he asked.

Fenella smiled. She was finally getting used to the word, at least. "I'm too full for pudding," she said, although in her head she thought "dessert."

"We could split something," Peter suggested. "They do a wonderful jam roly-poly."

"Which is what?" Fenella asked.

"Suet pudding, spread with jam, and then rolled up and steamed," he told her.

"That doesn't sound especially nice," Fenella replied.

"They'll serve it with a generous helping of custard," he added.

"Still not terribly tempting," Fenella laughed. "But as I'm quite full, that's probably good."

"I'll get it and you can take a bite or two; how about that?" Peter offered.

"I suppose I should, just for educational purposes," Fenella agreed.

When the pudding was delivered a few minutes later, it looked considerably better than Fenella had expected. Peter pushed it into the center of the table and handed Fenella a fork.

"Take a bite," he urged her.

She scooped up a small piece and popped it in her mouth. "Delicious," she said, embarrassed that she sounded so surprised.

"Have as much as you like," Peter told her as he took his first bite.

"I am rather full," she protested as she forked up a slightly larger mouthful.

The pudding was gone in very short order. Fenella was just scraping up the last of the custard when Peter's phone rang. He frowned at it and then answered the call. After a short conversation, he dropped it back in his pocket and sighed deeply.

"Something's come up," Fenella guessed.

"Yes, and it's rather important, actually," he told her. "I'm going to have to get back to Douglas, I'm afraid."

"It's fine," Fenella insisted. "I'll get to the House of Manannan another day. I'm sure I'm too stuffed to appreciate it anyway."

"I can leave you there and you can get a taxi home," Peter suggested.

Fenella thought about it and then shook her head. "I left Katie some extra dry food, but knowing her, she's eaten that and won't be happy being left until dinner time for more. I'd better get back as well."

They were back in Peter's car before Fenella had a thought. "But what about paying for lunch?" she asked.

"I paid when I ordered," Peter explained.

"But I was going to pay for lunch," Fenella complained.

"You'll have to pay next time," Peter told her with a grin.

The drive back seemed to go by very quickly. When they reached the promenade, Fenella insisted that Peter drop her off at the far end so that he could get to his office. "I'm more than happy to walk home," she told him. "I ate far too much lunch."

"Maybe we can go to the pub tonight," he said. "I'll stop by later, if I can."

Fenella walked slowly, enjoying watching and listening to the sea, until a light rain began to fall. As she picked up her pace, the rain seemed to pick up as well. Feeling too full to walk any faster, she resigned herself to getting soaked and tried to enjoy the experience.

She was mostly unsuccessful, however, and when she finally walked into the lobby of her building she was feeling quite cross with the world. The elevator seemed to take forever to arrive and Fenella was very conscious that she was dripping all over the lobby floor as she waited.

As she walked down the corridor to her apartment, she could hear a telephone ringing. At her door, as she dug around for her keycard, she realized it was her phone that she could hear. Of course, that made it nearly impossible for her to find the stupid card. Sighing deeply, she finally dug out the card as the phone went silent.

9

Of course, whoever it was didn't bother to leave a message. Fenella kicked off her shoes and frowned at the answering machine. What was the point in having the device if people weren't going to use it?

"Your phone has been ringing all afternoon," Mona said crossly from her seat near the window. "It's incredibly annoying."

"You bought the phone," Fenella pointed out. "And the answering machine that no one uses."

Mona shrugged. "The phone wasn't nearly as annoying when I could answer it," she said. "Although I must say, I wasn't often home when it rang. My friends used the answering machine, of course."

"As I've no idea who has been calling, I can't possibly be expected to apologize for their behavior," Fenella said. "I suspect they've all been insurance salesmen or some such thing."

"How was your trip to Peel, then?" Mona asked. "I wasn't expecting you back until later."

"Peter got a phone call and had to come back to sort something out for work," Fenella explained. "But Peel Castle was wonderful."

"Maybe I'll have to go and have another look at it," Mona said. "I haven't been out there in years."

Fenella wanted to ask her aunt a dozen questions about how that would work, like could she fly or just magically transport herself or what, but whenever she asked Mona about being a ghost, Mona always teased her with her answers. Instead, she shrugged and went into the kitchen to make sure that Katie had something to eat and water in her bowl. She'd just refilled Katie's water when the phone began to ring again.

"Hello?"

"May I speak to Fenella Woods, please," a voice on the other end of the line said.

"Speaking," she replied, readying herself to politely refuse whatever the caller was selling.

"This is Jessica Harris with the Isle of Man Ferry Company. How are you today?"

"Fine," Fenella said hesitantly. What did the ferry company want?

"Excellent, that's good to hear. I know that the unpleasantness on Saturday must have been upsetting for you. I'm just ringing to make certain that you're okay," the woman said.

Fenella raised an eyebrow. Surely the ferry company wasn't worried about her suing them, were they? "I'm fine," she said slowly.

"Captain Howard is, of course, conducting his own internal investigation into what happened," Jessica continued. "He was hoping you might be willing to attend a small meeting tomorrow morning to discuss the matter."

"I thought the police were handling the investigation," Fenella said.

"Of course, the police are investigating the murder," Jessica said. "But Captain Howard is quite concerned as to how Mr. Grosso managed to be on board the vessel well before passengers were meant to be admitted. He also wants to determine how the man came to be in someone else's cabin. I'm sure you can understand that there are several issues that are of interest to the ferry company that are not of interest to the police as they investigate the man's unfortunate death."

"I suppose so," Fenella said, knowing she sounded as doubtful as she felt.

"Very good," Jessica said briskly. "So you'll come to the meeting and help us with our investigation?"

"When is it?" Fenella asked.

"Tomorrow morning at eight," the girl said. "It will be here, at the ferry terminal building. Just tell the girls in the ticket office that you're here to see Captain Howard and you'll be shown to the right place."

"Will there be any police officers there?" Fenella asked.

"As I said, this is an internal investigation. There's no need for the police to attend."

Fenella agreed to be there and then disconnected, wondering whether she should let Daniel know about the meeting.

"What was all that about?" Mona asked.

Fenella explained about the internal investigation and the meeting set for the next morning. "The question is, do I call Daniel and tell him about it or not?" she asked her aunt when she was finished.

"I think you should ring him," Mona said. "If nothing else, it gives you a good excuse to talk to the man."

"I'm not looking for excuses," Fenella said, blushing.

"Of course not," Mona said with a wink.

"I'm not," Fenella said, feeling cross. "I'm just concerned that the ferry company and the captain are poking their noses into a murder investigation. I know from my own experience how dangerous that can be."

"Yes, I see your point," Mona said. "I think you should ring him straight away."

Fenella rolled her eyes at Mona and went back into the kitchen, more to get away from the woman than for any other reason. She added more fresh water to Katie's bowl and put a fresh handful of dry food out as well.

"Where's Katie?" she asked her aunt, as she realized that she hadn't seen the kitten since she'd been home.

"I didn't realize I had to look after her," Mona said. "I think she's in your bedroom."

Fenella walked into the large master bedroom and gasped. Katie wasn't anywhere visible, but she'd clearly been there. It looked as if the kitten had found the toilet paper roll in the adjoining bathroom and decided to play with it. The bedroom floor was covered in tiny bits of toilet paper, ranging in size from entire squares to nearly microscopic pieces.

"Katie!" Fenella shouted.

"Merow," a muffled voice replied.

"Where are you?" Fenella demanded.

"Meeeoowww," was the muted reply.

"Whatever happened?" Mona asked from the doorway.

"I think she decided to have some fun with the toilet paper," Fenella replied. "It might be best to leave the bathroom door shut in the future."

"Yes, indeed," Mona said. "For once, I'm not sorry that I'm intangible. Otherwise, I would feel as if I should help with the clearing up."

"First I need to find Katie, though," Fenella said. She looked under the various pieces of furniture but couldn't spot the little black cat. "Okay, Katie, where are you?" she asked again.

After a moment, Katie's little head appeared from behind one of the thick curtains at the window. "Merow," she said softly, hanging her head.

"You know exactly what you did wrong and that I'm quite cross, don't you?" Fenella said sternly.

Katie looked up at her and then quickly looked back down at the ground.

"No special treats for a week," Fenella said firmly. "And no new toys, either."

Katie stared at her for a moment and then glanced around the room at the mess. "Yooowww," she said, sounding surprised.

"It's no good pretending you didn't do it," Fenella told her. She turned and went to get trash bags and the vacuum cleaner. Half an hour later, the mess was gone, but Fenella was still feeling cross.

"It was only half a roll of paper," she said to Mona. "Imagine if it had been a full roll."

"Perhaps keeping a kitten isn't the best idea," Mona said. "She was probably just bored, but you can't be expected to keep her entertained all of the time."

"Maybe I was out for too long," Fenella said thoughtfully. "Especially after leaving her with Shelly the other morning. The poor little thing is probably just confused."

"Have you talked to the veterinarian lately?" Mona asked. "It isn't outside the realm of possibility that someone has been looking for Katie."

"I need to speak to him, actually," Fenella said. "I've brought her up-to-date on her vaccinations, but now I have to make arrangements to have her spayed. I'm not looking forward to that."

"No, but it's the responsible thing to do," Mona replied. "If you have any doubts, go and visit one of the local animal shelters. There are far too many animals that need loving homes."

"I really must do that, actually. Not for that reason, but to help Shelly find a kitten of her own."

"Maybe she'd just like to take Katie," Mona suggested.

"You don't mean that," Fenella said.

Mona opened her mouth to reply and then shrugged. "What are you doing with the rest of your evening?" she asked after a moment.

"I don't really know," Fenella told her. "Why? Did you want to do something?"

"I'd love to do something," Mona replied. "I miss having a body to use. Still, I mustn't complain, really. I've a pretty good afterlife, at least so far. Not like some people, I must say."

"Really? What do you mean?" Fenella asked.

"Not everyone has the same choices," Mona told her. "I'm not planning on staying here forever, but it is nice that I've had the chance to get to know you."

"It's kind of nice, sharing the apartment with you," Fenella admitted. "Nice, but strange."

"Anyway, if you aren't doing anything interesting, I have been invited to a party tonight," Mona said. "A few of the other ghosts from the building are having a small gathering in what used to be the ballroom."

"Seriously?" Fenella asked skeptically.

"This time I'm totally serious," Mona said. "There are quite a few of us, you know, still living here, even though we're dead."

"So you have ghost friends?"

"I suppose you could call them that, although I wouldn't."

"What do you all talk about when you get together?" Fenella asked.

"Our lives and our families, mostly," Mona said. "It isn't much different to being alive."

"If I came down, I wouldn't be able to see you, would I?"

"I don't know," Mona replied. "You might be able to see me, but you probably wouldn't be able to see the others. I'd look like a sad and lonely woman, sitting all by myself in what used to be a grand ballroom but is now a bunch of boring old offices."

"Maybe I'll just make myself some dinner and watch some television," Fenella said.

"I'll give Winston Churchill your best, shall I?" Mona asked.

"Winston Churchill is going to be there?"

"Probably not, but you never know," Mona said.

Before Fenella could ask her any more questions, Mona faded away. Fenella frowned. "I never know when she's telling me the truth and when she's lying," she complained to the kitten.

"Meemmeow," Katie said.

Fenella went into the kitchen and got Katie a small treat. "Here you are," she told the pet. "But just the one, as I'm still quite cross with you."

Katie rubbed her head against Fenella's hand and then gobbled down the treat. When she disappeared into the master bedroom, Fenella was quick to follow her. Katie blinked at her from the middle of the huge bed and then shut her eyes and curled up in a ball.

"You aren't fooling me," Fenella said. She crossed the room and pulled the bathroom door shut. "That might just protect my toilet paper," she said. Katie didn't look up as Fenella left the room.

Having eaten too much at lunch, Fenella made herself a light dinner. Going to the pub on a Monday night seemed a bit too indulgent, so she curled up in front of the television with a bag of microwave popcorn. Katie still hadn't moved when Fenella took herself to bed a few hours later.

"I guess shredding toilet paper takes a lot out of you," she said to the slumbering animal.

While Fenella had a restless night, she was grateful that the nightmare didn't return. As she switched off her alarm, she realized that she'd never talked to Daniel about the meeting she was going to that morning. Katie jumped off the bed and raced into the kitchen, with Fenella following at a more leisurely pace. She gave the kitten her breakfast and then headed for the shower. Maybe she'd try reaching the inspector when she was ready to go.

Time and the morning didn't want to cooperate with Fenella, though. First she dropped a bottle of shampoo on the bathroom floor and had to clean that up, then she couldn't find a matching pair of socks anywhere. She managed to spill her handbag when she picked it up to move its contents to a different bag. Crawling around on the floor to find everything she'd dropped left her with dusty knees on the black pants she'd been planning to wear.

Sighing deeply, Fenella went back into her bedroom and took off the now dirty bottoms. Of course, then she couldn't find anything else in the wardrobe that would be a suitable replacement. Finally pulling on a black skirt, she wasted several minutes more looking for a pair of pantyhose that didn't have a run in them. It was ten to eight when she finally made her way out of the apartment, all thoughts of calling Daniel Robinson completely forgotten.

She walked briskly along the promenade, not wanting to be late. Of course, once she arrived at the sea terminal, there was a long line of people waiting in the ticket office. While she was tempted to push her way to the front, as she simply needed directions, she'd already lived on the island long enough to know that that sort of behavior was inappropriate. Instead, she stood patiently behind a young couple with two toddlers who were taking it in turns to see which could shout the loudest.

"It was Fenella, wasn't it?" a voice said from somewhere behind her.

Fenella turned around and smiled at Sarah Grosso who was three people behind her in the line. "My dear, I'm so very sorry for your loss," she said quickly.

"Thank you," the woman replied. "I've been trying to keep busy and not think about things, but today seems like it's going to be difficult."

"I'm sure it will be," Fenella said. "You should have refused to come."

"Oh, I couldn't do that," Sarah said. "I want to do everything I can to help solve Robert's murder."

The man between Fenella and Sarah was clearly listening intently. He looked shocked and took a large step backwards when he heard the word "murder."

"Are you two together?" he asked Sarah. "Because I don't mind if you want to move up to be with your friend."

Sarah smiled and moved up to stand next to Fenella. The woman who had been between them gave her a nasty look. She was on her phone and clearly hadn't heard the exchange between Sarah and the man.

"We're together," Sarah said apologetically to the woman.

"Hmph," the woman said. She glanced at the man, but he was staring off into the distance, looking as if he was trying to pretend he was anywhere but there.

"Do you think they've asked everyone who had a cabin to come in?" Fenella asked Sarah.

"I don't know," Sarah replied. "I didn't realize that anyone else would be here until I saw you."

"What time were you supposed to be here?" Fenella asked.

"Eight o'clock, but I was running a little late." Sarah glanced at her watch. "It's only ten past, though, and I might even have been on time if the queue wasn't so long."

"Yes, I hate being late for anything, but I didn't anticipate there being this many people here," Fenella agreed.

A moment later a door opened behind the customer service desk and a woman peered out. She frowned at the crowd and then stepped forward.

"If Fenella Woods, Sarah Grosso, or Nick and Brenda Proper are here, please make yourselves known," she announced.

Fenella glanced at Sarah and then they both raised their hands. From the back of the room, a loud voice shouted.

"We're here. Parking was horrible and then we got stuck in this queue," Brenda Proper announced. "We'd have been on time if you'd simply told us where to go instead of insisting that we check in here first."

The woman frowned again and then sighed. "Right, if you'd all like to come with me, please?"

Feeling slightly self-conscious, Fenella walked around the other waiting customers to join the woman at the desk. Sarah and the Propers were right behind her. The woman opened the door between the desk and the waiting area and motioned for them all to walk through.

"Right this way," she said, leading them through another door and into a long corridor. At the end of the corridor, she stopped and opened a door. The large room had a single long table that stretched nearly the entire length of the space. At least twenty chairs were spaced around the table. Captain Howard was sitting at the head of the table, scowling at the new arrivals.

"Sit," he barked at them.

Fenella and the others quickly took seats. While she was tempted to apologize for being late, she bit her tongue. It only took a moment for her to look around the table and see that all of Saturday's cabin passengers were there.

"As we are all finally here," Captain Howard said, "perhaps we can begin."

"We'd have been on time if you hadn't had such a long queue at customer service," Brenda told him. "I told Nick that we should simply walk to the front of the queue and explain why we were there, but he insisted on waiting for our turn."

"I'd like to go over the events from Saturday morning," Captain Howard said, ignoring Brenda's words. "I'd like to try to work out where everyone was and how Mr. Grosso came to be in the wrong cabin."

"I believe you would be better off talking to the police about such things," Stanley March said. "It is their job to investigate, after all."

"I hope that you're all willing to cooperate," the captain said. "We've reviewed the security camera footage, so I believe I know in what order everyone collected their keys from the customer service desk. Let's work in that order."

"I thought the poor man was dead before we even started boarding," Charlotte Masters said. "What difference does it make who collected their keys first?"

"I'm not looking for a murderer," the captain told her. "I'm trying to work out what everyone saw and how Mr. Grosso ended up in the cabin that was assigned to Ms. Woods, that's all."

"This seems very irregular," Charlotte said. "I thought you told me that the police were going to be here. That's the only reason I came."

"Yes, well, the police have been informed that we are conducting our own investigation. They declined an invitation to join us this morning," the man replied tightly.

"I still don't see what we can tell you that will help in any way," Charlotte said tartly.

"Let's get started and see, shall we?" the man asked.

Charlotte sighed deeply and then sat back in her chair with her arms tightly crossed. Fenella doubted that the captain would get any useful information out of Charlotte, based on her expression.

"There are a few gaps in the security camera footage," the man said. "And it only becomes active on the passenger decks when we begin loading passengers onto the vessel. Unfortunately, as Mr. Grosso appears to have managed to get on board before that time, we don't have any video footage of his arrival. We aren't sure who he was with or what he did on the ship before his unfortunate demise."

"What could he have been doing?" Charlotte demanded. "Did he have criminal intent?"

"No," Sarah said firmly. "He probably arrived early and didn't realize it wasn't time to board yet. If he was too early, the ferry staff probably wasn't in place yet, so he probably just walked onto the ferry without even realizing they weren't ready for passengers yet."

"Didn't you have passengers getting off the boat?" Harry Hampton asked.

"It was the first sailing of the day," the captain explained. "The ferry arrived at Douglas last night around seven o'clock and all passengers disembarked. The cleaning crew went through, finished around ten, and then the ship was shut down for the night. The early morning staff arrived around six on Saturday morning to begin checking in freight passengers."

"So the man could have snuck onto the ferry at any time in the night," Charlotte suggested.

"He was at work," Sarah objected.

"The police have verified that Mr. Grosso finished his shift at six," the captain said. "He only worked a short distance from the ferry terminal and could have arrived there within minutes of leaving his office."

"And you think he snuck onto the ship?" Stanley asked.

"We know he must have done," the captain said. "The time of death indicates that he was on the ship not long after six, which means he either snuck in or someone from my crew let him board without proper authorization."

"I hope you're taking a good look at your crew," Sarah snapped. "Robert had no reason to sneak onto the ship."

"We are, of course, investigating the crew," the captain replied.

"But what was he doing on the ship early?" Charlotte asked.

"He'd just finished work," Sarah said quickly. "He was probably tired and wanted to get to our cabin and get some sleep before I got there. He probably thought it would be a nice surprise for me."

"I've heard there was a massive smuggling operation going on," Charlotte announced. "Someone told me that when they unloaded the ferry, they found three containers full of stolen property that weren't even meant to be on the ship."

The captain flushed. "Those sorts of rumors don't help matters any," he said. "I can assure you that nothing was found on the ferry that didn't belong there."

Fenella narrowed her eyes at the man. Something about the way that he'd said that had her doubting his words.

"Are there criminal reasons why someone might want to get on the ferry early?" she asked. "I mean, surely Mr. Grosso was simply an innocent victim, but what possible reasons could someone else have for trying to board an empty ferry?"

The captain shrugged. "I could give you a long list," he said. "Starting with teenagers who think it's something to try to get away with when they're bored, through to career criminals who are smuggling things across."

"What sort of things?" Fenella asked.

"Drugs usually come from the UK to the island," the man said. "And I've never seen people being smuggled between the two countries. Mostly, as Ms. Masters suggested, stolen property gets sent both ways."

"None of this has anything to do with Robert," Sarah said insistently.

"Perhaps he saw something he shouldn't have," Stanley suggested.

"Did he know anyone on the crew?" Charlotte asked Sarah.

"He used to spend a lot of time at the terminal," Sarah told her. "His company ships things back and forth all the time. I'm sure he knew some of the people who work at the terminal. He sometimes helped the guys who loaded or unloaded their containers off the ferry. I'm sure he knew crew on the ferry itself as well."

"So, if he turned up and he was tired, he might have just asked a friend to let him on board and into his cabin early," Captain Howard said. "We just have to find which member of staff let him do that. Can you suggest any names?"

Sarah shook her head. "He didn't talk about his work very much," she said apologetically. "He might mention that he spent the day at the terminal or that someone called off and he had to load the containers himself, but I can't recall him ever mentioning the names of anyone particular."

"If he was killed before the ferry started loading, why are we even suspects?" Stanley demanded. "None of us were on board when he died. The killer must have been one of your crew."

Captain Howard shook his head. "The police have reason to believe that he met someone in that cabin, someone else who was due to sail that morning and had a cabin booked."

"That's just stupid," Charlotte snapped. "What possible reason could they have for thinking that?"

"I don't know," the captain admitted. "But they seem pretty certain. They've questioned the crew extensively, but it seems as if they are only trying to find out who let Mr. Grosso on board, rather than anything further."

"They should be trying to figure out who let the killer on board early, instead of focusing on Mr. Grosso," Fenella suggested.

"Yes, well, perhaps they're working on that," the captain replied.

"So why did you ask us all here?" Stanley asked. "I'm sure you weren't expecting anyone to confess to murder."

"No, not at all," the captain said quickly. "I'm more interested in hearing about your interactions with the crew. I'd like to work out the order in which you all arrived and approximately what time you each arrived at your cabin."

"Surely your cameras and computers can tell you all of that," Stanley said. "Our tickets were scanned when we were checked in. Of course, then we had to wait in a ridiculously long queue for quite some time before we were allowed onto the ferry. No doubt you have a camera pointed at the customer service desk where we eventually collected our cabin keys. This is a complete waste of time."

"As I said, there are gaps in the camera footage," Captain Howard said. "We can't accurately place everyone."

"What caused the gaps?" Fenella asked.

"We aren't sure," the captain told her. "There appears to have been some sort of problem with the camera that day."

"Is that usual?" Fenella wondered.

"No, not at all," the captain said quickly. "When such things are discovered, they are fixed immediately, as well. It's just unfortunate that it happened on the one day when we really needed the footage."

"From what you've said, no matter what time we arrived, it was after the poor man was dead," Stanley said. "Come on, Florence, we're leaving. I won't waste another minute of my day talking about a crime I couldn't possibly have committed."

He got to his feet and pulled Florence out of her chair. "I did want to help," she protested as he marched her across the room.

"We can't possibly help, as we had nothing to do with it," Stanley said. "We arrived far too late to have been involved. The police have it all wrong if they think someone from one of the other cabins had anything to do with the murder. Captain Howard is just hoping to pin it on one of us so that his crew is in the clear."

"I most certainly am not," the captain snapped. Stanley ignored him, and he and Florence swept out of the room.

"I'm not," Captain Howard said insistently to the men and women who remained behind. "I do think one of my crew let Mr. Grosso on board, and maybe he or she let the killer on as well. I've been doing everything I can to find that person and get them to tell me what they know."

"And the police," Fenella suggested.

"Oh, yes, of course, and the police," the man agreed. "But thus far, no one has stepped forward to admit their involvement."

"So maybe Mr. Grosso snuck on board and his killer did the same," Nick Proper suggested.

The captain frowned. "I'd like to think our security is better than that," he said. "But that may be possible, I suppose."

They were interrupted by a knock on the door. Captain Howard crossed the room and pulled the door open.

"I'm sorry to disturb you, sir." It was the girl who had escorted Fenella and the others from customer service to the conference room. "But Inspector Robinson from the police is here. He said he must speak with you immediately."

The man glanced around the room and then sighed. "I suppose he found out about our little meeting," he said. "Bring him back here."

The woman nodded and then walked away. A moment later, she was back with Daniel Robinson on her heels.

"I should have let you know about our internal investigation," the captain said as soon as Daniel reached him. "But I didn't think it was relevant to anything."

"We can discuss this gathering later," Daniel said. "For now, we need to talk about another murder."

❧ 10 ❧

Several people, including Fenella, gasped. Nick started to get to his feet and then sat back down quickly. Charlotte was the first to speak.

"Who has been murdered?" she demanded loudly.

Daniel shook his head. "I'm glad you're all here," he said. "It will save me a great deal of driving around. I'll speak to you each in turn, after I've talked with Captain Howard."

"Mr. and Mrs. March left a few minutes ago," the captain told Daniel.

"I actually saw them in the car park," Daniel said. "They're giving a statement to one of my constables now."

"If you've come to see me, it must be one of my crew that's been killed," Captain Howard said.

Daniel held up a hand. "Let's have this conversation in private," he said. He glanced around the room. Fenella thought he smiled at her briefly as their eyes met, but she wasn't sure. "I'm going to leave a constable in here with you. Feel free to talk amongst yourselves, though."

"That's hardly likely," Charlotte said. "Not if we're being listened to."

"I would hope that you don't have any secrets from the police, at least in terms of the two murders," Daniel said.

"Of course I don't," Charlotte snapped. "But that doesn't mean I want the police listening to my conversations, either."

Daniel smiled stiffly and then turned back to Captain Howard. "If you're ready," he said.

"I'm not, but we may as well get it over with anyway," the captain said in reply.

Fenella felt herself let out a long breath as the pair left the room. A moment later the door opened again and a young uniformed constable walked in. She glanced around the room and then stood with her back to the door watching everyone. For the next several minutes, the silence in the room was almost unbearable.

"Hi," Justin Newmarket finally spoke. "I'm Justin."

The woman gave him a cool look. "I'm Constable Richards," she replied.

"Oh, come on," Justin said. "What's your Christian name?"

"You can call me Constable," the woman told him.

Sherry Hampton laughed. "She's immune to your questionable charms," she called to Justin. "But do continue trying. It's incredibly entertaining for the rest of us."

"I was just being friendly," Justin protested. "It was too quiet in here. It was uncomfortable."

"I was enjoying the quiet," Charlotte said. "I don't understand why people can't simply sit back and enjoy silence."

As Charlotte had been the one who'd insisted on everyone talking the first time they'd all been together, Fenella found her complaint odd. Before the uncomfortable silence could descend again, Brenda Proper spoke up.

"But who's dead?" she asked. "The police inspector seemed to think that there's some connection between this murder and what happened to poor Robert, but I don't understand how that's possible."

"I'm afraid I can't possibly comment," Constable Richards told her.

"Whoever it is, the inspector came to see Captain Howard about it," Sarah said. "I think it was someone from the ferry crew."

Fenella was watching the constable's face and she was sure she saw a flicker of something flash across it at Sarah's words.

"That's a very clever idea," Fenella told Sarah. "I wouldn't be surprised if you're right."

"It must have been whoever let the killer board the ferry early," Charlotte said. "Let's just hope he or she was killed while we were all here, having this pointless meeting."

Fenella doubted that it would be that easy, but she didn't say anything. For a few moments everyone went silent again.

"Are you single?" Justin tried again.

Sherry burst out laughing as the constable frowned at the man. "I'm not," she said eventually.

Justin nodded. "I didn't think so," he said. "You're too pretty to be single."

The woman stared at him for a moment and then shifted her gaze to look around the room. Sherry was still chuckling to herself as the door opened behind the constable.

"I'd like to speak to Charlotte Masters first, please," Daniel said in the doorway.

The constable whispered something to him and he nodded. They left the room together before Charlotte had even stood up. A moment later they were back.

"Ms. Masters?" Daniel said.

Charlotte picked up her handbag and walked out of the room with her head held high. The constable shut the door behind her and resumed her post.

"Can't you tell us anything now that we've worked out most of it?" Nick asked after a moment.

"I'm sorry, sir, but I'm not able to answer any questions," the woman said.

"What does your boyfriend do?" Justin asked after another silent minute.

"I'm sorry, but I'm not able to answer any questions," the constable said again.

Sherry laughed loudly. "I'm going to try that the next time I'm out and someone tries to chat me up," she said.

"You can just tell them you're married," Harry reminded her, giving her hand a pat.

"Oh, yes, of course," Sherry said, frowning.

"I can't imagine where you'd be that I wouldn't be with you, though," Harry continued.

"No, no, of course not," Sherry muttered.

It was Justin's turn to laugh. "Nothing like spending time with a happily married couple to remind you of the joys of being single," he said.

Daniel was back a moment later, and Fenella wasn't sorry when he took Justin away this time. Without him or Charlotte in the room, she thought she might have a very quiet wait for her turn.

"You can stop that any time," Sherry said sharply.

Fenella looked at Harry, who blushed. "I'm sorry," he said, removing his hand from where he'd rested it on hers. "I thought you might be worried about talking to the police, that's all."

"I have nothing to hide," Sherry replied. "You seem incredibly nervous, though."

"Not at all," Harry said. "Why would I be nervous?"

"I don't know. Maybe you're involved in smuggling or something," Sherry said with a yawn.

"I don't think that's at all funny," Harry snapped. "And you shouldn't suggest such things about your own husband."

"Well, you do have an awful lot of money," Sherry said. "How am I supposed to know where you got it all?"

"I earned it," Harry said tightly. "My first wife and I both worked very hard for a great many years. And we were very frugal as well. We never took lavish holidays or bought brand new cars. We saved up for a comfortable retirement."

"And then she went and died and never got to enjoy life," Sherry said.

"She enjoyed her life a great deal," Harry argued. "It is unfortunate that she never got to enjoy retirement, but no one is promised tomorrow."

"Well, I intend to have holidays and new cars," Sherry told the man. "You can afford it, and you want to keep me happy, don't you?"

Harry studied her silently for a moment. Fenella watched as Sherry realized the man's answer wasn't immediate.

"Harry? Darling?" she simpered. "You do want me to be happy, don't you?" She leaned over and whispered something in his ear that made him blush.

"Yes, dear, of course I want you to be happy," he said softly, patting her hand.

Sherry smiled faintly and then suddenly stood up. "I need to stretch my legs," she said, glancing around the room. She'd only taken a handful of steps when the door swung open again.

"Mr. and Mrs. Proper, if I could talk to you next, please?" Daniel said from the doorway.

Nick and Brenda exchanged glances and then got up wordlessly and followed Daniel out into the corridor. Sarah looked over at Fenella and shrugged.

"I wish I knew if it was better to be left for last or not," she said.

"As we haven't a choice, it might be better not to think about it," Fenella suggested.

"The inspector's awfully good-looking," Sherry said. "If I weren't happily married, I'd be trying to get myself arrested."

Sarah smiled at her. "He is rather handsome," she agreed. "I didn't notice the other day. I was too worried about Robert, and then once I was told that he was dead, I was too upset to pay any attention to anything. But you're right, the inspector is quite handsome."

Fenella felt a pang of jealousy, which she knew was totally misplaced. Sarah was a new widow and certainly not looking to replace her husband so quickly, and Sherry was married. Neither of the women were a threat to her relationship with Daniel, which was only a friendship anyway. She had no business being jealous no matter what. She was just done reminding herself of all of that when the door opened again and Sherry and Harry left for their turn with the inspector.

"That just leaves us," Sarah said to Fenella.

"Yes, perhaps he's simply saved the best for last," Fenella suggested.

Sarah smiled. "I cried so much when he tried to interview me last time, I suspect he's left me until he can get in a supply of tissues."

"You had every reason to be upset," Fenella told her.

Sarah nodded. "Robert and I weren't always the happiest couple on the planet, but we were bumping along, doing our best." She got up from her seat and sat down next to Fenella.

"Do you think he might have been involved in something criminal?" she asked in a whisper.

"He was your husband," Fenella said, surprised by the question. "Surely you'd be in a position to know."

"He was paid well," Sarah said, almost talking to herself. "Maybe too well for what he did, or what he told me he did. And he worked a lot of odd hours, late nights and early mornings and whatnot. I never thought anything of it. I work all sorts of hours myself. That's nursing for you. I keep wondering about this holiday we'd won, though."

"What about it?" Fenella asked.

"I don't know, it was just odd," Sarah said. "I never win anything, for one thing. And we only just found out about it last week and had to go right away. That isn't much good as a prize. What if I couldn't have found someone to cover all my shifts? Robert kept insisting it was all wonderful, but I thought it was strange."

"It does sound a little odd," Fenella agreed. "Did you talk to Inspector Robinson about it?"

"He was going to talk to Robert's supervisor," Sarah replied. "But I don't know what he found out. I don't imagine he'll tell me, either. The police never want to share anything."

She glanced at the constable by the door and then blushed. "I mean, I know they mustn't talk out of turn, but I feel as if I have a right to know if my husband was doing something illegal, don't I?"

"Maybe once they've arrested someone for the murder, they'll be able to tell you more," Fenella said.

"I certainly hope so," Sarah replied.

A moment later, it was Sarah's turn to leave with Daniel. Fenella was left alone with the police constable.

"Am I allowed to use my phone?" she asked the woman.

"I'd rather you didn't," the constable told her. "I wouldn't want you to accidentally see something in the news that the inspector doesn't want you to know."

Fenella nodded. "I was just going to play a game," she said.

"I'm awfully sorry," the constable said.

"So, do you like being a police constable?" she asked the woman.

When Daniel came back into the room several minutes later, Fenella and the constable were sitting together and chatting about cats.

"I moved her food dish twenty-five times before I found the perfect spot for it," the constable was saying as the door swung open.

"I haven't had that problem with my kitten," Fenella told her. "She seems happy with her dish wherever I put it."

"You were smart, getting a kitten," the woman replied. "When you adopt older cats, you get all of their quirks."

"I hate to interrupt," Daniel said. "But I really do need to question this witness."

Constable Richards blushed. "I'm sorry, sir," she said, standing up straight.

"It's not a problem," he said easily. "I know Fenella is easy to talk to."

Fenella found herself blushing as the constable gave her an appraising look.

"You can let the woman at customer service know that I'm done on-site," Daniel told the constable. "I'll talk to Ms. Woods at her flat, as I'm more than ready to get away from the Sea Terminal."

"Yes, sir," the woman said.

"Are you ready?" he asked Fenella.

"Definitely," she said quickly. After picking up her handbag, she followed Daniel out of the room and then through the building.

An unmarked car was parked in the "no parking" zone right in front of it. Daniel smiled ruefully as he pulled the parking ticket out from under his windshield wiper. "I forgot to put my police card in the window," he told Fenella as they both buckled their seatbelts.

"Will you have to pay the fine?" she asked.

"No, but I'll have to make a dozen phone calls," he told her. "It would probably be easier to just pay the fine, but that brings up its own set of problems."

Fenella thought about asking, but decided against it. Daniel seemed distracted, and she wanted to let him focus on driving them the short distance to her apartment building. He pulled up in front of the building and sighed. "I'll probably get a ticket here, too," he said.

"Can you park in the underground lot?" she asked.

"Not without a resident's card," he told her.

"Would mine work?" she wondered.

He grinned at her. "We could try," he said.

He put the car back in gear and drove to the entrance to the parking garage. When he put his window down, Fenella handed him her keycard. He waved it in front of the black box by the gate, and after a moment, the gate slowly opened.

"Will I have to come back to let you out?" she asked him as he pulled into a parking space that was marked "visitors."

"No, there's a button to push on the inside," he told her. "I know someone who rented a flat here for a few months. He got into some trouble because he used to have parties and invite several dozen friends. He'd stand at the gate and let them all in on his card."

"How many visitors' spots are there?" Fenella asked.

"Not enough," Daniel chuckled. "That's why he got into trouble. His friends usually just parked wherever they found a space, and then when the residents who owned the spaces came home, they weren't able to park. I believe owners are limited to a single guest parking space at a time now, thanks to my friend."

Fenella smiled. "That won't be a problem for me," she said. "Nearly all of my friends live in the building."

When the elevator opened on the sixth floor, Fenella led the man down the corridor to her door. "Merow, merowwwww, mmmmeer-rrooowwww," greeted them as Fenella pushed the door open.

"Katie?" Fenella called. "Where are you?"

A round of unhappy sounds followed. Fenella stood very still in the center of her living room and tried to figure out where the sounds were coming from.

"I think she's in the bedroom," Daniel said after yet another loud cry.

Fenella crossed to the master bedroom and pushed the partly shut door open. She took one look at the mess on her floor and briefly considered not looking for her pet. As Katie had been unable to get into the bathroom, she'd obviously amused herself today by helping herself to every tissue in the box that was next to Fenella's bed. There were tissues everywhere, most of them shredded into tiny pieces.

"Meeroww," Katie called from somewhere.

"She's under here," Daniel told Fenella as he looked under the bed. "She's seems to be tangled up in something."

With Daniel's help, Fenella pulled Katie out from under the bed. "She must have jumped inside the tissue box once she'd emptied it," Fenella said as she rescued the kitten. "And then she managed to get herself tangled in the plastic sheet that keeps the tissues in place."

"She seems to have had a pretty good fight with it," Daniel said, chuckling.

The kitten had managed to shred most of the tissue box, leaving herself wrapped in bits of plastic with only two corners of the box still intact. Fenella gently unwound the plastic that was around Katie's neck. "I hope you've learned a lesson," she said sternly. "Stop playing with my things."

Katie stared at her for a moment and then tossed her head and walked out of the room.

"I don't think she's learned anything," Daniel said with a laugh.

"Would you like a kitten?" Fenella asked as she surveyed the room.

"Maybe, but not that one," Daniel told her.

Fenella sighed. "I'm starting to see why her previous owner didn't come looking for her," she complained.

"It isn't that much to clear up," Daniel told her. He started rolling all of the tissues into a large ball. Fenella went to get the vacuum, and only a few minutes later the bedroom was clean again.

"See, that wasn't so bad," Daniel said.

"I'm so sorry," Fenella told him. "I'm sure you have better things to do than clean my apartment."

Daniel shook his head. "I'm counting that as a break," he told her. "My brain needed to shut off for a few minutes, and clearing up after Katie's mischief was the perfect tonic. Now I feel ready to talk to you about the murder."

"Coffee?" Fenella asked.

"Can't hurt," Daniel winked at her.

He sat at the counter in the kitchen while Fenella started a pot of coffee. She found some cookies in the cupboard and handed them to him.

"They're chocolate-covered," she said. "They'll help, too."

Daniel didn't speak until he'd had a few sips of coffee and several cookies. "Thank you," he said. "It's been a very long day."

"I'm sorry," Fenella said. She glanced at the clock. "It's time for lunch," she exclaimed. "Would you like a sandwich?"

Daniel opened his mouth and then shut it and shook his head. "You're still a suspect, at least on paper," he said. "Coffee is just about okay, but I can't let you make me lunch."

Fenella sat down next to him with a frown on her face. "How can I be a suspect? I don't even know who's dead."

"Have you ever met a man called George Mason?" he asked.

"I don't think so," Fenella said. She sipped her coffee and tried to think. After another minute, she shook her head. "It doesn't ring any bells. I'm assuming you mean here on the island. It seems a common enough name that I might have met someone in the US with that name."

"Yes, I did mean on the island," Daniel agreed. "I know you haven't been here that long and you've not met that many people. The name isn't familiar to you?"

"I'm sorry, but it isn't. Is that who died?"

"Yes, he was found in his flat this morning," Daniel told her.

"And he was murdered?" Fenella asked.

"He was," he confirmed. "Where were you last night between midnight and six this morning?"

Fenella blinked at him. "In bed," she said.

"Alone?"

She knew she was blushing as she replied. "Yes, alone."

Daniel nodded and then pulled out a notebook. He wrote in it for a moment and then looked up at her. "Please think back to Saturday. Do you remember speaking to any of the ferry crew?"

"So he was someone from the ferry," Fenella exclaimed.

Daniel sighed. "Constable Richards told me that you and the others had worked out that much," he said. "Yes, he was an employee of Isle of Man Ferries. Do you recall speaking to him?"

"I may have said a few words to the security people as I went through the gate," she said. "But the only other person I remember speaking with was the woman at customer service."

"Mr. Mason was working on the car decks, so it's unlikely you would have encountered him," Daniel told her. "But I had to ask."

"And I'm still a suspect, as I don't have an alibi," Fenella said.

"You're fairly low on my list," Daniel told her.

"Why do you think that someone from one of the other cabins killed Robert Grosso?" she asked.

"I can't tell you that," Daniel replied. "And that's only one possible angle that we're investigating."

"What can you tell me?" Fenella demanded.

"About the investigation? Nothing," he said. "Even if you weren't involved, I can't talk about open investigations with anyone."

"Well, I find it odd that you suspect the cabin passengers," Fenella said. "They all seem like perfectly ordinary people."

"And most of them probably are. But I have reason to believe that one of them is hiding a secret."

"What sort of secret?" Fenella asked.

Daniel smiled at her. "I wish I could tell you everything that I know," he said. "But satisfying your curiosity isn't worth my job."

"Shall I tell you what I think?"

"Go ahead, then," he said.

"I think Robert Grosso was involved in all the burglaries that have been taking place in the area recently. I think he was using his connections through his job to sneak stolen objects onto the ferry and get them across. He must have had an accomplice on the ferry, which is probably where poor George Mason fits in. I'm guessing he also had another accomplice and that's who killed both men." Fenella sat back and took a sip of coffee, watching Daniel closely.

"That's certainly one theory," he said. After a moment he sighed. "And it makes excellent sense," he said. "If we could identify the third man, I think we'd be well on our way to solving the two murders."

"Or woman," Fenella suggested.

"Yes, of course, or woman," he agreed. "Or couple," he added.

"You think it's a married couple that are in on it together?" Fenella asked.

"I'm not ruling anything out," he said. "A number of the suspects are married. In my experience it's hard to hide secrets in a marriage, and being involved in a burglary and smuggling ring is a pretty big secret to try to keep."

"Stanley and Florence March seem to have a lot of money," Fenella said speculatively.

"Stop," Daniel held up a hand. "I'm not going to discuss the suspects with you," he said firmly. "Rest assured that we are looking into the finances of everyone who had a cabin booked."

"Even mine?"

Daniel hesitated and then nodded. "I'm sorry, but we have to be thorough."

"And I did just come into a large amount of money," Fenella said.

"Lucky for you, your advocate can account for every penny of it," Daniel told her.

"So Aunty Mona wasn't smuggling stolen property across the Irish Sea?" she asked.

"Certainly not," Mona sounded indignant from across the room.

Fenella glanced at her and then bit her lip to keep from laughing.

"While her source of income is something of a question mark," Daniel said, "we're fairly certain she wasn't doing anything criminal."

Not wanting to press that particular subject any further, Fenella got up and topped up her coffee. "Would you like more?" she asked Daniel.

"I'd better not," he said, sounding sorry. "I need to get back to the station and wade through all of the paperwork from today's interviews. I'll need you to sign your statement. Can I stop back later today?"

"If you stop around six, you can share my dinner with me," Fenella invited him.

He nodded. "If I were to accidentally interrupt your dinner, I suppose it wouldn't be breaking any rules if I were to have something to eat," he said.

"Excellent, I'll make enough spaghetti for two," Fenella told him.

"I'll be back around six," he said. "And Katie," he added, "see if you can be good until then."

Katie was sitting on her favorite chair. When she heard her name, she looked up, and when Daniel finished speaking she gave him a soft "mew" as a reply.

"Time for us to solve these murders," Mona said as soon as Fenella had shut the door behind Daniel. "I'm starting to worry about you. What if the killer thinks that you saw something you shouldn't have?"

"Don't be silly," Fenella snapped. "There wasn't anything to see."

"There's something that makes Daniel think that the killer was one of the other cabin passengers," Mona pointed out. "Maybe he or she is worried that something else was left behind as well."

"If something had been, the police would have it now and the killer would be behind bars," Fenella said.

"Unless the killer thinks you've taken it," Mona said. "Maybe he or she is waiting for you to try to blackmail them."

"That's crazy. I can't blackmail anyone because I don't know who they are, and if I did know who they were, I'd tell the police."

"Yes, but you don't have a criminal mind. Whoever is behind these murders is probably running some sort of massive burglary and smuggling operation. If they found evidence that someone had murdered someone else their first instinct would probably be blackmail, not to ring the police."

"Aunty Mona, you aren't making me feel any better," Fenella said.

"Once we solve the case, you'll be fine," Mona said airily. "Tell me about the suspects. What happened today?"

Fenella sighed deeply, but didn't have the energy to argue. While she made herself some lunch, she told her aunt all about the meeting at the Sea Terminal.

"So Sherry Hampton accused her husband of smuggling; that's interesting," Mona said.

"She was just being awful," Fenella told her.

"I wonder what she means by a lot of money," Mona mused.

"Probably not all that much. Young people don't seem to appreciate how much everything costs these days. My students were always talking about how they could live on virtually nothing as if it were a great virtue. I always pointed out to them that it wasn't too hard to live on a small income if your parents were paying for tuition, room, and board."

Mona chuckled. "Yes, that's true," she said. "I'm sure Harry has saved up a decent little nest egg, but if that's all he has to support himself through retirement, he may have to get rid of his expensive trophy wife."

"I'm not sure either of them would mind that," Fenella muttered.

"I can't believe Stanley and Florence could be involved in anything criminal," Mona said. "There was tons of money on both sides, anyway, and Stanley has always been good at making more. As much as I'd like to see them both in trouble with the law, I don't think they're involved."

"What about Justin Newmarket?" Fenella asked.

"He'd be easy to recruit to do some light burglary and heavy lifting, but if we're looking for the criminal mastermind behind the crimes, I don't think he fits," Mona said.

"Maybe he's just pretending to be dumb," Fenella suggested.

"I suppose it's possible. We'll keep him on the short list. What about the Propers?"

"I don't know. I've only spoken to them a few times. They aren't my favorite people, but they don't seem like criminals."

"Also on the short list, then," Mona said. "Nick cheated on his wife, after all. Perhaps he's dishonest in other ways."

"So you think it was Justin or Nick and Brenda that killed Robert and George Mason?" Fenella asked.

"You didn't mention Sarah Grosso," Mona said. "We can't rule her out."

"The widow? But why would she have killed her own husband?"

"Maybe she was just tired of him and decided this was the perfect time to get rid of him," Mona suggested. "Maybe his death doesn't have anything to do with burglaries or stolen property."

"She was so upset on Saturday."

"She seems to be getting over it, though," Mona pointed out. "You said she was quick to agree with Shelly about how handsome Inspector Robinson is."

"Well, yes, but she didn't ask him out or anything. It was just a conversation between women."

"You don't know that she didn't ask him out," Mona said. "Anyway, it hardly matters. What does matter is that she's on the short list as well."

"I forgot about Charlotte," Fenella exclaimed. "I can't see her strangling anyone with a rope, though."

"She could do it," Mona said. "She's just nasty enough."

Fenella grinned. "I nearly forgot that you didn't like her," she said.

"Yes, well, she's definitely on my list, as well."

"I think just about everyone is on your short list," Fenella said.

"And that's why you have to start doing some investigating."

"Because we were so successful last time," Fenella said sarcastically.

"Oh, don't be like that," Mona said. "It isn't like you're working on your book. You've nothing better to do."

"That's a good point, actually," Fenella said. "I should be working on my book."

She got up from her seat and put her dirty dishes in the dishwasher before she headed into the master bedroom. Sitting down at the desk, she glanced around the room.

"Maybe I should make the other bedroom into a proper office," she said thoughtfully. With that thought in the back of her mind, she opened the biography of Henry the Eighth that was on the top of the pile and began to read. While she struggled to keep focused on the words on the page, she managed to kill a few hours. She was just getting to the part where Henry met Anne when she decided to stop.

That was the material that needed her complete attention, and she couldn't provide that at the moment. A glance at the clock told her that it was only a little bit too early to start on dinner. Deciding she could drag her preparations out, she headed for the kitchen to make dinner for herself and Daniel.

B y the time Daniel arrived, the water was boiling and the meat sauce was dangerously close to burning. Fenella turned off the heat under the sauce as she headed for the door.

"I'm sorry I'm a little late," Daniel said as a greeting. "Paperwork is the bane of my existence."

Fenella laughed and led him into the kitchen. "Sit down and have a glass of wine," she suggested.

"I'd better not," he replied. "Technically, this is probably a working dinner rather than a social one."

"I'll put the wine back in the fridge, then," Fenella said, annoyed with herself for sounding disappointed.

"You're welcome to have some," Daniel told her.

"No, that's okay," she said. "I'll have a soda. I love them and I try not to drink too many."

As Daniel sipped on his own soft drink, Fenella dumped dried pasta into the boiling water. She slid the baguette that she'd smothered in garlic butter into the oven and then shrugged. "I think that's everything," she said.

"It all smells wonderful," Daniel told her.

"The sauce is from a jar," Fenella admitted. "Although I've improved on it, or at least I hope I have."

"After the day I've had, I'll eat anything," Daniel said. "I never got any lunch."

"You need to take better care of yourself," Fenella told him. "Eating is important. You need to keep your body fuelled."

"Yes, I know. My ex-wife used to nag me about meals as well," Daniel told her.

Fenella took a deep breath. "Maybe she wasn't nagging," she suggested. "Maybe she was worried about you because she loved you."

Daniel looked at her in surprise and then frowned. "Maybe I could go out and come back in again," he said. "I could try harder not to say stupid things."

"Let's just pretend you did," Fenella said. "There's no point in you walking back and forth. We'll just start over."

"Dinner smells wonderful," Daniel said.

"It's only jar sauce, but I've tried to improve on it."

"I'm sure it will be delicious. I was too busy with reports to get myself any lunch today, so I'm starving. I'm going to have to start taking better care of myself, really."

"Yes, you are," Fenella agreed.

Katie wandered into the kitchen and nibbled her way through her bowl of dry food. When it was empty, she glanced up at Fenella, who shook her head at the tiny kitten. "Meowww," Katie said, looking away. She walked over to the counter and jumped up onto the empty stool next to Daniel. Before Fenella could say anything, Katie made the leap onto Daniel's lap. She rubbed her face against his chest and then snuggled down on his lap, giving Fenella a smug grin before she rested her head on her front paws.

"Put her on the floor if she's bothering you," Fenella told Daniel.

"Puurrrrrrrr," Katie said as Daniel began to rub behind her ears.

"She's fine," Daniel said. "A little affection after a long day helps no end."

"You could give him a cuddle," Mona suggested as she appeared on the couch across the room.

Fenella very nearly spit out a reply to her aunt, biting her tongue at the very last moment and covering herself with a forced cough.

"Are you okay?" Daniel asked.

"Fine," Fenella said. "Just, um, I'm fine." She glared at Mona and then turned her attention back to dinner. It wasn't long before the pasta and garlic bread were ready. As Daniel kept Katie happy, Fenella served up generous helpings of spaghetti and piled the garlic bread onto a large serving platter.

For several minutes the pair was quiet as they ate.

"Once you're finished eating, you need to ask him about the suspects," Mona said as she crossed the room to stand at Fenella's elbow. "Ask him who has more money that he or she should have. I still think the widow is a suspect. I'll bet, if she wasn't involved in anything criminal, she knew what her husband was up to."

Fenella stood up suddenly, forcing Mona to take a step backwards. "Would you like more of anything?" she asked Daniel.

"Another drink would be great," he said.

Fenella glared at Mona as she stepped past her.

"I think that's just rude," Mona said. "You nearly stepped on me. You wouldn't behave like that if I were still alive."

"I wouldn't be here," Fenella hissed back.

"Yes, that's true, but still," Mona said. "Ask the gorgeous inspector about Charlotte, too. I never did like that woman."

Fenella carried two more cans of soda to the table and filled up the inspector's glass and her own.

"I'm sure you don't want to talk about work," she said. "So what shall we talk about?"

Daniel shrugged. "How are you finding the island?" he asked. "I've been here for three months or so and I still feel like everyone treats me as an outsider. I've been told I can expect that to improve in another ten or fifteen years."

Fenella laughed, but Mona shook her head. "Maybe twenty," she said.

"It's different for me," Fenella said. "I was born here, for one thing, and I don't get out much, either. Shelly and Peter have been very welcoming and I don't know very many other people."

"Whereas I meet new people every day, usually under the worst possible circumstances," Daniel said. "I sometimes feel as if they'd be more honest with me if I were a Manxman."

"Goodness, I hope not," Fenella said. "I can't imagine lying to a policeman simply because he isn't a local."

"I didn't mean lying, exactly," Daniel said. "It more like they answer my questions but don't ever elaborate. I feel as if I'm missing out on a lot of local gossip because I'm a stranger."

"No doubt that's true," Fenella said. "But surely there are some men and women at the station who are local and don't have that handicap."

"Maybe, but I'm CID," Daniel explained. "I knew moving to the island would be a big adjustment, but I suppose I'm surprised at how very different it is from everywhere else I've ever worked."

"I hope you aren't thinking about leaving," Fenella said quickly. As soon as the words were out of her mouth, she blushed. Goodness knows what Daniel would think of her now.

"I like it here a lot," Daniel told her. "The island is beautiful and the crime rates are low. It's only when I'm in the middle of an investigation like this one that I start to feel like I'm at a disadvantage."

"Hopefully, this will be the last murder investigation for a long while," Fenella said.

"The murder investigation isn't as difficult as the investigation into the burglaries," Daniel replied. "It's a small island and I can't help but feel that there must be people who know something about what's happening, but I can't get anyone to talk to me."

"And now it looks as if whoever is behind the burglaries is eliminating his or her accomplices," Fenella said.

"Exactly," Daniel said. "I knew when we spoke to the men and women who work for the ferry company that someone was hiding something. I actually had a list of three or four people that I was going to talk to again because I was suspicious of them. George Mason was on that list."

"How frustrating," Fenella said.

"That's one word for it," Daniel replied.

"Not to change the subject, but I have ice cream for dessert,"

Fenella said. "I can't seem to bring myself to call it pudding, as pudding is a very specific thing in the US. I don't have any of that, although it does sound good, now that I've mentioned it."

Daniel smiled. "Ice cream sounds good," he said. "I won't argue with you, whatever you want to call it."

"Mint chip or chocolate chip cookie dough?" Fenella asked.

"After my day, I think I deserve a scoop of each," Daniel told her.

"I think that's an excellent idea," Fenella said.

"For goodness sake, the man was telling you all sorts of things about the case and you interrupt for ice cream?" Mona demanded. She stomped back and forth across the kitchen, waving her arms. "Get him talking about the case again. Find out who the main suspects are. I'm dying of curiosity."

"You're already dead," Fenella said.

"I'm sorry?" Daniel asked.

"Oh, I was just, um, fighting with the ice cream, or rather, it's fighting with me," she stammered. "It doesn't seem to want to scoop nicely, that's all."

Daniel raised an eyebrow and gave her a faint smile. Fenella ignored Mona, who was laughing loudly, and got the ice cream into bowls.

"Here we are," she said. "After we've finished, maybe we should take a walk on the promenade and enjoy the spring weather."

"That isn't nice," Mona said.

Fenella smiled at her aunt. It wasn't her fault that Mona couldn't come along, was it?

"I think I'd better head for home after this," Daniel said between mouthfuls. "I have a very busy day tomorrow, starting with talking to the dead man's parents."

"Oh, dear, that doesn't sound pleasant," Fenella said.

"They're across in Manchester," he told her. "Someone from their local constabulary had to share the news with them. Tomorrow I have to question them to see if they knew anything about their son's job here on the island."

"And to see if they knew that he was involved in criminal activity," Fenella said.

"Yes, well, I won't quite put it like that," Daniel said. "From everything I've heard about them, they are a lovely older couple who live very quietly within their means. George was the youngest of three, and from all accounts his older brother and sister are model citizens. I'm just going to ask them a few soft questions about the man's job and his friends. I'm hoping he might have said something to them about the people he worked with, and maybe he gave them a name or two of people who aren't ferry company employees."

"That would be too easy," Fenella said.

"Yes, I know, but I have to try. A lot of police work goes like that. You never know where or when you might get an unexpected break."

"You're certain he was involved in the burglary ring?" Fenella asked.

"We have several reasons to believe that he was involved in something criminal, not least because he was murdered," Daniel corrected her. "It's far too early in the investigation to be certain exactly what he was involved with, though."

"Surely someone else must know something," Fenella said thoughtfully. "The two dead men can't be the entire burglary and smuggling ring, can they?"

"We're pretty sure the murderer is also involved," Daniel said dryly.

Fenella laughed. "I've been assuming the murderer is the mastermind behind the scheme," she said. "But there must be other people involved as well."

"I suspect so, based on the number of homes that have been hit and the scale of the suspected operation," Daniel said. "But it's really all just speculation at this point."

"If I were involved and two of my associates had been murdered, I'd be at the police station begging for help," Fenella said.

"I can only assume that their fear of the murderer is greater than their desire to see him or her behind bars," Daniel said. "Or their fear of going to prison themselves is greater than their fear of the murderer."

"Prison sounds lovely and safe, really," Fenella said.

"But not as pleasant as being free and able to spend your ill-gotten gains," Daniel pointed out.

Fenella nodded reluctantly. "I'd still go to the police," she said.

"Which is why you're never going to make it as a career criminal," Daniel said with a laugh. He got to his feet, gently setting Katie on the floor as he did so. "And now I need to go home and try to get some sleep. Tomorrow is another day."

Katie walked between his legs, rubbing her back against him as he headed for the door.

"I think she likes you," Fenella said.

"She's a sweetheart," Daniel replied.

Fenella opened the door for him. He turned and stared into her eyes for a moment. "Thank you for dinner," he said quietly. "And for the conversation. I feel better about, well, everything now."

"I'm glad I could help, although I don't feel as if I did anything," Fenella said.

Daniel smiled and then took a small step closer to her. Feeling as if the whole world had suddenly stopped, Fenella held her breath and waited for the kiss she was sure was coming. The sound of a door opening in the corridor had Daniel taking a step backwards.

"Ah, Daniel, I wasn't expecting to see you here," Shelly said brightly. "I was just coming to see if Fenella wanted to go to the pub."

Fenella sighed deeply. What she really wanted was to have two more minutes alone with Daniel.

"I was just leaving," Daniel explained. "I came over to get Fenella to sign her statement."

"Which I never did," Fenella reminded him.

Daniel flushed and put his hand in his pocket. He pulled out a folded sheet of paper and handed it to Fenella. She read through the brief statement that said nothing more than that she did not know George Mason and had been alone and asleep in her residence the previous evening. "I'll just find a pen," she said, retreating into her apartment.

"Are you sure we can't persuade you to join us for one drink?" Shelly asked Daniel as he waited. "I'm buying, as I have spring fever."

"Thank you, but no," Daniel said. "I'm exhausted."

"You do look rather tired," Shelly said, sounding concerned. "I was hoping you'd have this latest murder solved by now, but I suppose you haven't."

"There was a second murder today," Daniel said tightly.

"Are they connected?" Shelly asked.

"We believe so," Daniel said.

"My goodness, what is this island coming to?" Shelly demanded. "I can't remember the last time we had a murder before those awful ones last month, and now two more? I do hope Fenella hasn't brought bad luck to our beautiful little island."

"Gee, thanks," Fenella said as she handed Daniel her statement.

"I didn't mean it," Shelly said quickly. "It's just so unfortunate that you've been caught up in both cases. I can't imagine how awful you must feel. Which is why you need to come with me to the pub."

Fenella grinned. "I'd come with you to the pub anyway," she said. "But after today, I really feel that I could use a drink."

"Thank you for this," Daniel said, sliding the folded paper back into his jacket pocket. "I'm sure I'll see you around."

Fenella swallowed a sigh at his words. No doubt he would have said something else if that kiss had actually happened. She couldn't blame Shelly, though. The other woman couldn't have known what was happening in the corridor, after all.

"Ready for the pub?" Shelly asked brightly.

"Give me two minutes to touch up my makeup and find some shoes," Fenella told her.

"I'll just go and see if Peter wants to come as well," Shelly told her.

Fenella pushed her door shut and turned around to head to the bedroom. She jumped when she saw Mona was right behind her.

"You should have kept the door shut until after he kissed you," Mona said.

"I didn't know he was going to kiss me," Fenella argued. "And anyway, maybe he wasn't going to kiss me."

"Oh, he was definitely going to kiss you," Mona told her. "Now, don't make the same mistake with Peter. Have him come in for a coffee after the pub and let him kiss you in private."

"I'm not trying to get Peter alone for a kiss," Fenella said crossly. "And I think you should stay out of my love life."

"If you had a love life, maybe I'd try to stay out of it," Mona told her. "As it is, I'm simply trying to help you get one."

Fenella didn't answer. Instead, she went into the bedroom and shut the door behind her. It was a pointless gesture, as Mona seemed to be able to materialize wherever she wanted in the apartment, but it made Fenella feel better. She brushed her hair, added a fresh coat of lipstick to her lips, and spritzed on a light spray of perfume. That will do for the pub on a Tuesday, she told herself. Especially as you know Daniel won't be there, a little voice teased. She ignored the little voice as she found comfortable shoes. Her handbag was on the table near the door. Grabbing it, she pulled the door open, startling Shelly, whose hand was poised to knock.

"Oh, goodness," Shelly gasped. "There you are."

"Here I are," Fenella agreed ungrammatically.

"And here I are," Peter added as he locked his door behind him. Fenella was quick to follow suit and then the trio headed for the elevators.

"It's definitely getting warmer," Shelly remarked as they made their way the short distance to the Tale and Tail.

"It has a long way to go, though," Peter said as a cool breeze blew through them.

The pub was mostly empty. After the friends got drinks, they headed for the comfortable couches on the upper level. The windy spiral staircase always felt almost magical to Fenella. It seemed like something out of a storybook, rather than something that was used daily in a local pub.

"So who was murdered today?" Shelly asked after they'd settled in.

"Oh, dear, was someone else murdered?" Peter asked. He took Fenella's hand. "Don't tell me you found another body."

"No, I didn't," Fenella assured him. "But the police think today's murder is connected with Robert Grosso's, so I had to answer more questions."

"At least it was Daniel who was doing the asking," Shelly said. "I'd be quite happy talking to him for hours, even though he's quite a bit too young for me."

"I didn't mind," Fenella said. "But it was sad."

"Of course it was," Peter said, squeezing her hand. "If you don't want to talk about it, Shelly and I totally understand."

"I totally don't," Shelly argued. "I want the skeet."

"Skeet?" Fenella asked.

"It's the Manx word for gossip or news," Peter told her.

"I see," Fenella said. "But I don't know how much I'm allowed to share of what I know."

"Let's talk about the football," Peter suggested. He squeezed Fenella's hand again, which was oddly comforting to her, and then launched into a twenty-minute discussion of football scores for teams that Fenella had never heard of. Shelly made a few comments, but Fenella was silent. While she appreciated what Peter was doing on her behalf, she couldn't help but wish that he'd chosen a different subject, maybe one that she could talk about as well.

"I believe it's my round," he said as he finished the last of his glass of wine. "You two sit tight. I won't be long."

He was gone before Fenella could object. She had come out intending to stop after a single glass of wine, but maybe a second one would help her sleep. She definitely didn't want any more nightmares.

It was unusual for people to use the spiral staircase to go down. Most people went up the stairs and then took the elevator down, having had a few drinks along the way. That was probably why Peter wasn't expecting to bump into anyone on his way back up with the second round of drinks. The young man who was going down also clearly wasn't expecting there to be anyone in his way. He went down the stairs far too quickly, and Fenella and Shelly could only watch in horror as he collided with Peter at around the halfway point.

Fenella was on her feet, rushing to Peter's aid, almost before he'd hit the ground. People were coming from every direction to try to help, and Fenella found herself caught on the stairs, unable to reach her friend.

"Fenella, come back up and we'll take the lift down," Shelly called to her.

Pushing her way through the people behind her on the stairs, Fenella made her way back up and then followed Shelly to the elevator. A few moments later they were able to see for themselves what had happened to their friend. He was lying on the floor surrounded by broken glasses and spilled drinks. The young man who had run into him was standing next to him.

"I'm so sorry," he kept muttering over and over again.

Peter groaned and then tried to push himself into a sitting position.

"Maybe you should lie still and we should get an ambulance," one of the waitresses suggested.

"I'm fine," Peter said in a weak voice. He cleared his throat and tried again. This time the "I'm fine" sounded slightly stronger.

"You've a huge lump on your head," the waitress told him. "You need to get that checked out."

Peter put his hand up to his head and winced. Fenella took a step closer.

"It is a big lump," she said. "I think you need a doctor."

"I'm really, really sorry," the young man said. "Are you his wife? I didn't mean to run into him. You can't see anyone on the stairs, because of the twists and turns. I shouldn't have been going so fast, though. I've not even been drinking, you see. My sister is having a baby and she just texted me to come to the hospital and I just ran as fast as I could. I'm going to be an uncle."

Fenella stared at him for a minute. She wasn't sure he'd taken a breath during the entire monologue. "Congratulations," she said after a moment.

"But I can't leave, not after I've caused all this trouble," the man said anxiously.

"I'm fine," Peter said crossly. He got to his feet and then swayed markedly and put his hand to his head. "Just a little dizzy," he muttered.

"I'll pay for the broken glasses," the young man told the man from behind the bar who'd walked over as Peter stood up.

"I'll put it on your bill," the man replied. "Now you get out of here and go see Bev. I know where to find you if I need to."

"Are you sure?" he asked, looking from the man to Fenella and back again.

"Go and see your sister," Fenella told him. "I'm sure Peter will be fine."

The man opened his mouth and then clamped it shut and headed for the door.

"Hey, Jake, take a taxi," the bartender called after him. "I don't think you should be driving."

Jake gave him a thumbs up as he dashed out the door.

"He's very excited about becoming an uncle," Fenella remarked to the bartender.

"Oh, aye, his sister is quite a few years older than him and she more or less raised him after their parents split up. She's been trying for a baby for the last five or six years, and I think they tried nearly everything before they finally found something that worked for them. This is probably the most wanted baby on the island," he told her. "Jake is just over the moon for her and her husband."

"How wonderful," Fenella exclaimed. "I hope everything goes well for them."

"I think maybe I need a doctor," Peter interrupted. "I'm seeing a few more of you than I think there are."

Fenella smiled, and she and Shelly each took one of Peter's arms and led him toward the door.

"Let me know how he is," the bartender said. "We like to keep an eye on our regulars."

Outside, Shelly looked at Fenella. "Maybe we should get a taxi," she said. "It might be faster than trying to walk all the way home to where my car is."

"I think a taxi is a good idea," Fenella said as Peter lurched sideways and then stopped and groaned.

The taxi rank was only a few steps away, and the trio piled into the nearest car. Fenella sat with Peter in the back while Shelly sat next to the driver. Within minutes, they were on their way to Noble's, the island's main hospital.

"You're very pretty," Peter said as they went. "All three, no, four, no five, well, however many of you there are, they're all very pretty."

"Thank you," Fenella said, stifling a nervous giggle.

"I might try to kiss one of you," Peter said in a loud whisper. "But I'd probably miss your lips."

"Never mind, maybe when you're feeling better," Fenella replied.

"My head hurts a lot, anyway," Peter told her. "I was trying not to spill the drinks, but I should have been protecting my head instead, I think."

"I'm sure the doctor will be able to give you something for the pain," Fenella said, although she wasn't sure at all. She could vaguely remember something about people not being allowed any medication after a head injury, but she wasn't about to tell Peter that.

Fenella found herself looking around eagerly as the taxi approached the hospital. She hadn't seen it before and she was curious how it would compare to hospitals in the US. The sign over the door where the taxi dropped them off read "Accident and Emergency." She and Shelly helped Peter out of the car. Shelly paid the driver as Fenella helped Peter through the sliding doors and into the brightly lit lobby.

"My head hurts," Peter said as they walked.

"I'm sure it does," Fenella said soothingly. "Let's see what the doctor says."

The woman behind the reception desk smiled brightly at them. "How can I help?" she asked.

"He fell down some stairs and hit his head," Fenella explained.

"And how much has he had to drink this evening?" the woman asked. "I'm not suggesting that was a factor in the accident," she added quickly, "but it can make a difference in our treatment plan."

"I can talk for myself," Peter said testily. "And I had one glass of wine. If I smell like I've been drinking for days, that's because several additional glasses of wine spilled on me as I fell."

"What a waste," the woman said with another smile.

She handed Peter a clipboard. "If you could just fill these out, we'll get you in to see a doctor as soon as possible."

Fenella and Shelly sat on either side of Peter as he answered questions about his overall health, who his general practitioner was, and what he'd had to eat and drink that day. When he was done, Fenella took the clipboard back to the counter.

"There wasn't a single question about insurance," she said as she sat back down. "In the US, the very first and most important question would have been about that."

"I find it odd that a country like the US doesn't have a National Health Service like ours," Shelly said.

"It is odd," Fenella agreed. "But that's a conversation for another time."

Peter put his hand to his head and moaned quietly. "This is really painful," he complained. "I hope they can see me quickly and get me something for the pain."

It was only a few minutes later that a woman walked out and called his name. He got to his feet and then swayed back and forth for a moment. Fenella stood up quickly and took his arm.

"Maybe you should escort him back," the woman told her. "Or we can get a wheelchair."

"I'm fine," Peter snapped. "But I'm happy for Fenella to come along. I'm not sure I'll remember what the doctor says tomorrow."

The pair followed the woman down a short corridor and into a small exam room.

"You can just lie on the bed," the woman said. "I'll take your vital signs while we wait for the doctor."

While Peter was being checked over, Fenella studied the floor and the ceiling and read the titles on the collection of brochures that were hung in a display case on the wall. She felt slightly out of place being there, but she didn't want Peter to be left alone, either. Shelly probably should have come with him, she thought, he and Shelly had been friends for years.

"Thank you for coming back with me instead of Shelly," Peter said after the woman left the room. "Her dress was making my head hurt more."

Fenella grinned. Shelly loved bright colors and bold patterns, and the dress she was wearing tonight was the perfect example of both. Even without a head injury, it was slightly painful to look at.

"Ah, Peter Cannell? I'm Sarah Grosso," the woman said from the doorway. She took a step into the room and then stopped and stared at Fenella. "But what are you doing here?" she demanded.

"Peter is a friend of mine," Fenella explained. "But I wasn't expecting to see you here. I thought someone told me you worked on the surgical ward."

"I switched to A&E a few weeks ago," Sarah told her. "It pays better, and with the hours that Robert worked, it didn't much matter if I had to work a lot of nights and weekends."

"Are you okay?" Fenella asked, studying the woman. She looked as if she'd been crying.

"Oh, I'm fine," Sarah replied with a wave of her hand. "It's just, well, as if losing Robert wasn't hard enough, I lost a close friend today."

"I am sorry," Fenella said.

Sarah nodded. "Thank you," she said. "I almost didn't come into work tonight. George's murder was almost enough to push me over the edge."

"I didn't realize you knew George Mason," Fenella blurted out.

Sarah nodded and Fenella could see tears in the woman's eyes. "He was, well, a close friend," she said in a soft voice.

Peter shifted on the bed and Sarah looked over at him. "I'm sorry," she said quickly. "I should be concentrating on you and not worrying about my problems."

Fenella sat and wondered exactly what "close friend" meant as Sarah poked and prodded Peter. She seemed nearly as upset at his death as she had been when her husband had died.

"The doctor will be in shortly," she said, straightening up from where she'd been bending over Peter. "I'm sure you have a terrible headache. I'll check with her about getting you something for the pain."

"Thank you," Peter said.

Sarah glanced over at Fenella and then headed for the door. She stopped as she pushed it open. "Robert didn't know that I knew George," she said over her shoulder to Fenella. "I was worried that he'd found out and they'd had a fight. I thought maybe George had accidentally killed Robert. George texted me yesterday morning and wanted to see me. I didn't reply. Maybe if I had, George would still be alive."

"You can't blame yourself for the actions of a murderer," Fenella said firmly. "Maybe if you had been there, the killer would have killed you both."

"Maybe," Sarah said doubtfully. "I wish I knew why my friends are being targeted."

"I'm sure Inspector Robinson is working on that right now," Fenella said.

"I hope so," Sarah said.

She walked out, the door swishing shut behind her.

"I hope she's warned all of her other friends," Peter said from the bed. "It sounds as if she's dangerous to know."

"I don't think either man's death has anything to do with her," Fenella told him. "I think they were both involved in criminal activity that led to their deaths. Their personal involvement with Sarah is merely coincidental."

"Or maybe she's having an affair with a third man and he's eliminating the competition," Peter suggested. "Maybe he set them both up to make it look like they were doing something illegal, but really they weren't."

Fenella frowned. The idea seemed crazy, but she wondered if Daniel had given it any thought. Was it possible that Sarah was the motive for both murders and the burglary ring was just a red herring? She sighed as the door swung open again. This time the new arrival was a middle-aged woman with tired eyes. She was reading the notes on a clipboard as she walked into the room.

"Mr. Cannell? I'm Elaine Gifford, the doctor on duty tonight. How are you feeling?" she said.

"My head hurts," Peter told her. "But lying down seems to have helped with the double vision."

"You had double vision?" she asked.

"Yes, or maybe triple vision," he told her. Fenella was only half listening as Peter talked about the accident and its aftermath. Her brain was puzzling over the exact nature of Sarah's relationships with both murdered men and wondering about Peter's theory. She was startled when the doctor turned to her.

"I'm sorry, but we're going to want to keep him overnight," the woman said. "Someone needs to check on him regularly and I'd prefer for that to be someone with medical training. Head injuries can be tricky and I don't like to take chances."

"That's fine," Fenella said quickly.

"We'll get him up to one of the wards, then," the doctor said. "You can visit him in the morning any time after nine."

"I expect I'll come out with our other neighbor, Shelly, first thing, then," Fenella said. "Do you need anything?" she asked Peter.

"Headache tablets," he said grumpily. "But no, nothing else. I think I'll probably just sleep. You don't need to come back in the morning. I'll get a taxi home when I'm discharged."

"Nonsense," Fenella said. "I'll be here, although we'll still have to get a taxi home, as I don't drive yet."

Peter tried to smile. "I will get you my friend's card," he said. "We'll get you behind the wheel yet."

"Let's get you better before we worry about that," Fenella told him. She gave him an awkward hug and then followed the doctor into the corridor.

"It doesn't seem too bad, although I'm sure it's painful," the doctor told Fenella. "We'll give him something for the pain and check on him through the night. If nothing changes, he can go home tomorrow, although he won't be able to drive or drink alcohol for a week, I'd suggest."

Fenella checked that Peter had given them her phone number in case of emergencies before she walked back into the lobby where Shelly was waiting. Shelly crossed the room rapidly when Fenella emerged from the back.

"How is he?" she asked anxiously.

"He's going up to a ward for the night," Fenella told her. "We can visit tomorrow morning and if nothing has changed, he'll be allowed to go home."

"That's good news," Shelly said.

The pair walked outside and found the hospital's taxi rank. It was nearly midnight and Fenella felt the day's events catch up to her as they rode back to their apartment building. She was barely keeping her eyes open when they arrived. The fresh air was cold and woke her up enough to pay the taxi driver, but the walk back to her apartment was a blur. She and Shelly hugged in the corridor and then Fenella stumbled into her home.

"Where have you been?" Mona demanded. "I've been worried sick about you."

"Peter fell down the stairs at the pub and hit his head," Fenella told her. "Shelly and I took him to the hospital."

"How is he?" Mona asked anxiously.

"They think he's going to be fine," Fenella replied. "But they've kept him overnight, just to be sure."

"The poor man," Mona said. "I must go and visit him. Maybe he's hit his head hard enough that he'll be able to see me."

Fenella was too tired to question her aunt's words. After dumping a handful of dry food into Katie's bowl and giving the kitten a pat, Fenella got ready for bed. She was asleep the minute her head hit the pillow and didn't move again until her alarm went off at seven.

As the clock buzzed insistently, Fenella tried to remember how to switch it off and why she'd set it in the first place. Katie picked up her head and glared at her owner until Fenella finally found the right switch to silence the noise.

"I'm sorry," she said to the kitten. "I don't even know why I set it." Katie shrugged and then put her head back down and went back to sleep. Fenella was thinking about doing the exact same thing when her phone rang. Grumbling to herself, she climbed out of bed and padded over to the nearest receiver.

"Hello?"

"Ah, Fenella, it's Peter," a voice said. "I was just ringing to let you know that the doctors have assured me that I can go home today. They should be letting me out around ten. Maybe you and Shelly could collect me?"

"Someone will be there," Fenella promised.

"Thank you so much," Peter said.

"Are you feeling better?"

"I am, although I still have a painful headache," he told her. "The doctor I saw this morning said that I have a very hard head, but that it will be several days before I'm back to normal."

"I'm glad it wasn't anything serious," Fenella told him. "I'll see you around ten."

"Thank you," Peter replied.

Fenella thought about calling Shelly, but decided to leave it for an hour. There was no need for both of them to be dragged out of bed at seven. Ten o'clock was three hours away. She was halfway back to her own bed when the phone rang again.

"Hello?" she said tiredly.

"Fenella? It's Donald Donaldson. How are you?"

Suddenly feeling wide-awake, Fenella swallowed hard. The handsome and successful businessman had made something of an unpredictable habit out of calling Fenella when she least expected it. He was traveling around the US, taking care of some sort of business dealings, but he called Fenella just enough to keep her from forgetting about him and the handful of kisses they'd shared before he'd left.

"I'm fine, although I'm tired," she said honestly.

"Have I rung you too early in the morning?" he asked. "I'm in California, so it's late at night and I wanted to catch you before I headed to bed."

"I was just up too late last night," Fenella explained.

"Doing something exciting or just enjoying our local pub?" he asked.

"I was at the pub with Shelly and Peter, but Peter fell down the stairs and hit his head," she told him.

"Oh, dear, he is okay, isn't he?" Donald asked, sounding concerned.

"He's fine. I just got off the phone with him and they're letting him go home this morning after a night in the hospital. We took him to the emergency room last night."

"Tell him I hope he feels better soon," Donald said.

"I will."

"You two aren't getting seriously involved, are you?" Donald asked. "Because I want to ask you for a favor, but I don't want to upset Peter."

"We're just friends," Fenella said, not letting herself think about the conversation she'd had with the man in the car on the way to the hospital.

"That's good," Donald said, sounding just a little bit smug. "I'm

166

flying back to the island tomorrow. There's a huge charity fundraiser on Thursday evening that I simply must attend. I was hoping you would do me the honor of accompanying me to the event."

"A charity fundraiser," Fenella echoed.

"Yes, at the Seaview in Ramsey. It's one of those events that everyone who is anyone on the island will be at, and I can't miss it," Donald explained.

"It sounds very fancy and not at all like me," Fenella said honestly.

"It is rather fancy, but I promise we'll have fun," Donald told her. "Unfortunately, I need to fly back to New York the next morning; otherwise, I'd take you out for a rather more enjoyable evening straight away. Instead, I shall just have to promise you something fabulous in the near future in exchange for your time on Thursday."

"What would I wear?" Fenella asked.

"It's black tie, so something formal is needed," Donald told her. "Let me give you my credit card number. You can go shopping and buy whatever you want."

"I couldn't possibly use your credit card," Fenella said quickly. "I'm sure I can find something affordable." Her eyes wandered over to the wardrobe that was still full of Mona's gorgeous clothes. Surely her aunt must have owned an appropriate gown.

"Is that a yes, then?" Donald asked in a teasing voice.

"I suppose so," Fenella said, sighing.

"You don't sound excited," he said.

"I just hope I can get some sleep between now and then," she replied. "I'm sure I'll have more fun if I can keep my eyes open."

Donald laughed. It was a sexy sound that made Fenella feel slightly tingly. "I'll see you Thursday night around seven, then," he said.

Fenella put the phone down, feeling slightly on edge. There was something about Donald that made her nervous and slightly giddy, but she also worried that she couldn't trust the man. A night out at a charity fundraiser wasn't a big deal, she told herself firmly. She took two steps toward the bed when the phone rang a third time.

"What?" she said this time, feeling quite fed up with all of her callers.

"Maggie? Are you okay?" Jack asked.

"I'm fine," she said, feeling even more exhausted.

"It isn't like you answer the phone like that," he said. "Are you quite sure you're okay?"

"I'm just tired. A friend of mine had an accident last night and I spent several hours in the emergency room with him. I didn't get home until well past my usual bedtime."

"Him?" Jack said. "What sort of accident?"

"He was accidentally knocked down a flight of stairs," Fenella said. "But he's fine now. In fact, I have to leave soon to go to the hospital to pick him up."

"Why isn't his wife doing that?" Jack asked.

"He isn't married," Fenella replied.

"How old is he?"

"He's a few years older than me, he's single, he's good-looking and we've been on a few dates, but it isn't anything serious," Fenella told the man.

"I don't think you should be dating other men," Jack said. "It doesn't seem fair to them, really, seeing as you're still recovering from our break up."

Fenella nearly laughed out loud. "That's a decision for me and for Peter," she said after a moment. "And Donald and Daniel," she added impulsively.

"You're dating three different men?" Jack asked, his voice rising to an angry squeak.

"Jack, what do you want?" she asked.

"I want, well, that is, I was calling to see how you are," Jack said. "I worry about you, and clearly for good reason."

"Yes, well, you've no real cause to worry about me. I'm fine and I'm enjoying life, thank you very much."

"Yes, well, I suppose I'm happy for you, although I think it would be more seemly if you were a little bit more upset about the unexpected demise of our relationship," he said stiffly.

"I hope you're moving on as well," Fenella said. "How are Hazel and Sue?"

"They aren't speaking to one another," Jack said, sounding bewildered. "Hazel brought some homemade cookies to my office yesterday, and while she was there Sue stopped by with a box of chocolates that she thought I might like. They started shouting at one another, and in the end the dean had to step in to separate them. I don't know what they were fighting about, really. Something to do with buying affection with laundry, from what I could make out."

Fenella thought about trying to explain it all to the man, but she simply couldn't find the energy. "It might be safer if you stopped accepting presents from both of them," she suggested. "And stopped getting them to do your laundry and grocery shopping."

"Yes, well, I don't know. It's ever so much easier this way."

"Well, good luck, then," Fenella said. "I have to go."

"Wait," he said quickly. "It's the middle of the night over here and I simply couldn't sleep. I had this idea, you see, that it's my sister's birthday soon, but I can't remember exactly when."

"Your sister's birthday is in June," Fenella said.

"Oh, so I haven't missed it? Excellent."

"It's your mother's birthday that's in April," she added. "You did remember to send her a card, didn't you?"

"When in April?" Jack asked.

"The tenth," Fenella said. "You've missed it."

Jack sighed. "I can't believe that you abandoned me like this," he said. "How am I supposed to keep track of such things?"

"You know the calendar in the kitchen?" she asked the man. "The big one on the wall next to the refrigerator?"

"Yes," he replied.

"Before I left I wrote the birthdays of everyone you know on that calendar," she said.

"Oh," Jack said.

"I have to go," Fenella told him. "It's nearly time for me to head to the hospital."

She hung up the phone before he could protest. Every time Jack called she wondered again why she'd stayed with him for so long. And she remembered why they'd each had their own little houses rather than moving in together. While she'd sometimes stayed at his home and he'd often stayed at hers, that was as far as she'd been willing to go. "And that should have told you something about the relationship," she said to her mirror image. Her reflection stuck out her tongue, making Fenella laugh.

After a shower and some breakfast, she called Shelly, who sounded far more awake than Fenella felt. They agreed to go together to pick up Peter from Noble's. Fenella did a bit of tidying around her apartment while she waited for Shelly. When the other woman knocked, Fenella was quick to lock up and follow her to the elevator.

"I'm so glad Peter is okay," Shelly said as they rode down to the parking garage. "It could have been so much worse."

"Yes, he sounded pretty good on the phone this morning," Fenella said. "I just hope he takes it easy for a few days until he's back to normal."

"I'm not sure Peter was ever normal," Shelly said with a laugh.

The day was sunny and bright and the drive to Noble's didn't seem to take long at all.

"I hope he can walk a bit better than he was doing last night," Shelly said once she'd found a parking space. "It's a long walk to the car park here."

"But it's a beautiful day for walking," Fenella said. Spring was finally in the air. Fenella was wearing a light jacket, and for the first time in a long while, she didn't feel chilled when a breeze blew past.

"We need to get out this afternoon and enjoy this weather," Shelly said.

"I'm up for a long walk on the promenade," Fenella said.

"Oh, let's do something more interesting than that," Shelly replied.

They'd reached the front door of the hospital now and took turns to get through the slowly revolving door.

"Did Peter tell you where to find him?" Shelly asked.

"No, and I didn't think to ask," Fenella said.

The woman behind the reception desk was happy to point them in the right direction. "Take the lift to the second floor and follow the signs," she said cheerfully.

A few minutes later, they were greeting their neighbor who was sitting in a chair in his room.

"Someone is supposed to be here any minute now to give me my instructions and let me go," he told the women. "I hope you don't mind waiting."

"Of course not," Shelly said. "But how are you feeling?"

"Quite a bit better," Peter said. "And I'm only seeing one of each of you, as well."

"That is good news," Fenella laughed. "I do think one of me is quite enough, anyway."

"Before I forget, I must tell you about the very strange dream I had," Peter said. "Your Aunt Mona came to visit me."

"Did she?" Fenella asked.

"Yes, and I have to say, she looked wonderful. She didn't look a day over thirty. It's odd that I dreamt of her being younger, as I didn't know her in those days, but it was definitely her."

"How nice," Fenella said faintly.

"We had a lovely long chat, all about you," Peter continued. "And that was odd as well, because she knew all about everything you've been doing since you arrived on the island. Isn't it strange what the brain does when it's asleep?"

"Especially after a bump on the head," Fenella said.

"Yes, especially then," Peter agreed.

The nurse who arrived a moment later had several photocopied sheets of instructions for Peter. Shelly and Fenella waited patiently while she went over them with the man. When she was satisfied that he understood all of the necessary precautions for dealing with his head injury, she smiled.

"You can go, then," she said. "I'm sure you're eager to get out of here."

Peter grinned. "I'm sorry to say it, but yes, I am."

"Everyone always wants to leave," the woman said. "I think it's the food that puts them off."

They all laughed. Fenella wasn't sure how steady Peter was on his feet, but he did well walking to the elevators.

"I should go and get the car," Shelly said as they rode down. "It's miles away."

"I'm quite happy to walk," Peter said. "They kept me in bed all night and most of the morning. Some fresh air and exercise will do me a world of good."

"If you change your mind when we're halfway across the car park, do let me know," Shelly said.

The pleasant morning was turning into a very nice afternoon. The sun was shining and it definitely felt like spring or even summer was right around the corner. Although they walked fairly slowly, Peter did well. The drive back to the apartment building didn't take long and Shelly insisted on dropping Fenella and Peter at the front door.

"I'll go and park the car," she said. "You get Peter up to his flat and get him settled."

"I'm quite capable of looking after myself," Peter said.

"But you'll let us fuss over you, because you know we're worried about you," Shelly replied cheerfully.

Fenella kept out of the argument, but she stayed close to Peter's side as they crossed the lobby and rode the elevator to their floor.

"You really don't need to come in," Peter said as he unlocked his door.

"I could make you a sandwich or some soup," Fenella offered.

Peter opened his mouth, and then shut it and swallowed hard. "That was me, swallowing my pride," he told her. "If you're sure you have the time, I would be grateful if you could heat me up a tin of soup or something. My head is pounding again and I really just want to sit down."

Peter's apartment was similar to Fenella's, but on a smaller scale. From what she could see, it only had one bedroom, and while the kitchens were virtually identical, Peter's living room was noticeably smaller. Everything she could see was clean and tidy, with only an odd book and a few pieces of mail lying out. It didn't take long for Fenella to put together a sandwich and to heat up some soup. Shelly joined them in time to help and they had Peter sitting down to lunch within minutes. He ate everything he was given.

"Would you like something else?" Fenella asked as she cleared away the dirty plates.

"No, I'm nicely full, thank you," Peter said. "It was lukewarm oatmeal for breakfast, so I didn't eat. I didn't think I was hungry, but clearly I was."

"Would you like us to stay and keep you company?" Shelly asked as Fenella loaded the dishwasher.

"I'm going to take a nap," Peter said. "And then I think I'll watch some mindless television for a while. You two go and enjoy the beautiful day."

Shelly and Fenella exchanged glances. "We'll come back and make you something nice for dinner," Shelly said. She opened Peter's refrigerator and studied the contents. "Maybe a nice shepherd's pie, as you seem to have the ingredients."

"That sounds wonderful," Peter said. "I love your shepherd's pie."

"We'll be back in a little while then," Shelly told him. "You get some rest. Would you like to give one of us your spare key so we can let ourselves in, just in case you're still sleeping?"

"I suppose I should," Peter said. "One of you should have a spare anyway, in case I lock myself out."

He disappeared into the bedroom and came back out with a key on a ring. "I lost the spare keycard ages ago," he told them. "But the old key still works in the lock." He looked at Shelly and then Fenella. "I don't know which of you wouldn't mind having it," he said.

"Give it to Fenella," Shelly suggested. "I think she's home more than I am."

Fenella took the key and dropped it into her bag, feeling slightly uncomfortable about the whole thing. Hoping she'd never need the key, she snapped her bag shut and then followed Shelly into the corridor.

"Do you have things you need to do?" Shelly asked after Peter had shut the door behind them. "Or should we go and enjoy a few hours in the sun together?"

"Oh, let's do that," Fenella said quickly. "That sounds much better than doing laundry or research."

"I was thinking we should go to Onchan Park," Shelly said. "We could get lunch in their café and play some crazy golf, maybe even go for a boat ride if they're running."

"I'm not sure about the boat ride," Fenella said. "I'm not a good sailor, remember?"

"These are tiny little motorboats on a very small pond," Shelly said with a laugh. "We won't be moving enough for you to get seasick."

Fenella wasn't sure about that, but she was eager to get out and enjoy the weather. Seeing more of the island was another bonus. After Fenella stopped home to give Katie some lunch, Shelly drove them to the park, which wasn't very far away.

"I thought there would be a noticeable divide between Douglas and Onchan," Fenella said as they got out of the car.

"Oh, no, they run right into one another," Shelly told her. "It might simplify things if they merged into one large city, but there are all sorts of reasons why they never have."

Shelly led her through a large playground full of various equipment for children of all ages and abilities.

"I've never seen such wonderful playground equipment," Fenella said. "It sure has changed a lot since my childhood."

"Some of the swings are specially designed for special needs children, and the roundabout is wheelchair compatible," Shelly said, pointing out the items.

"I think we'd call that a merry-go-round in the US," Fenella said. "I can't remember what I called it when I was little, but we had them in all the parks. I remember them being situated on concrete pads. Nothing like tripping and falling and being dragged over concrete because you didn't let go of the bars."

"Well, they're a good deal safer now, being built over foam or rubber pads, and that one is completely flat to the ground. When I was still teaching I used to come over with the special needs children, and it was lovely that the children in wheelchairs were able to enjoy themselves as much as their peers."

Shelly led Fenella to the café, where they both enjoyed baked potatoes stuffed with cheese. When they'd finished those, Shelly easily persuaded Fenella to indulge in some local ice cream.

"Now I'm too full to want to move," Fenella complained as she wiped her mouth and her fingers after the ice cream.

"Then let's sit in a boat," Shelly suggested.

Fenella eyed the small lake warily. The park was fairly quiet and most of the other visitors were mothers with small children. Only two boats were puttering their way around the lake. Both boats had older couples in them, riding around and enjoying the nice weather.

"Come on," Shelly urged. "You can see how small the lake is. We can stop at any time if you start to feel sick. You're never more than two minutes from the dock, even at the incredibly slow speed these boats travel."

Fenella laughed. "Okay, we can try," she said.

Shelly paid for twenty minutes of rental time and then she and Fenella made their way to the small dock.

"Here we are, ladies," the man on the dock said. "We've just finished getting the boats cleaned up and freshly painted for the new season. You're the first passengers in this one."

He steadied the boat with his foot while Fenella gingerly stepped inside. The boat rocked back and forth a bit, but it wasn't as bad as she'd feared. Shelly climbed in next to her and then sat behind the steering wheel.

"Did you want to drive?" she asked Fenella as the man pulled the cord to start their engine.

"Oh, goodness, no," Fenella said.

After a few minutes, Fenella was relieved to find that Shelly had been right. She felt absolutely fine as they slowly circled the small lake. As they went along, Fenella enjoyed the scenery, which mostly consisted of views of the café, the putting green and the miniature golf course.

"Isn't this nice?" Shelly asked after about ten minutes.

"It's lovely," Fenella told her. "And the perfect weather for it."

"That's because there isn't any wind," Shelly said. "You wouldn't believe it, but it can get quite windy out on this tiny lake."

"It certainly feels like spring today."

"I think they're giving rain for tomorrow, unfortunately," Shelly told her. "And for the weekend as well."

"I'm surprised the park isn't busier, then."

"Most people have to work," Shelly said with a laugh. "The mums will all be leaving soon as well, as they'll need to collect their older children from school before too much longer."

"It will probably get busy once school is out for the day," Fenella speculated.

"I'm sure lots of neighborhood mums will stop here on their way home from school," Shelly agreed. "Nothing better than letting the kids have a run around before you take them home for dinner and homework."

"Do all the kids get picked up at the end of the day?" Fenella asked. "I mean, I know you don't have school buses, but what happens when both parents have to work?"

"Schools have after-school care," Shelly told her. "And lots of mums use childminders who collect all of their charges from school at the end of every day. There are all sorts of options for child care. A lot of women take extended maternity leave as well. I believe women can get up to a year of paid leave."

"Wow, that doesn't happen in the US," Fenella said.

They made another leisurely circuit of the lake, and Fenella looked again at the miniature golf course. It looked like fun with its odd obstacles and ramps. As the boat turned back toward the dock, Fenella noticed a young couple playing the course. As the man leaned into to whisper something to his companion, Fenella gasped.

"What's wrong?" Shelly asked.

Fenella turned in her seat and watched as the man kissed the top of the woman's head. "I know those two," she whispered to Shelly.

"Who are they?"

"Justin Newmarket and Sherry Hampton," Fenella said.

❧ 13 ❧

Shelly drove the boat around the lake another time, giving Fenella a chance to get a better view of Justin and Sherry.

"They look like a couple," Shelly said.

"Poor Harry," Fenella replied.

"It's time to head back to the dock," Shelly told her after a glance at her watch. "And then I think we should play crazy golf."

"I don't know about that," Fenella said.

"Just pretend you didn't see them," Shelly said. "Act surprised and see what sort of explanation they offer."

Shelly pulled the boat up to the dock, hitting it a little bit harder than she probably should have. The man laughed and then helped them both out of the boat. "Did you have fun?" he asked.

"It was lovely," Shelly told him.

"We're here all summer," he said. "Make sure you come back to see me again."

Shelly blushed and glanced at Fenella, who wasn't really paying attention.

"Do you think he was flirting with me?" Shelly demanded as they walked away.

"I don't know, maybe," Fenella said.

"He's probably around my age," Shelly said. "And he was sort of cute. He's probably retired and works here in the summer just to get out of the house."

"Maybe he's married and he works here to get away from his wife," Fenella said. Shelly's face fell. "I'm only teasing," Fenella said quickly. "Why don't we come back again the next time it's nice and you can talk to him a bit more."

"We'll see," Shelly said.

They bought tickets for the golf and picked out clubs and balls.

"Maybe they won't notice us," Fenella said as she put her ball on the first tee.

"Except the course goes up one side and down the other," Shelly pointed out. "And they're just about halfway done."

Fenella forced herself to concentrate on playing the game and tried hard to ignore the couple who were now slowly making their way toward her. They were only a few feet away when she looked over and made eye contact with Justin, who had his arm around Sherry. As their eyes met, Justin jumped and then took a large step backwards, nearly tripping over the small stone castle that was an obstacle on his previous hole.

"Careful," Sherry laughed. She looked at Justin's face and then looked over at Fenella. "Oh, hello," she said lightly.

"Hello," Fenella replied. "I wasn't expecting to see you here."

"It's far too nice a day to be stuck inside," Sherry said. "Harry had a meeting with his financial advisor, so I told him I was going to come down here and play some crazy golf like I did when I was a kid."

"It's the perfect day for it," Fenella said.

"Yes, isn't it?" Sherry replied.

Fenella looked over at Justin, who was studying his shoes intently. After a moment, he looked up and found her staring at him. "Oh, I was, um, that is," he stammered.

"I rang Justin and asked him if he wanted to meet me for a round of golf," Sherry said. "We knew each other at school and we have lots of friends in common. In fact, I told him to round up a whole group of people, but no one else was free this afternoon."

"Well, enjoy your game," Fenella said. She put her ball down and lined up a shot, conscious that Sherry and Justin were still watching her. After a moment, though, they went back to their own game. Fenella and Shelly were nearly halfway around the course when Sherry strolled over.

"You're friends with the police inspector, aren't you?" she asked Fenella.

"I'm not sure that we're friends," Fenella replied. "I mean, I don't know quite what we are."

Sherry nodded. "I was just wondering whether Harry is a real suspect or not," she said. "I mean, he does have a lot of money in the bank. I never thought about it, but I'm not sure exactly where he got it all. He doesn't seem the type to be involved in anything criminal, but you never know, do you?"

"I'm sorry, but I've no idea who the police suspect," Fenella said. "Inspector Robinson doesn't discuss police business with me."

"Sure, but you must get some interesting pillow talk. I just want to know if my husband is going to be arrested or not."

Fenella shook her head. "We aren't that good of friends," she said emphatically. "Maybe you should be having this conversation with your husband. Perhaps you should ask him where all of his money came from."

"He'll just fob me off with the same answer he always gives. He never stops banging on and on about how hard he and his wife worked for their entire working lives. He seems to think that I should go out and get a job to bring in even more money. It gets quite tiresome."

"A job would get you out of the house," Fenella pointed out.

Sherry shrugged. "I don't know. I'm not sure I'm well-suited to marriage anyway. And I don't really think Harry would miss me if I went. The problem is, he isn't going to want me to take any of his money with me."

"I can see his point," Fenella said dryly.

"Anyway, I'd better get home. He'll be done with his financial advisor by now. I'm hoping his investments are doing well and he'll be in a generous mood. I saw this gorgeous bracelet in the jeweler's window..." she trailed off and walked away, leaving Fenella staring after her.

"Poor Harry," Shelly murmured.

They finished their round of golf and then headed for home. While Fenella wasn't actually worried about Peter, she knew she'd feel better once she and Shelly had checked on him again.

He answered her soft knock within seconds. "I gave you a key," he reminded her. "I'm sure I didn't dream that."

Fenella laughed. "I didn't feel right just barging in," she said.

"You'd have been welcome," he said. "I had a nap and I was just getting fed up with the drivel on daytime telly. Your timing is perfect."

"I hope you're also getting hungry," Shelly said. "We've been at the park and all that fresh air has given me quite an appetite."

She went to work in the kitchen, getting the shepherd's pie ready for the oven while Peter and Fenella chatted in the comfortable living room.

"Tomorrow you can cook," Shelly said to Fenella as she settled onto the couch next to Peter. "Tonight's dinner is in the oven."

"I wish I could, but tomorrow night I'm supposed to be going to some fancy charity fundraiser with Donald," Fenella replied.

"Donald Donaldson?" Peter asked. "I didn't realize he was back on the island."

"He's flying in today for the event tomorrow," Fenella explained. "And then he has to leave again, I understand."

"Wow, must be nice to be able to afford to fly back and forth for just one day," Shelly said.

"Is it the event out at the Seaview?" Peter asked.

"I think that's what he said," Fenella replied.

"Oh, that's very posh," Shelly said. "Only a few very select people get invited to that."

"I was invited," Peter said. "I used to go sometimes, but this year, I decided not to spend the money. Tables run into the thousands of pounds and there are other charities that I'd rather support."

"What should I wear?" Fenella asked Shelly.

"You'll have to raid Mona's wardrobe," Shelly told her. "After dinner, I'll come over with you and help you choose, if you'd like."

"Oh, yes, please," Fenella said quickly. "Donald said long gowns were appropriate. I'm not sure Mona even had anything like that."

Shelly looked at Peter and they both laughed. "Mona had some of the most gorgeous gowns I've ever seen," Shelly told her. "She went to a great many very fancy events over the years. I've no doubt you'll find several things to choose from in her wardrobe."

The shepherd's pie was delicious and the threesome chatted easily about nothing and everything as they ate. After dinner, Peter decided that he was too tired for company and headed for bed. Shelly and Fenella went back to Fenella's apartment to look at Mona's dresses.

The light was blinking on her answering machine as Fenella let herself and her friend into the apartment.

"It's Donald. I just wanted to let you know that I'm in New York now and should be back on the island around eleven tomorrow morning. I plan on sleeping from then until time to get ready for the party. I'll see you around seven," was the first message, which made Fenella smile.

The second message made her less happy. "Yes, Ms. Woods, it's Jessica Harris from Isle of Man Ferries. As the last meeting we had with you had to be cut short, Captain Howard would appreciate your attending another session on Friday at one o'clock. This time the police will also be in attendance. Please let me know if you can not attend."

Deciding to simply ignore the message for now, Fenella led Shelly into her bedroom and threw open the doors to Mona's wardrobe. She kept meaning to go through everything in it, but it felt intrusive, especially with Mona's ghost wandering in and out all the time.

"This one," Shelly said, pulling a long red dress off of the rack. "Or no, this one," she said quickly, adding a blue gown to her hand. "Or you could go with classic black," she added, pulling a third dress from the wardrobe.

"Oh, goodness," Fenella said. "How can I ever choose?"

"Try them all on," Shelly suggested. "And while you do that, I'll see what else I can find."

Fenella took the dresses into the adjoining bathroom and slipped into the red one. It fit perfectly.

"I look glamorous," she said to Shelly as she walked out of the bathroom.

"You look amazing," Shelly cooed. "That one would be perfect, but try the others, too."

Fenella changed into first the blue and then the black dress. While they both fit her well, neither made her feel as gorgeous as the red one had.

"It's the red one," Shelly said definitely, after she'd seen the other two options. "Although I did find a few others, if you're interested."

Fenella glanced at the dresses on Shelly's arm and shook her head. "I think I'll just go with the red one. I feel fabulous in it, even though I didn't shave my legs today. Imagine how wonderful I'll feel tomorrow night with smooth legs."

Shelly laughed. "There are some fabulous silver shoes in here that will be perfect with that dress," she said. "And a matching evening bag."

"That was easier than I thought it would be," Fenella said a short time later. She and Shelly were curled up on the couch sipping soft drinks, with Katie between them.

"Are you excited about seeing Donald again?" Shelly asked.

"Excited? I don't know. Nervous might be a better word. He's out of my league, really."

"He isn't," Shelly laughed. "And don't you let yourself think that way. He's rich, but that doesn't make him any better than you."

After Shelly left, Fenella got ready for bed. She gave Katie fresh water and a handful of dry food and then switched off the lights in the kitchen.

"I loved that dress," Mona said softly from somewhere behind Fenella.

"It's beautiful," Fenella said, after her heart rate returned to normal.

"I wore it for several very special occasions, including the wedding of a man who'd treated me very badly," Mona said. "His wife-to-be nearly didn't go through with the ceremony when she saw me."

"I'm just going to a charity fundraiser with Donald," Fenella said.

"You'll be the best dressed there," Mona predicted. "And the subject of a great deal of conversation."

"Why?"

"Donald is well-known and important on the island," Mona told her. "Who he chooses to spend his time with is of interest to many people with nothing else with which to entertain themselves."

"It's going to be awkward and awful, isn't it?" Fenella asked.

"You must simply rise above it," Mona counseled her. "Spend time with Donald, have fun, and ignore the looks and the whispering."

"I'll try," Fenella said.

"Channel your inner Aunt Mona," Mona advised. "I never went anywhere without getting talked about. It can be quite fun in a way. Just act as if you don't care, and after a while you'll find that you actually don't."

"Did you go and visit Peter?" Fenella asked.

"I told you I was going to," Mona replied.

"But he could see you," Fenella said. "And I thought you couldn't go anywhere outside of the apartment, anyway."

Mona sighed. "I really don't have the time to explain the entire spirit world to you right now," she said. "There are limits to where I can go, but a quick trip to Noble's to see Peter didn't use up too much energy. And it was worth it. I miss him and Shelly quite a lot."

"You get to see them nearly every day," Fenella pointed out.

"But I don't get to talk to them," Mona said. "It was lovely to talk to him. He's quite taken with you, by the way. You must take care not to break his heart."

"As if I could," Fenella said. "But what did he say about me?"

Mona didn't reply. After a minute, Fenella switched the lights back on. Katie looked up from her water bowl but Mona was nowhere to be seen. Frowning, Fenella turned off the lights again and took herself off to bed.

"Meerrrooowww," Katie said, patting Fenella on the tip of her nose. "Mmmeeeerrrrooooowwwwww."

Fenella opened one eye and squinted at the clock. It was six and far too early to think about getting up. "Go away," she muttered to the kitten. Rolling over, she pulled the duvet up over her head and tucked it in around her nose.

"Yooowwww," Katie said. A moment later, Katie jumped squarely onto Fenella's head. When Fenella didn't move, she began to walk down her neck and onto her shoulder. By the time she reached Fenella's hip, Fenella was laughing.

"Okay, you win," she said. Katie jumped down and Fenella rolled out of bed. After giving the kitten her breakfast, Fenella took a shower and got dressed. She made herself some toast with jam for her own breakfast before wondering if she should check on Peter.

After several minutes of indecision, she decided to try knocking gently on his door. The door swung open almost immediately.

"I just wanted to check on you," she stammered, surprised to see the man fully dressed and looking back to his old self.

"I'm fine," he said with a sigh. "But I'm also tired of being an invalid. I want to get out somewhere and do something."

"Why don't we go to ShopFast?" Shelly suggested in a bright voice from behind Fenella. "I noticed yesterday that you were out of nearly everything. If you think you're up to it, I'll take you over and you can get what you need."

"I think I'm up to it," Peter said. "And you're right. I had stale cereal for breakfast."

"You should have come next door," Fenella said. "I have stale bread for toast."

"So you need a shopping trip, too," Shelly said. "We'll leave in five minutes."

It was closer to ten minutes before everyone was ready to go, but the shopping trip itself didn't take long. Peter got tired quite quickly, but as it was early, the store wasn't busy and they managed to get everything on his list before he needed to head for home. Fenella got everything on her list as well, and she felt better a short time later when her shelves and refrigerator were fully stocked.

"Lunch in my flat at twelve," Peter told them both as they carried his shopping into his kitchen for him. "I'll heat soup and put out everything for sandwiches. I just need a short nap first."

After lunch Fenella and Shelly took a long walk on the promenade before Fenella returned home to soak in her tub for a while.

"It's exactly what you need before your big night out," Shelly had told her during their walk. "A long, leisurely bath will get you in the right frame of mind for tonight. Take a glass of wine in with you."

"I'm only following Shelly's advice," Fenella told her reflection as she slipped into her bubble-filled tub with a glass of wine in one hand and a book in the other. Half an hour later, she remembered why she never took long baths. The wine was delicious, but the book was a problem. She didn't want to get it wet, but holding it above the bubbles made her arms tired. Besides, she kept slipping further into the water and having to use one hand to stop herself, which meant turning pages was impossible. With a sigh, she put the book as far from the tub as she could and settled back to relax.

"I'm bored," she said after a moment. "I don't think baths are really my thing."

With that thought in mind, she finished her wine and climbed out of the tub. When she was dry, she watched some pointless television until it was time to start getting ready for the evening ahead.

The butterflies in her stomach threatened to make her sick as she dropped the red gown over her head. Once she'd fastened the zipper, however, she found that she felt calm and collected. Really, this dress is magical, she thought, as she pinned up her hair and applied her makeup. The silver shoes looked wonderful with the dress and it only took her a moment to move what she needed from her everyday handbag into the small evening bag that matched the shoes. She was ready to go with two minutes to spare.

"You look stunning," Donald told her when she opened the door to his knock. "I can't tell you how much I wish I didn't have to fly back to New York tomorrow."

"You look pretty good yourself," Fenella said, taking in the handsome dark-haired man's perfectly fitted tuxedo.

"Shall we?" he invited her, offering his arm.

Fenella took it and let him lead her out into the corridor. When they reached the lobby, she was surprised to see a limousine at the door.

"I wasn't expecting this," she murmured as Donald helped her into the car.

"Everyone will be arriving by limo tonight," Donald said. "It's that kind of evening."

A few butterflies flitted through Fenella's stomach, but she managed to ignore them and focus on Donald. He made her tell him what she'd been doing since he'd left the island and then told her a few stories about his travels and business dealings. They drove to Ramsey along the coast road and Fenella could barely take her eyes off the scenery as they went.

"I can't believe how beautiful the island is," she told Donald. "Or rather, I can't imagine why it isn't overpopulated. Who wouldn't want to live here?"

Donald laughed. "It is special, but there are many other islands with gorgeous views and much nicer weather," he said. "I have a little house in Tortola in the Virgin Islands. I need to take you there one day."

Fenella was glad she was looking out the window. Hopefully, Donald couldn't see her blushing that way. The thought of traveling with him to a Caribbean island was slightly overwhelming, even in her magic red dress.

Outside the huge hotel, a red carpet had been laid out. As Fenella stepped out of the car, flashbulbs popped and someone shouted. "Donald, who's your friend?"

Donald smiled as he took Fenella's arm and led her into the hotel's vast lobby. "We're down here," he said, leading her through the lobby and down a long corridor. The thick carpeting made walking in her heels slightly difficult, but with Donald's arm to lean on, Fenella made it to the huge ballroom unscathed.

Gorgeous crystal chandeliers sparkled above tables set with cut crystal wineglasses and shining silver cutlery. There were fountains dispensing drinks scattered around the room and formally dressed waiters and waitresses seemed to be everywhere with trays full of delicious-looking tidbits.

"Wow," Fenella breathed.

"It is lovely," Donald said. "Let's get some champagne."

With glasses of champagne in hand, the pair began to circulate. Fenella quickly gave up on trying to remember all of the names of the people to whom she was introduced. She met many members of the island's government, company CEOs, and a few minor celebrities who she suspected had been flown to the island especially for the event.

"That's one circuit of the room done," Donald said some time later as they found themselves back at the champagne fountain where they'd started. "I need another drink before we start over again."

"Must we?" Fenella blushed as she realized she'd spoken out loud.

Donald grinned. "We can stand here for a short while," he said. "Maybe people will come and find us, instead of us having to go and find them."

A moment later, Fenella heard a familiar voice.

"My goodness, what are you doing here?" Florence March said in a shocked voice.

Fenella forced herself to smile as she turned to face the woman and her husband.

"Mrs. March, this is a pleasant surprise," she lied brightly.

Stanley frowned. "It's Fenella something, isn't it? From the ferry? I wasn't expecting to see you here."

Donald slid an arm around Fenella's shoulders. "Fenella is a very dear friend of mine," he said smoothly. "She was kind enough to agree to accompany me tonight."

Stanley looked at Florence, who frowned. "Donald, it's always nice to see you," she said after a minute.

"It's always lovely to see you as well," Donald said. "You and Stanley seem to travel almost as much as I do. We're hardly ever on the island at the same time."

"Except you travel for business and we travel for pleasure," Florence said. "I'm not sure we'll be taking the ferry again, though. Not after the unpleasantness last weekend."

"Yes, of course, that's where you met my Fenella," Donald said. "I can't imagine how difficult that must have been for you all."

"We had to cancel all manner of plans," Stanley complained. "It was incredibly inconvenient."

"And poor Robert Grosso died," Fenella reminded them.

"Yes, but I can't help but think that he was doing something criminal, sneaking on board the boat early like that," Florence said. "We boarded early, of course, but only because it's so much more convenient that way."

"You boarded early?" Fenella asked.

"Not terribly early," Florence said quickly. "Just a little bit before we were technically supposed to. Our driver takes the car on, you see, and we travel as foot passengers. One of the staff was kind enough to let us get on board and collect our cabin keys before it grew busy."

"I see," Fenella said thoughtfully. "I don't suppose you saw Robert Grosso or any of the others on the ship?"

Florence shook her head. "It's all something of a mess, really," she said.

"We'd rather not talk about it with the ferry captain," Stanley said. "We don't want the poor young woman who let us on early to lose her job. She was only trying to be nice."

"I assume you've told the police," Fenella said.

"Oh, no, we can't do that," Florence said. "They'll tell Captain Howard and the poor girl will be let go for sure."

Fenella wanted to argue, but she bit her tongue. The couple had empty glasses in their hands, and Fenella was pretty sure those hadn't been their first drinks of the evening. It was unlikely that they would have shared that information with her if they'd been sober.

"So, how's business?" Donald asked Stanley.

"Oh, you know, I just dabble a bit now to keep my hand in," Stanley said. "I've been thinking about getting involved in that project that Peter Cannell has been working on, but I'm not sure."

"That's a beautiful dress," Florence said as the two men began to discuss things that Fenella knew nothing about.

"Thank you," Fenella replied.

"Where did you find it?" Florence asked.

"Oh, it's something from back in the US," Fenella found herself saying. "I brought a lot of clothes with me."

"I'm sure," Florence said. "What did you do in the US?"

"I was a professor of history at a university there," Fenella replied.

"Really?" the other woman said. "I never would have suspected."

"What do you do?" Fenella asked, wondering if the question was rude.

"Me? I look after Stanley. The children are grown, of course, and quite capable of looking after themselves, but Stanley enjoys me fussing over him."

"I had a partner like that once," Fenella said. "After a while, I got tired of looking after a grown adult."

Florence shrugged. "I've been doing it for a great many years now," she said. "I can't imagine doing anything else."

"Maybe you should go back to school," Fenella suggested.

"I never really enjoyed school," the woman told her. "It took up far too much of my time. My mother used to take me out for a day and we'd go across to Liverpool and shop." She glanced around and then stepped closer to Fenella and lowered her voice.

"I was raised to be a rich man's wife," she said. "My mother came from a very poor background, but she managed to marry well above her station. She was determined that I'd find a wealthy man and never have to work."

"And she got her wish," Fenella said.

"Oh, taking care of Stanley is hard work, make no mistake about that," Florence said. She smiled, presumably to make it seem like she was joking, but the smile looked bitter to Fenella.

"It's never too late to start a new life for yourself," Fenella said. "What would you do, if you could do anything?"

Florence blinked at her. "I've no idea," she said after a minute. "No one ever asks me what I want to do. My mother managed my childhood and I married Stanley at eighteen."

"But are you happy?" Fenella had to ask.

"Happy?" the other woman echoed, as if the word was unfamiliar to her.

"Florence, we need to go and speak to Michael," Stanley said suddenly.

"Oh, but, I mean, I'm enjoying talking to Fenella," Florence said.

"That's nice, but I need to speak to Michael." Stanley held out his hand and Florence took it.

She turned back to Fenella as they walked away. "It was nice seeing you," she said quickly before Stanley pulled her into a large crowd.

"That poor woman," Fenella said as the crowd swallowed up the Marches.

"Stanley isn't that bad," Donald said. "He spoils her, and as far as I know, he's never looked at another woman. She could have done much worse."

"But she isn't happy," Fenella argued.

"Isn't she? I didn't realize," Donald said.

Fenella opened her mouth to explain, but sighed instead. "Maybe she is, in her own way," she conceded. "Just because her life isn't one that I would be comfortable with doesn't make it bad."

"And on that note, I think they're ready to serve dinner," Donald said.

The food was delicious and Fenella felt lucky that the other men and women at their assigned table were interesting and friendly. After eating and drinking far too much, Fenella settled back in her chair for the charity auction.

"You must let me buy you something to thank you for coming with me tonight," Donald told her.

Rather than argue, Fenella shrugged. "When I see something I want, I'll let you know," she said. He could hardly blame her if she never saw something she wanted, could he, she thought as the first item came up on the auction block.

It was harder than she thought it would be, trying to act like she didn't want anything, though, as some of the items were amazing. A fortnight's holiday in France sounded incredible, but Fenella forced herself to feign indifference. She wasn't ready to spend two weeks with Donald in a foreign country where she didn't speak the language, she reminded herself.

An hour later the auction was over. Donald had bought several pieces of artwork, explaining to Fenella that he liked to support local artists and always displayed their art in his offices around the world.

"But I really did want to buy you something," he said after he'd written a huge check for his purchases. "Now I will have to send you something from New York."

"Don't be silly," Fenella told him. "I don't want anything."

"We'll see," he said. The drive home was less interesting, as it was very dark and rainy. When they reached Fenella's apartment building, Donald sighed.

"I'll walk you to your door, but I really can't stay," he told her.

"You don't need to," Fenella told him. "You go home and get some sleep. It took me weeks to get over my jet lag. I don't know how you're functioning."

"Not very well," he admitted. "And tomorrow I'll be back on New York time. Maybe that will be easier, though. I don't know."

"Go home," Fenella said sternly.

He smiled and then pulled her close. "Not without at least one kiss," he said softly. One kiss turned into several as Fenella felt herself getting lost in an almost overwhelming physical attraction. When Donald finally lifted his head, he stared at her for a moment.

"Maybe I should come up for coffee, after all," he said.

Knowing he wasn't talking about coffee, Fenella shook her head. "I don't think so," she said, annoyed with herself for sounding uncertain.

"I'll be back on the island by the end of May," he said. "I'll ring you."

"Thank you for an interesting evening," Fenella said.

Donald kissed her very gently on the lips and then nodded at his driver. The man got out of the car and quickly opened Fenella's door for her. She felt slightly giddy as she walked across the lobby and into the elevator.

"I did warn you about Donald," Mona said as Fenella let herself into the apartment. "You look like a teenaged girl who's just had her first kiss. That simply won't do."

Fenella shook her head. "I remember the warning," she said. "And I'm taking it slowly and being careful. But I have to tell you, that man can kiss."

Mona frowned, but Fenella ignored her and took herself off to bed.

❧ 14 ❧

Katie didn't let Fenella oversleep the next morning. After she tried patting Fenella's nose, to no avail, she jumped up on Fenella's chest and bounced up and down several times.

"Really?" Fenella said. "I had a late night and a lot of wine. I don't want to wake up."

"Meerroow," Katie said, sounding almost sympathetic. She jumped off the bed and raced out of the room. A moment later Fenella could hear her shouting loudly from the kitchen.

"You won't starve to death if you have to wait another hour for breakfast," Fenella called loudly.

A moment later she could hear Katie walking back toward the bedroom. When everything went oddly quiet, Fenella sat up in bed. It took her a minute to realize that the faint noise she could hear was the toilet paper being unwound. She'd forgotten to close the bathroom door last night when she went to bed.

"Katie!" she shouted. The kitten's small head peered around the bathroom door.

"Errowwoww?" she said in a quizzical tone.

"Get out of the bathroom," Fenella said sternly.

Katie stalked out of the bathroom and through the bedroom back into the kitchen. Fenella sighed as the small animal began to loudly complain about her lack of breakfast again.

"Maybe I should give you to Shelly," Fenella muttered under her breath as she climbed out of bed. In the bathroom, the entire roll of toilet paper had been unwound onto the floor. Fenella rolled it back up, thankful at least that Katie hadn't had time to shred it. With that job done and the bathroom door firmly shut, Fenella went into the kitchen and gave Katie her breakfast.

"And now I'm going back to bed," she told her pet. "And I don't want to be disturbed."

She was just climbing back under the duvet when someone knocked on her door. Suddenly aware that she hadn't given poor Peter a single thought since dinner yesterday, Fenella rushed to answer it.

"I've woken you," Shelly said apologetically.

"No, Katie woke me," Fenella told her. "She's very good at it."

Shelly laughed. "I just finished making a nice breakfast for Peter and I thought I would see if you wanted to go on an errand with me."

"How is Peter?" Fenella asked.

"He's doing well. He has some business associates visiting this morning and then they're meant to be taking him out for lunch. He has promised me he won't make any important decisions for a few days, regardless."

"That's probably wise," Fenella said.

"Yes, so I told him that I'd come over in time to make him something for dinner. I didn't know what you had planned for today," Shelly said.

Fenella frowned. "I know there's something, but I can't think what," she said. "Maybe it will come back to me after I get showered and dressed."

"Did you have a nice time last night?" Shelly asked.

"I did, thanks," Fenella said. "It was an interesting evening, but I met far too many people and I don't remember anyone's name."

Fenella invited the other woman inside, and Shelly played with Katie while Fenella got herself ready for the day. As she walked out of the bedroom, she glanced at the answering machine and remembered her appointment.

"I'm supposed to go back to the Sea Terminal to meet with Captain Howard this afternoon," she said with a sigh. "I'm not looking forward to that."

"Do you have to go?" Shelly asked.

"I don't know. The woman from the ferry company did say that the police were going to be there. I don't know if that means it's an official meeting or not."

"Ring Daniel and ask him," Shelly suggested.

Fenella frowned. She hadn't seen Daniel in several days; calling him seemed awkward. "Maybe I'll just go," she said.

"Does that mean your morning is free?" Shelly asked.

"Yes, I think so," Fenella replied.

"Would you like to come with me to the animal shelter, then? I think it's time I found myself a kitten."

Fenella grinned. "I'd love to," she said.

The nearest shelter wasn't far away, so the pair decided to walk.

"I want a white kitten," Shelly told Fenella. "Or maybe white and black. And I definitely want a kitten. Older cats have their own sets of challenges. I want to be able to bring up a kitten myself, rather than worry about what my cat's previous owner might have done."

"I do think kittens are wonderful, but they can be incredibly mischievous," Fenella said, thinking about rolling up the toilet paper.

"I'm home nearly all the time," Shelly pointed out. "She won't have the opportunity to cause any mischief."

Inside the shelter, dozens of cats of all ages were spread out around the room. Some were lounging on chairs or couches and others were curled up in cat beds that seemed to be nearly everywhere.

"How can we help you?" the woman behind the desk asked as Fenella and Shelly approached.

"I've decided I want to adopt a kitten," Shelly said.

"How nice," the woman exclaimed. "Have a good look around. We have a few kittens scattered around the place. Give them all a good look and then let me know which one you like best."

Fenella looked around. "I don't even know where you should start," she told Shelly.

Shelly went over to a nearby couch and sat down. "Maybe I'll see if anyone comes to me," she said.

Fenella joined her, looking around at all the beautiful animals. "I'm glad I already have my Katie, otherwise I might be tempted," she said as she watched two kittens wrestling with one another.

A moment later a large grey cat jumped down off of a high platform and strolled across the room. Her eyes were focused on the large picture window at the front of the building. Seemingly accidentally, she reached the couch and then jumped into Shelly's lap.

"My goodness, but you aren't at all what I'm looking for," Shelly said to the animal. The cat blinked at her and then settled into her lap. "Just a quick cuddle, then," Shelly said. "But then I'm going to find a kitten to take home."

Half an hour later, paperwork complete, Shelly was ready to carry the grey cat back to her apartment.

"I can't believe I'm doing this," she said for the third time as she and Fenella walked out of the adoption center. "She weighs a ton, too."

"Yowl," the cat said as she shifted herself in Shelly's arms.

"She's gorgeous," Fenella told her. "And she chose you. I don't think you had much choice."

"No, I really didn't," Shelly agreed happily.

They parted ways outside of Fenella's door. "I don't think we want to introduce Smokey to Katie just yet," Shelly said. "I think I need to get her settled in at home first."

"You have everything you need for her, right?" Fenella checked.

"Yes. I bought a lot of it when I was going to be cat-sitting for Katie, and then I never used it," Shelly said. "I'm all set."

Fenella let herself into her apartment. When Katie came to meet her, she scooped her up and gave her a big hug. "You've nothing to worry about," she told the kitten. "I wasn't even a little bit tempted to replace you with someone else."

"Merow," Katie said, nuzzling Fenella's face.

After making herself some lunch, Fenella changed into clean clothes for her meeting at the Sea Terminal. The black pants and navy sweater she'd been wearing earlier were covered in cat hair. She left a few minutes earlier than she needed to for the walk, expecting to spend time waiting at customer service again. Instead, as she entered the building this time, she was greeted by name.

"Ms. Woods," Constable Corlett said. "Inspector Robinson is waiting for you in conference room two."

A second uniformed constable escorted Fenella down the corridor. Daniel was sitting at the head of a long table with Captain Howard next to him. They were talking intently as Fenella entered.

"I hope we'll get those answers today," Daniel said.

"If we don't, maybe you can just arrest them all," the captain replied.

"Ah, Fenella, er, Ms. Woods, thank you for joining us," Daniel said as he looked up. "Captain Howard, you remember Ms. Woods?"

"She's the one who caused all of the trouble," the other man growled. "She rang you instead of informing a member of my staff about the body."

"I believe the murderer should be getting the blame, not me," Fenella said crossly.

Before the captain could reply, Stanley and Florence March were escorted into the room. As they found seats, the other cabin passengers seemed to arrive all at once. Within minutes everyone was seated around the table, looking expectantly at Daniel.

"Thank you all for coming," he said. "Your meeting with Captain Howard was unfortunately interrupted the other day. When he explained to me why he'd wanted to speak with all of you, it seemed that it might be beneficial to reschedule the meeting with myself in attendance."

"So what do you want?" Stanley snapped.

"We're trying to work out the order in which everyone boarded the ferry," Daniel explained. "But the statements we've taken don't seem to match the footage from the security video. I'd like to suggest that if any of you would like to amend your statements, now would be a good time to do so. Keep in mind that we do have some video footage and that we've been comparing that with what you've all told me. I have constables outside who can take any new information you'd like to share."

"I think people are worried that they might get others into trouble," Fenella said tentatively, not looking at Stanley or Florence.

"I want to assure you all that we, as a company, recognize that it is more important to solve these murders than to worry about minor infractions of the rules. If someone let you on the ferry early and you're worried about that person's job, please don't be. I won't be firing anyone for having done that."

"We boarded early," Florence said. "A very nice young lady at customer service arranged it for us. She had a member of the security staff walk us through security and onto the ferry. The girl at customer service sorted our cabin keys for us as well."

"How early did you board?" Daniel asked.

Florence glanced at Stanley. "Maybe about an hour before they started letting everyone else on," she said.

Daniel raised an eyebrow and then made a note in his notebook. "Did anyone else board early?" he asked.

"I did, but only a few minutes early," Justin said. "I went to school with one of the girls who works in the gift shop on the ferry. I bumped into her as she was walking through the terminal building and we were chatting. She said I could walk on with her, as I had a proper ticket and everything. Once I got there, she dug out my cabin key for me."

"I see," Daniel said. "Anyone else?"

"Brenda and I boarded early, too," Nick said. "Like the other couple, we asked at customer service and they said that we could. The girl there had someone walk us through and that person got us our cabin keys."

"Do you know who it was who escorted you onto the ferry?" Captain Howard asked.

"It was some man," Brenda said. "He was about twenty-five and his head was shaved."

Daniel flipped through a file in front of him and held up a photograph. "Is this the man?" he asked.

Brenda shrugged. "It could have been," she said. "I know that's the other man who was killed, but I'm not sure if that's the man who took us onto the ferry or not. It looks like him, but I wasn't really paying attention."

"Mr. Proper, do you recognize the man in the photo?" Daniel asked.

Nick shrugged. "Maybe," he said. "If it wasn't him, it was someone who looks quite like him."

"But you didn't think to mention that to me when we talked earlier," Daniel said as he made notes.

"You asked if I knew the man in the photograph," Nick said. "His showing us onto the ferry a few days earlier isn't exactly the same as knowing him."

"What time did you arrive on the ferry?" Daniel asked.

"I don't know, not too early," Nick said. "Just long enough to get ourselves settled into the cabin. We were quite happy to just wait out the journey there."

"But I saw you," Fenella blurted out.

Daniel looked over at her and she blushed under his stare. "You saw them?" he asked after a moment.

"Yes, when I first walked out of my cabin, I saw them. They came up the stairs and looked at me and then let themselves into one of the other cabins."

"We went down to get a newspaper," Brenda said quickly.

"Did they have a newspaper?" Daniel asked.

"It was in my bag," Brenda snapped.

"I don't like the direction this is going," Nick said. "I think Brenda and I have had quite enough for today." He stood up and motioned to Brenda, who jumped to her feet.

"Just a few more questions, please," Daniel said.

"I don't think so," Nick replied.

"We can continue the conversation in my office, if you'd prefer," Daniel said in a pleasant voice.

Both Nick and Brenda sat back down, but neither looked happy about it. "Fenella," Daniel said, "who else did you see in the corridor while you were waiting for the police?"

Fenella closed her eyes and tried to think. She'd told Daniel all of this on the day it had happened. He had to have it all in his notes. "Mr. and Mrs. March came up the stairs as well," she said after a minute.

"We did," Florence agreed. "I wanted to change some of my Manx money for English, so we went down to see about that, but they weren't open yet."

"I see," Daniel said. "And why did you both need to go?"

"I wasn't letting my wife wander around the ferry with several thousand pounds in cash in her pocket," Stanley said tersely.

Daniel made another note and then looked at Justin. "And you were safely tucked up in your cabin while all of this was going on?" he asked.

"I suppose so," Justin said. "Once I got in there, I didn't leave until we were ordered out by the police. I was, um, going to wait until we were underway before I went out to see if there were any pretty girls around."

Fenella knew he was lying, but she bit her tongue. That he was prone to seasickness didn't seem relevant at this point.

Nick had relaxed slightly while Daniel had been talking to the others; now Fenella watched him tense up as Daniel looked at him. "Mr. Proper, your wife said you went down to the gift shop to get a newspaper. Is that correct?"

Nick swallowed hard. "I don't recall," he said after a moment. "We got on the ferry and into our cabin. After a while, Brenda said something about going to the gift shop, so we went. When we got back up the stairs by the cabin, Ms. Woods was standing outside her door, looking all pale and upset. The next thing we knew, we were being escorted off the ferry."

"You didn't try to speak to Ms. Woods, in spite of seeing that she was upset?" Daniel asked.

"I, er, no," Nick replied. "That's more Brenda's line than mine, and she was eager to lie down."

"Mr. and Mrs. March, do you remember seeing Ms. Woods on the ferry?" Daniel asked.

"I'm pretty sure it's in my statement," Stanley said. "We were getting ready for the ship to sail and when we went up to our cabin, Ms. Woods was standing in the corridor."

"And did you also see Mr. and Mrs. Proper?" Daniel asked.

Stanley frowned. "I don't think so," he said.

"I saw them," Florence said. "I didn't pay any attention at the time, but now that you've mentioned it, I saw them in the passenger lounge.

They were talking to that man in your photograph about something. He didn't look very happy."

"This was after the ferry was boarding?" Daniel asked.

"Yes," Florence said. "After we boarded and went to our cabin, we didn't want to leave until other people were being let on board. We were worried that someone might question us about being on the ferry early."

Daniel looked over at Nick. "Do you remember talking to Mr. Mason again, after boarding started?" he asked.

"Yeah, but I didn't want to mention it," Nick said. "The thing is..."

Daniel held up a hand. "I think we might be better off having this conversation in my office, privately," he said. As he stood up, Nick continued.

"It wasn't a big deal," he said. "He wanted some money from me, that's all."

Daniel frowned. "As I said, let's take this down to my office," he said. He had his phone in his hand, and a moment later the door opened and two uniformed constables walked in.

"Please take Mr. Proper down to my office. I'd like Mrs. Proper escorted to the station as well, but they need to go in separate cars," Daniel said.

"I'm sure Brenda remembers exactly what happened," Nick said quickly. "How the man asked for a hundred pounds and I said..."

"That's quite enough," Daniel said loudly. "If you say one more word, I'll arrest you for obstructing justice."

"You can't do that," Brenda said. "I do remember, Nick said..."

"The same goes for you," Daniel told her. "No one says anything, do you understand?"

Nick and Brenda exchanged glances. Before they could do more than that, Constable Corlett escorted Nick out of the room. Daniel waited until he'd received a text to follow with Brenda.

"Well, this has been interesting," Stanley said after the door shut behind Daniel and Brenda. "I never would have suspected Nick Proper of murdering two men. Not that I know Nick, particularly, but he doesn't seem the type, really."

"It's a lot more complicated than just murder," Captain Howard said. "Someone was masterminding a huge stolen property ring between here and Liverpool."

"Well, that wasn't Nick," Stanley said. "He's not smart enough to manage something like that."

"On the contrary," Florence said. "I think he is quite capable of that very thing. No doubt Brenda helped him. She's very clever."

"I thought you didn't know them," Charlotte said.

"It's a small island," Florence said with a shrug. "Everyone meets everyone if they live here their entire lives."

"And you think they were the brains behind the burglary ring?" Charlotte asked.

"I think that seems like the most likely solution," Florence said. "Of course, that's for the police to work out, really."

"I don't know," Stanley said. "I suspect the police will still be looking for the person behind it all."

"Perhaps that person is across," Florence said. "Maybe the operation was being managed out of Liverpool. That's where the stolen property was going, wasn't it?"

"I suppose that's possible," Captain Howard said. "Maybe the Propers were simply in charge of the island side of the operation."

"I don't know that Nick could have even managed that," Stanley said scornfully.

"No one has offered a motive for Robert's murder in any of this," Sarah said quietly.

"I think it's pretty obvious that he was involved in the burglary ring," Stanley said. "He was probably responsible for getting the stolen property off the island. It wouldn't have been difficult for him to add a few things here and there to the containers his company was shipping across, I'm sure."

"I don't believe it," Sarah said.

"You'll see, when the Propers go to trial," Stanley predicted. "It will all come out."

"Maybe I should take a long holiday," Sarah muttered.

"I was thinking the same thing," Florence said. "I think Stanley and I might go away in the next day or two, actually."

"I'm not sure the police are finished with everyone," Captain

Howard said. "And I'd still like to talk to you more about the young woman who let you board early."

"You said no one was going to lose their job," Florence reminded him. "It doesn't matter who she was."

"There is going to be some significant retraining going on, that's for sure," the captain said.

"At least now the crime rate on the island should drop," Harry said. "I was thinking about putting in a security system. Now I won't bother."

"Many of the burgled homes had systems," Stanley said. "Another reason why I can't picture Nick behind the operation. He'd have no idea how to disarm a security system."

"You seem to know an awful lot about a man you claim you don't know," Charlotte said.

Stanley shrugged. "I've spent my life learning how to read and understand people on very short acquaintance. You have to do that to run a business. I knew everything I needed to know about Nick when I shook his hand for the first time."

"When was that?" Fenella asked.

"Oh, I, that is, I can't remember. It would have been at some charity function that my wife dragged me to, no doubt," Stanley said.

"What about Brenda? What did you think of her?" was Fenella's next question.

He glanced at Florence. "She wasn't the criminal mastermind type," he said dryly.

"I think you underestimate the woman," Florence said sharply. "She may well have been the driving force behind everything that's happened. I will be telling the police that, the next time I speak to them."

"Nonsense," Stanley said. "They need to look elsewhere for the person responsible."

"No, they don't," Florence said sharply.

"We'll have to agree to disagree, my dear," Stanley said. "Perhaps I know Nick and Brenda better than you do."

"Or maybe not," Florence said. "Anyway, what matters is what the police believe, not you."

"Yes, well, I suppose we'll all have to talk to the police again, won't we?" Stanley said.

"What does that mean?" Florence demanded.

"It means that I shall have to share my thoughts on the matter with the police, that's all," Stanley told her.

Florence's cheeks turned red and she got to her feet. "I think that's quite enough," she said. "I'm going home."

"At least the police won't have any trouble finding you there," Stanley said.

Florence picked up her handbag and stormed out of the room, leaving the others staring after her. After a moment Stanley shrugged.

"I suppose I should go with her," he said. "She hates when I disagree with her, but I had to share my thoughts on Nick and Brenda. I'm sure they're in all manner of trouble, but I still think someone else was behind it all."

"Do you think Nick and Brenda killed the two men?" Fenella asked.

"Probably," Stanley said. "But only on orders from someone else. Nick wasn't much more than hired muscle."

"I hope you talk to the police soon about your theory," Fenella said. "I'm sure Inspector Robinson will be interested."

"I'll ring him from home and share my thoughts," Stanley told her. "I assume we're done here for today?" he asked the captain.

"We might as well be," the man replied with a sigh. "I don't think we've accomplished anything, but I suppose the police have arrested someone, so it wasn't a total waste."

Fenella was hoping that some of the others might want to talk more, but as soon as Captain Howard stood up, everyone in the room seemed to be on their feet. In less than a minute, the room was nearly empty as people rushed out the door. Only Fenella and Charlotte remained behind. Fenella dawdled over picking up her handbag, waiting to see if the other woman would speak.

"That was very odd," Charlotte said as she dug her car keys out of her bag. "It was almost like Stanley was trying to start a fight with Florence."

"Perhaps they're not getting along well at the moment," Fenella said.

"Clearly they aren't," Charlotte said. "But I wonder why?"

"I was talking to Florence at a charity event last night and she seemed, well, unhappy," Fenella said. "I think she spends too much time looking after Stanley."

"She needs a hobby," Charlotte remarked. "I sew and knit, and those keep me quite busy when I'm not traveling. Actually, they keep me quite busy when I am travelling as well. There's nothing better than a knitting project to fill the time on a ferry journey."

Fenella nodded. "I was planning to read," she said. "After years of teaching and researching, it's wonderful to read strictly for pleasure again."

Charlotte nodded. "Must be off," she said. Before Fenella could reply, she swept out of the room, leaving Fenella on her own.

Picking up her handbag, Fenella followed slowly behind the other woman, not wanting to catch up to her. Outside, it was cool and overcast, and Fenella thought she'd better hurry to get home before the rain started. As she walked, with her jacket pulled tightly around herself, she found it hard to believe that the weather had been so pleasant lately. At least there was the prospect of many more spring days to come.

The rain was just starting to fall when she reached her building. While she'd been walking, her brain had been replaying the conversation that had taken place after Daniel had arrested the Propers. As she opened the door to her apartment, an odd thought sprang into her head.

"She needs a hobby," Fenella could hear the words replaying over and over again. Was it possible that Florence had a hobby, after all? But if that were true, it almost seemed as if Stanley was trying to get Florence into trouble, which made no sense at all. Fenella sat down and gave Katie a pat. The kitten curled up in her lap and Fenella petted her mindlessly while she tried to think.

"You're lost in thought," Mona said. "What happened at the Sea Terminal?"

Fenella gave her aunt a complete rundown of the afternoon's events. When she was done, she looked at Mona curiously.

"I had an odd thought," she said. "But I'm afraid you'll laugh at me."

"Tell me anyway," Mona said. "Ghosts can't laugh."

Fenella narrowed her eyes, not quite believing the other woman. "What if the mastermind behind the whole burglary ring is Florence March?" she asked.

Mona burst out laughing, leaving Fenella frowning at her. "I thought you couldn't laugh," she said when her aunt finally stopped.

"Only in extreme circumstances," Mona said, waving a hand.

"I don't think the idea is that funny," Fenella said crossly.

"I knew Florence March for a great many years," Mona said. "She's as bland and colorless a person as you can get. I can't see her having enough imagination to put something like a burglary and smuggling ring together."

"The more I think about it, the more it seems like Stanley was hinting at that, though," Fenella told her.

"He was hinting at something and no doubt he knows something he hasn't told the police, but it's a long way from that to Florence being behind the crimes," Mona said.

"So it's a crazy idea," Fenella said with a sigh.

"But it's one you should share with Inspector Robinson," Mona replied. "Maybe it will get him thinking outside the box, at least."

"I'm sure Stanley will give him ideas," Fenella argued.

"But he probably hasn't spoken to Stanley yet," Mona pointed out.

Knowing that Mona would nag her until she did, Fenella called the police station. She was put on hold for several minutes before Daniel came on the line.

"The conversation after you left was strange," she told the man. While he listened, she did her best to repeat what was said.

"So Mr. and Mrs. March aren't getting along very well," Daniel said. "I'm not sure why that's of interest to me."

Fenella took a deep breath. "I was wondering if there's any chance that Florence is the person behind the burglary ring and the murders," she said.

The silence on the other end seemed to drag on for a very long time. At least he isn't laughing, Fenella thought.

"I'm going to have both Marches brought in for questioning," Daniel said eventually. "If anything interesting comes of it, I'll let you know once it's set to hit the papers."

Fenella hung up and made herself some dinner. She fed Katie and then pottered around the apartment, wondering what was happening. When Shelly stopped by to suggest the pub, Fenella found that she wasn't in the mood, but she went anyway.

❧ 15 ❧

Daniel finally stopped by two nights later. Fenella was sitting on the floor playing with Katie and Smokey, while Shelly watched, when he knocked on the door. Shelly was closer, so she let the man in.

"This is a surprise," Fenella said, standing up quickly. She brushed cat hair off of herself, blushing as she realized how casually dressed she was. Her sweatshirt and jeans were covered in black and grey fur, and nothing she did seemed to help much.

"I hope it isn't inconvenient," Daniel said.

"Not at all," Fenella replied, wishing she'd taken the time to shower and fix her hair and makeup before Shelly had arrived.

"I just brought Smokey over for a kitty play date," Shelly told Daniel. "But it's just about time for us to head home for our dinner."

"MERROW," Smokey said emphatically.

"I think somebody is hungry," Shelly laughed. She picked up the cat and held her up, nose to nose. "Are you hungry, my precious?" she cooed.

"Merrow, merrr, merrr, yowww," Smokey said in a conversational tone.

"I believe that means yes," Fenella laughed.

"I'll stop back in a few hours," Shelly said. "I'll be on my way to the pub by then."

Fenella nodded. They'd fallen into the habit of going to the pub nearly every night. Sometimes Fenella opted for a soft drink, but a single glass of wine each evening wasn't going to hurt her. Some doctors even suggested that it was healthy.

"I don't want to get in the way of your dinner," Daniel said after Shelly and her pet had let themselves out.

"Have you eaten? We could order pizza or Chinese," Fenella offered.

"If you're sure I'm not in the way, I'd love Chinese," Daniel said.

There was a Chinese restaurant only a few doors away and they were happy to deliver to their neighbors. After a few minutes with the menu, Fenella called in the order for them both.

"So, how are things?" Fenella asked as she handed Daniel a can of soda.

"Things are good," Daniel said with a grin. "Tomorrow's papers will be full of news."

"Really? I kept expecting to hear things, but the usual gossips don't seem to know anything."

"Stanley and his advocate have been doing everything they can to keep things very quiet," Daniel explained. "I've been interviewing him and Florence at their home rather than the station and only formally arrested her earlier this evening."

"So Florence was involved in something criminal?" Fenella asked in surprise.

"She was behind the burglary ring, just like you suggested," Daniel confirmed.

Fenella glanced around the room, but Mona was nowhere in sight. She couldn't wait to tell her aunt that she'd been right.

"I'm shocked," Fenella said.

"But you suspected it," Daniel countered.

"But I thought I just have an overactive imagination," Fenella explained. "Tell me everything, please."

"I'll tell you what I can. As I said, a lot of this will be in the paper tomorrow. It all started some time ago. It seems that Florence found herself bored once her children left the nest. She tried doing more volunteer work, but found that wasn't fulfilling enough. At a party one night, one of her wealthy friends was talking about going away for several months and leaving her house empty. She asked Florence to stop by and check on the house for her. While she was doing that, Florence found a pair of diamond earrings she liked."

"Her poor friend," Fenella remarked. "Did she just help herself, then?"

"She did, but so cleverly that no one ever suspected. She found herself someone else to do the real dirty work."

"Nick Proper," Fenella guessed.

"Apparently she knew Brenda from one of the charities she was involved with," Daniel explained. "And she knew the couple needed a bit of extra money. She gave Brenda the code for the security system and told her that she and Nick could keep everything they took. By the time Florence's friend got back to the island and discovered that she'd been burgled, Florence had been wearing the earrings for several months."

"But surely her friend was suspicious?" Fenella asked.

"Florence was clever about it," Daniel explained. "She took the earrings within days of her friend leaving. About a month later she managed to 'accidentally' leave a tap running when she was there checking on the place. A whole crew of cleaners had to come in to clear up the mess and they were able to tell the police that there was no sign of a break-in when they were there. Just a few days before the friend was due back, the Propers went in and made a huge mess as they stole nearly everything of value in the house."

"That is clever," Fenella admitted.

"Yes, and it was enough excitement for Florence that she couldn't help but do it again a few months later when another friend went away. This time, she took a share of the proceeds rather than any one item, and her terrible partnership with Nick and Brenda was born."

A knock on the door interrupted the story. Daniel helped Fenella as she opened carton after carton of delicious-smelling Chinese food. When it was all spread out across the counter, the pair fixed plates and then dug in.

"This is excellent," Daniel said after a few bites. "I like it better than the food at the Chinese place near me."

"I love it," Fenella told him. "But you were telling me about Florence and the Propers."

"Yes, well, those first incidents were something like fifteen years ago," Daniel said. "It seems that Florence was very careful, only staging one or two break-ins a year. From what she's told us, some years she didn't manage any. Nick and Brenda took care of disposing of the stolen property at first, but Florence didn't trust them. After a while, she found a man across that was able to get her better prices. She still used Nick and Brenda for the burglaries here, though."

"So what happened?" Fenella asked.

"A few different things," Daniel said. "First, Stanley retired and started taking an active interest in how his wife was spending her time."

"Surely he'd noticed that she had more money than she should, didn't he?"

"Every penny she made went into a Swiss bank account that he knew nothing about," Daniel told her.

"Wow," Fenella said.

"That was another problem, as Swiss banks are working with UK tax authorities now. She started to worry about keeping that account hidden."

"So she had Nick start breaking into more houses?" Fenella asked.

"More or less," Daniel said. "They switched their focus from one or two big hits every year to several smaller ones. But that meant a lot more stolen property to get off the island. Robert Grosso was brought in to help, as he had access to large shipping containers and could conceivably get almost anything across. Robert used George Mason as his accomplice on the ferry. George would let Robert load his containers first and then George would sign off on the paperwork. But more accomplices meant more people to pay and that meant more burglaries had to happen. After a while, things started to get a little out of control. Nick started breaking into houses at random, which increased the chances of his getting caught. Apparently, Robert started demanding a larger cut of the profits, which was a problem as well."

"And poor Florence had to deal with all of this with Stanley watching her every move," Fenella suggested.

"Exactly," Daniel said. "When things finally got too out of control and Robert got too demanding, she told Nick to get rid of him. They were supposed to throw the body overboard once the sailing got underway. Of course, when the body was found, George worked out what had happened and tried to blackmail Nick."

"So Nick killed him."

"Actually, although she won't admit it, we think Florence killed George. A woman matching Florence's description was seen leaving the building where his flat was located on the night before the body was found."

"I never did hear how he died," Fenella said.

"He was poisoned," Daniel told her. "He was given a massive over-dose of medication that just happens to be a drug that Stanley March takes. It was in a bottle of expensive wine that was completely out of place in George's flat."

Fenella shuddered. "I'd suspected Florence of being involved in something criminal, but I never thought she'd killed anyone."

"As I said, she hasn't admitted it, but she has told us a lot of the story. She seemed weirdly proud of it, actually."

"Someone told me Florence needed a hobby," Fenella said. "Little did she know."

"Florence was far too successful, really," Daniel said. "We're going to be going back over the reports for every burglary on the island in the past twenty years. It bothers me that she and Nick were able to get away with it for so long."

"But you weren't here," Fenella pointed out.

"No, I would like to think I would have solved the case years ago," Daniel said with a laugh.

"I'm sure you would have," Fenella replied.

She served them both scoops of ice cream for dessert before putting all of the dishes into the dishwasher.

"Why did you focus on cabin passengers?" Fenella asked the question that had been bothering her since the investigation started.

"Robert had a note in his pocket that read, 'Once we are all in our cabins, we'll meet in 212 to talk.' It wasn't signed, but we're pretty sure Nick wrote it. It seems as if he tried to disguise his handwriting, though."

"So you knew it was a cabin passenger, but not which one," Fenella said. "And so many of the cabin passengers were on board early as well."

"Yes, Captain Howard isn't very happy about that. I suspect quite a few crew members were supplementing their income by letting passengers board early in exchange for a small gratuity. I hope that's going to stop now. Our investigation was raising questions about Nick and Brenda," Daniel told her. "I'd like to think that we would have found Florence eventually, as well, but I have to congratulate you for putting it all together like that."

"It was just dumb luck," Fenella said.

"I don't know about that. Some people just have good instincts for such things. Maybe it helps that you don't really know anyone here, so you can look at them all with the same critical eye."

"You haven't been here long, either," Fenella pointed out.

"No, but in this case I was told to go softly on Stanley and Florence, as they have friends in high places."

"Oh, dear, but it really did feel to me like Stanley was trying to implicate Florence when we were at the Sea Terminal."

"Yes, I think he was," Daniel agreed. "From what I can see, he's more than a little afraid of Florence. After the second murder, he started putting two and two together and he didn't like the answer he was getting. I was going to question them both again about the murders, and I suspect he would have dropped several very large hints into that conversation if we weren't already suspicious."

"Why didn't he just go to the police?"

"I think he was hoping he was wrong. He also probably felt some loyalty to his wife of forty years and the mother of his children. I'm not sure he even knows why he didn't, though, especially after the second murder."

"Are there any charges you can press against him?" Fenella asked.

"We're negotiating that," Daniel told her.

The next half hour of conversation was more general and by the time Shelly knocked on the door, Fenella was feeling incredibly at ease with the handsome police inspector.

"Pub?" Shelly asked.

"Oh, I suppose so," Fenella replied. She turned to Daniel. "You will come, won't you?"

"Not tonight," Daniel replied. "I have some paperwork to finish up at the office. Maybe another night."

Fenella was disappointed and sorry she'd agreed to go.

"You need to change," Shelly told her friend. "Maybe you can find something to put on that isn't covered in cat hair?"

Fenella looked down at her outfit and blushed. She should have changed for Daniel's benefit.

"I'll be back in fifteen minutes," Shelly told her before she turned and walked back to her own apartment. "Peter is feeling better, so he might be coming as well," she added over her shoulder.

Fenella shut the door and looked at Daniel.

"I'm sorry," he said, taking a step closer to her. "I really shouldn't have stayed as long as I have."

"It was nice, dinner and all," Fenella said.

"Yes, I enjoyed it a lot," Daniel told her. He took another step toward her. "As I said earlier, you did well to spot Florence as the culprit. You seem to have good instincts."

"Or I was just lucky."

"Maybe, but I have some cold cases that I'm working on. I was wondering if you'd be interested in going over them with me? Sometimes it's helpful to get the perspective of a complete outsider, especially with cases that are twenty or thirty years old."

"That sounds fascinating," Fenella replied.

Daniel took another step until he was only inches from Fenella. "I'll ring you before I come over next time," he said. "And I'll bring dinner as well."

"That sounds great," Fenella said, a little breathlessly.

Daniel stared into her eyes for a moment and then closed the small gap between them. The kiss set off fireworks in Fenella's brain. When he finally lifted his head, she felt as if her knees were only just barely supporting her body.

"I'll ring you soon," Daniel promised as he let himself out.

"Wasn't that romantic?" Mona said. "And look at the state of you. I'm surprised he wanted to get that close. You're covered in fur."

Fenella ignored her aunt and walked into the bedroom to change. When she looked into the mirror, she was surprised to find that she looked the same. She'd half expected to find scorch marks on her lips. Daniel's kiss had been that good.

ACKNOWLEDGMENTS

Another book that wouldn't exist without the hard work and talents of my editor, Denise, my cover artist, Linda, and my beta readers, Jennifer and Ruth.

As always, many thanks to you, my readers, for letting my characters into your lives. I hope you are as fond of them as I am!

Fenella's story continues in...
Cars and Cold Cases
An Isle of Man Ghostly Cozy

Fenella Woods is nervous but eager to start driving lessons on the Isle of Man. Having never driven a manual transmission before, she quickly finds herself struggling with having to change gears with her left hand while sitting on what feels like the wrong side of the car and driving on what seems to be the wrong side of the road.

Her friendship with CID Inspector Daniel Robinson is less stressful. He's going through some cold cases and he asks her to share her thoughts. Daniel seems to think that she'll have a different perspective on the investigations because she doesn't know any of the people involved. He's surprised to find that the first case he mentions, a missing person from thirty years earlier, involves Fenella's new driving instructor.

Fenella's aunt Mona, who is either a ghost or a figment of Fenella's imagination, has her own ideas about both the missing person and an unconnected thirty-year-old murder investigation that Daniel is also reopening. And, of course, she's eager for Fenella to get involved in both cases.

Fenella isn't sure she's ready to try to deal with driving lessons, two cold cases, one nosy aunt, a kitten who needs surgery and three different men who all appeal to her in very different ways. She knew her life was going to change when she moved to the Isle of Man, but she wasn't anticipating quite this much excitement.

ALSO BY DIANA XARISSA

ABOUT THE AUTHOR

Diana Xarissa grew up in Erie, Pennsylvania, earned a BA in history from Allegheny College and eventually ended up in Silver Spring, Maryland. There she met her husband, who swept her off her feet and moved her to Derbyshire for a short while. Eventually, the couple relocated to the Isle of Man.

The Isle of Man was home for Diana and her family for over ten years. During their time there, Diana completed an MA in Manx Studies through the University of Liverpool. The family is now living near Buffalo, New York, where Diana enjoys writing about the island that she loves.

Diana also writes mystery/thrillers set in the not-too-distant future under the pen name "Diana X. Dunn" and fantasy/adventure books for middle grade readers under the pen name "D.X. Dunn."

She would be delighted to know what you think of her work and can be contacted through snail mail at:
Diana Xarissa Dunn
PO Box 72
Clarence, NY 14031.

Find Diana at:
www.dianaxarissa.com
diana@dianaxarissa.com

Made in United States
North Haven, CT
04 June 2022

19860790R00127